ROBERT B. PARKER'S
BURIED
SECRETS

THE JESSE STONE NOVELS

Robert B. Parker's Buried Secrets
(by Christopher Farnsworth)

Robert B. Parker's Fallout
(by Mike Lupica)

Robert B. Parker's Stone's Throw
(by Mike Lupica)

Robert B. Parker's Fool's Paradise
(by Mike Lupica)

Robert B. Parker's The Bitterest Pill
(by Reed Farrel Coleman)

Robert B. Parker's Colorblind
(by Reed Farrel Coleman)

Robert B. Parker's The Hangman's Sonnet
(by Reed Farrel Coleman)

Robert B. Parker's Debt to Pay
(by Reed Farrel Coleman)

Robert B. Parker's The Devil Wins
(by Reed Farrel Coleman)

Robert B. Parker's Blind Spot
(by Reed Farrel Coleman)

Robert B. Parker's Damned If You Do
(by Michael Brandman)

Robert B. Parker's Fool Me Twice
  (by Michael Brandman)

Robert B. Parker's Killing the Blues
  (by Michael Brandman)

Split Image
Night and Day
Stranger in Paradise
High Profile
Sea Change
Stone Cold
Death in Paradise
Trouble in Paradise
Night Passage

For a comprehensive title list and a preview of upcoming books, visit PRH.com/RobertBParker or Facebook.com/RobertBParkerAuthor.

ROBERT B. PARKER'S

BURIED SECRETS

A JESSE STONE NOVEL

CHRISTOPHER FARNSWORTH

G. P. PUTNAM'S SONS • NEW YORK

PUTNAM
— EST. 1838 —

G. P. PUTNAM'S SONS
Publishers Since 1838
An imprint of Penguin Random House LLC
penguinrandomhouse.com

Library of Congress Cataloging-in-Publication Data

Names: Farnsworth, Christopher, author.
Title: Robert B. Parker's buried secrets / Christopher Farnsworth.
Other titles: Buried secrets.
Description: New York : G. P. Putnam's Sons, 2025. | Series: Jesse Stone novels
Identifiers: LCCN 2024018650 (print) | LCCN 2024018651 (ebook) |
    ISBN 9780593544761 (hardcover) | ISBN 9780593544778 (epub)
Subjects: LCGFT: Thrillers (Fiction). | Novels.
Classification: LCC PS3606.A726 R63 2025 (print) | LCC PS3606.A726 (ebook) |
    DDC 813/.6—dc23/eng/20240701
LC record available at https://lccn.loc.gov/2024018650
LC ebook record available at https://lccn.loc.gov/2024018651
    p.   cm.

Printed in the United States of America
1st Printing

Interior art: Rainer Fuhrmann © Shutterstock

To Philippa Buss Roosevelt,

in loving memory

ROBERT B. PARKER'S
BURIED
SECRETS

ONE

Jesse Stone was on his way home when his deputy chief, Molly Crane, interrupted him on the radio for a welfare check.

"A guy is worried about his friend. Says he hasn't seen him in a couple weeks and now he won't answer the door," Molly told him.

"Can't someone else do it?" It had already been a long day. Three of his officers were out sick—COVID again—which was why Molly was covering dispatch. Jesse himself had been on multiple patrol calls and was looking forward to sitting down and watching whatever ESPN had to offer.

"Suit's breaking up a fight at the Scupper. Everyone else is busy," Molly said. "Serve and protect. It's in the job description."

"Yeah, but I'm the chief. I'm supposed to tell you what to do."

"It's adorable that you think that," Molly said. "Anyway, it's not like you had plans. Your girlfriend left you for *The New York Times*."

"You know, I can fire you anytime I want," Jesse said.

"Good luck. You'd be lost without me."

"Fine. Where is it?"

"See?" Molly read him the address.

The house was in a nice neighborhood on the good side of Paradise, but it had seen better days. The paint was peeling, and the wood was splintered and rotting in places. The lawn was mostly weeds and crabgrass. Deferred maintenance, Jesse had heard it called. When the people inside the house had to choose between upkeep and property taxes. Even in a place with a median income as high as Paradise's, it happened to some of the older residents as their lives extended past their savings accounts.

As Jesse drove up, he saw a younger man in the driveway, his worried face framed by a thin beard. He wore a leather jacket, black jeans, and boots, despite the early-spring warmth. He looked like he was late for a club opening somewhere.

"Are you the police?" he asked, as Jesse got out of his Explorer. Not from around here, Jesse figured.

"I'm Chief Stone," Jesse said, showing the young man his badge.

He looked at the badge and then at Jesse, as if trying to make up his mind.

True, Jesse didn't really dress like a cop. Perks of being the chief of a twelve-person force. He wore jeans and a polo shirt and sneakers and a ball cap with PARADISE PD printed on it. Usually a jacket to hide the Glock on his hip, too, but again, today was warm.

"This is the part where you tell me your name," Jesse said helpfully.

"Oh, right," the man said. "Sorry. I'm Matthew. Matthew Peebles."

"Can I see some ID?" Jesse said. *Peebles? Really?*

Matthew Peebles appeared taken aback. "Why do you need to see my ID?"

"It's a cop thing." Jesse shrugged. "We like to make sure people are who they say they are."

"Oh. Of course," Peebles said. He handed over a driver's license from a thick wallet attached to a chain. It was from New York.

Despite the odds against it, Peebles really *was* his name. Jesse handed the ID back. "You said you were worried about your friend inside the house?"

"Well. My parents' friend more than mine, really," Matthew said. "His name is Phil Burton. He's old. I mean, he's an elderly gentleman. I come out from the city and check on him every now and then for my folks. We talk on the phone, too. But I haven't heard from him for a while, and I got worried."

The propensity of people who lived in New York to refer to it as "the city," as if there were no others, wasn't lost on Jesse. Nobody ever did that in Los Angeles when he lived there. He wondered if it was them overcompensating.

"You drove four hours up here to check on him?"

"He wasn't answering. And like I said, I was worried."

3

"Would you mind calling him again?"

Peebles called again, with his phone on speaker so Jesse could hear. There was a generic voicemail greeting, and the mailbox was full.

"Are you going to check on him or what?" Peebles asked. He seemed to be growing increasingly agitated.

"Let's go knock on the door," Jesse said.

He knocked on the door, which wasn't in any better shape than the rest of the house. Then he rang the bell. No answer to either.

"You're sure he's home?"

"Well, pretty sure," Matthew said. "He usually spends a couple weeks out of the country every winter. He doesn't like the cold much anymore. But I thought he was back now."

Jesse rang the bell again.

"Can you kick it in?" Matthew asked.

Jesse looked at him. "I'd rather not do that if he's just on vacation. I think your friend probably wants to come home to a door that works."

"Well, are you going to do *anything*?" Matthew asked, now clearly aggravated.

Jesse nodded. "I think I might try the back way first."

He went around the side of the house and found a gate. It was stuck, as if something was pressing against it. Jesse sighed. "Serve and protect," Molly said. *Let's see her come out here and do this,* he thought.

He hopped up, caught the top of the gate with both hands, and felt the familiar twinge in his bad shoulder, a relic of the injury that had ended his days playing baseball. He ignored it and scrambled up without looking too ridiculous, he thought. He swung his body over the gate and came down in the yard.

Which looked like it was auditioning for a landfill, Jesse thought. There was a pile of garbage under his feet heaped up against the gate. The random junk was holding it shut. Old tires, layers of cardboard boxes, plastic restaurant-sized jugs of condiments and sauces, both empty and full. A child's wagon. A stack of broken lawn furniture. Heavy black garbage bags.

Jesse shifted his balance, trying to stay upright, and picked his way toward the back.

He found a sliding glass door, half open, and put on the blue nitrile gloves he always kept in his pocket before walking inside.

The door opened into what must have been the kitchen, and the inside of the house was even more crowded with junk than the yard. The counters were hidden under boxes: cases of motor oil, unopened. Stacks of mail that must have gone back decades. Old phone books. *Where do you even get phone books anymore?* Jesse wondered. Fast-food wrappers and delivery bags in piles, most of them with rotting food and grease stains.

There was also a familiar smell. Jesse knew that odor. It was not a pleasant one.

He tried to breathe through his mouth.

There was a narrow path in among all the debris. It led to the living room, where Jesse found dozens of moldering cardboard file boxes, some stacked as high as his head, arranged in a semicircle around an old couch.

And the couch was where Jesse found the body.

TWO

Phil Burton—Jesse assumed that's who this was—had been there awhile.

It was like he'd built a nest in the living room, the one open space in the house that Jesse could observe.

The decomposition wasn't too bad. The house was dry, and it had been cold until recently. The skin had drawn back from the face, but there was still something recognizably human there. He'd been an old man, his hair strawlike and fried from multiple dye jobs. His eyes were sunken behind tinted aviator glasses, and he wore a button-down shirt with epaulets. He looked deflated, half melted.

Around him on the floor were paper plates and more fast-food containers. This was apparently his dining room as well as his bedroom.

In truth, this wasn't the first time he'd found a body

like this in Paradise. Older men, living alone, with no close friends or family nearby, occasionally ended up like this. Waiting for someone to discover them.

But Jesse had never seen a house this far gone before. He'd heard of hoarders, obviously, but he'd never seen one here. He wondered how it started—how you went from hanging on to an old phone book to living like this. What was the tipping point? When did you stop seeing the mess, start seeing it as your life?

Burton clearly wasn't going to tell him. Jesse took another look at the body. No obvious sign of foul play.

Apparently, he went to sleep here and never woke up.

There were worse ways to go.

Jesse carefully picked his way out of the house again, easing among the piles and stacks of junk. It had been years since Jesse was a prospect with a Major League career ahead of him, but he still moved with an athlete's grace.

In his mind, he was already making a list of everything that would need to be done. Notifying the coroner, a search for the next of kin, finding someone to come and excavate all the layers of garbage.

As he climbed back over the gate, he wondered how Matthew Peebles was going to take the death of his family friend. He seemed high-strung.

As it turned out, Jesse didn't have to worry about that. When he got back out of the house, Peebles was gone.

Jesse called Molly to report what he'd found, then Dev Chada, the medical examiner. Then he waited, leaning against a low stone wall that separated the property from the road. The air was better out here, and the day was cooling down nicely as the sun set.

Suit showed up before anyone else.

Luther "Suitcase" Simpson did not appear at all damaged, or even wrinkled, by his recent call to break up an argument between a couple of drunks. He was a big guy, one of the most solid cops—and friends—Jesse had ever known. Still, he'd always be a kid to Jesse. Seeing Suit in his plainclothes blazer, Jesse couldn't help thinking of a boy wearing his dad's clothes.

"You look pretty fresh for someone who just got out of a bar fight," Jesse said.

"Ah, it barely qualified as a fight," Suit said. "Two guys who could hardly stand up, getting angry over a woman. She didn't want either of them. Once they realized that, they began crying on each other's shoulders. I got them each a ride home."

"The path of true love never did run smooth," Jesse said.

"Especially when booze is involved."

"Don't have to tell me," Jesse said. He'd spent a few too many nights looking for answers at the bottom of a glass, and far too many years searching for love with the wrong woman.

Suit, at the heart of him, wanted only to do good. He was driven to help people, which is why he became a cop.

Jesse, on the other hand, was driven to make things right, which was not exactly the same thing.

Suit looked around. "Where's the good citizen who reported this?"

"Not so good would be my guess," Jesse said. "He scampered."

"'Scampered'?"

"That's a technical term. Look it up in your detective handbook."

"You call the crime scene people?" Suit asked.

"We might need an archaeologist," Jesse said. "Maybe a whole team of them. Come on. I'll show you."

Jesse got over the fence first.

"Pretty spry for a guy your age," Suit said.

Jesse waited until Suit came down on the piles of trash and slipped, nearly falling on his ass. "Careful there, Junior," Jesse said. "Wouldn't want you to get hurt."

Suit regained his balance and put on his own pair of nitrile gloves. They went in through the open sliding door.

Suit went red, then pale, as the scent hit him.

"Jesus," he said, taking in the view. "How does somebody live like this?"

"Well, in this case, he doesn't. Not anymore."

They made their way through the narrow path to the living room, Suit turning sideways in places to avoid touching anything. For someone his size, it was like navigating a maze of spring-loaded traps, like something out of an Indiana Jones movie.

Burton was right where Jesse had left him.

"Ugh," Suit said.

"'Ugh'? Is that your professional opinion, Detective?"

"Well, what would you say? Can you imagine? Just being left like this until someone remembers you exist?"

"Not everyone has someone who cares about them," Jesse said.

Suit took a KN95 out of his pocket and put it on. As his arm came up, he accidentally nudged one of the towers of file boxes stacked around the room. The tower shifted, and the old cardboard suddenly split open, sending a cascade of papers and folders to the floor.

"Ah, shoot," Suit said. "Sorry."

He tried to find a safe place to stand and took a step forward, and again nearly fell on his ass as a stack of magazines slid out from under his foot.

"It's like watching Baryshnikov dance," Jesse said.

"You watch a lot of ballet?"

"Sorry, I meant one of those dancing bears."

Then something caught Jesse's eye in the pile of papers released from the box. He kneeled down to take a closer look.

Suit was still staring at Burton's corpse on the couch.

"Well," Suit said. "At least he didn't suffer."

Jesse carefully picked up a Polaroid photo. He looked at the image, then showed it to Suit.

Suit went pale again.

"Maybe he should have," Jesse said.

THREE

The Polaroid was aged and a little faded, but preserved from its time in the box. It showed a man in what appeared to be an alley. It was hard to see the background; it was a tight shot, focusing mainly on the bullet wound in the man's forehead.

"What the hell?" Suit said.

Jesse stood.

"We should let the crime scene techs handle this. I don't want to disturb anything else."

But Jesse kept looking down at the floor, the Polaroid still in his hand.

There were dozens more among the papers and folders scattered on the floor. Suit was staring at them, too, breathing a little heavier in his mask.

From what Jesse could see, the pictures were all of dead men. Gunshot wounds. Blood. Some staring dead-eyed, some with their eyes closed as if they were blinking or sleeping. All starkly lit in the camera's flash.

The house suddenly felt much smaller, as if all the junk was pressing in on the both of them. Before, it was just sad. Now it seemed haunted.

"Let's go," he told Suit.

Jesse got to the fence before he realized he still had the first picture.

He slipped it into his pocket and climbed over, back into the everyday world.

Jesse made some more calls. First to Molly, to let her know that he and Suit would be out here awhile, and then to Dev. Then he called the state's crime scene technicians. They were going to need a lot of people for this one. The house was packed to the walls with junk, and all of it would have to be hauled out and cataloged.

He and Suit stood outside and waited. Dev showed up first. Jesse walked him, carefully, into the scene, leaving Suit outside.

"I don't want to trigger an avalanche," he told Suit.

"I'll just enjoy the fresh air out here," Suit said.

Even Dev, who spent most of his days up to his elbows in death, looked a little green when he saw the corpse.

"Damn, I hate these," he said.

"Can't blame you," Jesse said. "Look, I need you to be careful."

Dev made a face. "When am I not?"

"Sorry. Not what I meant. This isn't just a dead body."

He took the picture from his back pocket and showed it to Dev, then pointed to the others on the floor.

"My God," Dev said. "What do you think this means?"

"No idea," Jesse said. "There could be a lot of evidence buried around here. Any hope I have of getting answers is in all these boxes. That's why I need you to do your best to get the body out without disturbing—"

At that moment, another cardboard box sagged, then slid over on the other side of the pile, vanishing into the gloom.

"So that's what you meant by 'avalanche,'" Dev said. "I get it now."

"I know you've got to do your job," Jesse said. "But I don't want to lose anything in here, either."

"I don't think losing anything is the problem. I imagine it's going to take months to go through all of this."

"Probably," Jesse said and sighed. He felt the need for something simple, like a traffic violation. And a drink, which bothered him. He shoved the thought down.

"Don't worry," Dev said. "I'll be gentle. I don't want to be buried in here, either."

Dev picked his way through the photos, the piles, and the papers, stepping with the balance of an acrobat. He barely disturbed the dust on any of the surfaces. Jesse was legitimately impressed.

"Graceful," he said.

"Ten years of gymnastics as a kid, plus twelve years of stepping over corpses," Dev said.

Dev made a preliminary examination of the body, just looking, not touching. Then, clamping his jaw shut and putting his mask and gloves on, he gingerly reached out to the corpse.

"I think we're in luck," he said. "The body has mostly dried out. I think he's been dead for at least two months."

"You have a funny definition of luck."

Dev carefully rolled the body to one side. The cloth of the shirt stuck to a blanket covering the couch, then peeled away, along with a layer of other stuff that Jesse didn't really want to look at very closely. Dev made a frustrated noise.

"This is going to be ugly," he said.

Jesse's phone buzzed. A text from Suit, letting him know the State Police's crime scene team had arrived. Jesse didn't text back. He wasn't a teenage girl. He didn't text if he could possibly avoid it.

"What if we lift the blanket from the couch?" Jesse asked. "Move him to the floor?"

The blanket under the body extended from one end of the couch to the other. The body was on top of it. It seemed like it was all still in one piece.

"Worth a shot," Dev said.

They each took a position, Dev at the body's head, Jesse at its feet.

"Really wish I'd sent one of my assistants for this," Dev said.

"Come on. Isn't this why you went to med school?" Jesse grabbed his end of the blanket. Dev did the same. "On three."

Jesse counted. They lifted. The body was surprisingly light. The blanket didn't rip. Nothing else came loose.

They put it down on the floor.

Jesse spotted something under the couch cushions, which were flattened and thin from years of wear as well as sodden with dried fluids.

But there was definitely something underneath.

"Hey, Dev," he said. "Take a picture of this, will you? I want to move these."

Dev snapped a photo with his phone, then Jesse lifted one of the cushions carefully and set it aside.

Jesse and Dev both stared.

They didn't speak. They didn't have to.

Dev snapped another picture, preserving the scene. Jesse then moved the other cushions, exposing the bottom of the couch completely.

The photos, apparently, weren't the only secrets hidden in this house.

In the couch, filling the hollow space of the frame, were stacks and stacks of cash.

Thousands of dollars, easily. Hundreds of thousands, even.

"Well, shit," Dev said.

"That's what I was thinking," Jesse said.

FOUR

An hour later, Jesse was on the phone with Brian Lundquist, the head of the State Homicide Division. He and his team usually handled the big investigations for small towns like Paradise, but he'd known and worked with Jesse for years now, and if they didn't have the same relationship that Jesse had with his predecessor, Healy, they still respected each other.

"How much money?" Lundquist asked.

"They haven't got an exact count yet," Jesse said. "But they did a rough estimate. If they're all hundreds, about two million dollars in cash. Some of it was ruined, of course."

"Jesus," Lundquist said.

The crime scene techs had gone into the house and, under Dev's careful direction, managed to slide the body into a bag, which they hauled out and into a waiting ambulance. Then they'd gone back inside and begun the process of bagging the money and excavating the layers and layers of debris.

Dev had promised to call as soon as he'd done the autopsy, but he didn't think he'd have much to tell Jesse. "Advanced decomposition," he'd said, just before he left. "Unless I find a bullet inside the skull, I'm probably going to have to go with natural causes."

"You ever have any dealings with this guy before?" Lundquist asked.

"Nobody did," Jesse said. "He was a recluse. Neighbors barely saw him."

Jesse had sent Suit around to canvass the neighborhood. He'd come up with nothing.

"We've got a couple complaints about him with code enforcement for not mowing his lawn," Jesse said. "Other than that, he's a blank."

While they talked, Jesse watched the crime scene techs walking in and out of the house, laden with junk.

They laid it out, piece by piece, onto tarps they'd placed on the front lawn.

All of which they had to photograph and tag because of the photos of the dead bodies.

"Any chance the guy was just into true crime? Private investigator? Or maybe he just had a really sick fetish?" Lundquist asked. "Maybe that's why he had those pictures."

"That would make things easier, but I doubt it," Jesse said. "If I had to guess, I'd say he had something to do with every one of them."

"I really hate it when you get a hunch, Jesse."

"So do I."

"But you're probably right."

"I usually am."

"Well, let's not get crazy here. They find anything that links these pictures to any names? Or open cases?"

Jesse laughed. "Sure. They found a list, right next to a card with the killer's signed confession and his current address."

"Too much to hope for."

"I can't even tell you what else they've found yet. They're just doing their best to find the floor right now."

A few of the neighbors watched from their front doors or on their lawns. They weren't yet moving to the sidewalk or crowding the crime scene tape to get a better look, but it was only a matter of time. Jesse was surprised the media wasn't here yet, but the local stations were understaffed—budget cuts, he'd heard—and it was a Friday night.

Not that Jesse had a problem with it. He wanted to keep people as far away as possible until he could get a better handle on it.

"You thinking serial killer?"

Jesse considered the question. Serial killers were rare, but he'd run into a couple. They kept trophies. And contrary to all the movies, they were usually sloppy, disorganized, and isolated—just the kind of guy who'd die alone in his house, surrounded by trash.

But Jesse didn't think that he'd found one. He had a file, taken at random from one of the boxes inside the house, spread out on his dashboard in front of him. It had more Polaroids. These were different people from the first photos he'd discovered, and an entirely different era, judging by the clothes and hairstyles. Maybe the late eighties or early nineties. They were just as dead, though. There was a woman who'd been shot in the chest, lying prone on a kitchen floor, her eyes looking away from the camera, staring blankly at the ceiling. There was a man who'd been strangled—Jesse recognized the bruising around his neck as well as the distinctive bursting of blood vessels in his open eyes. Another guy with the tidy little gunshot wound in his forehead. And four more, all killed by varying methods, including one unidentifiable corpse that had been burned to a crisp on a concrete floor, scorch marks radiating from it in a circle.

The papers inside were old as well, brittle sheets of lined yellow from a legal tablet, covered in faded numbers and barely legible words. He couldn't make out much, and what he could seemed to be in some kind of code. Dates and locations, if he had to bet. It looked like some kind of recordkeeping system. Something far too impersonal for a serial killer.

And there was the money.

"I don't know," Jesse finally said. "If I were going to bet, probably not."

"Then why the photos of dead bodies?"

"Well, that's what they pay me to find out."

"Maybe you could hand this one off, Jesse," Lundquist said. "It already sounds like a mess, and it's not going to get any better."

"No," Jesse said simply. His town, his responsibility.

"I should have known better than to ask."

"You really should have."

There was a sigh over the line. Then Lundquist said, "All right. I'll send more people."

"Thanks," Jesse said.

"You're lucky it's getting close to the end of the fiscal year and I need to spend some of my budget or I'll lose it. We can hire one of those cleanup crews to help out."

Jesse knew about those crews. Relatives who discovered bodies in a house full of accumulated trash would hire them to sort through the mess, dump everything out, so they could salvage the house.

"Still hard to believe that's an actual business," Jesse said. "I mean, how many people are found like this every year?"

"Lot of it going around, I guess," Lundquist said. "Too many sad and sick and lonely people in this world."

An evidence tech passed by Jesse with a child's tricycle over one shoulder. Jesse felt a pang of something he couldn't name.

And that same need for a drink.

"Well," he said. "One less of them now."

FIVE

"Good morning," Molly said.

"That is a matter of opinion," Jesse said.

"Aw, is hims gwumpy?"

Jesse just stared back at her. He was, in fact, more irritable than usual this morning. He chalked it up to not enough coffee and too little sleep. He'd been out late at the Burton house. Suit was there again this morning, with Gabe Weathers. The media had finally shown up, and the pile of junk on the front lawn was growing. They were going to need to haul some of it away soon.

"Can you get Peter Perkins to head over to the Burton place?" he asked Molly as he made himself a fresh cup. Peter had been set on retirement, but with the department's recruiting and staffing issues, Jesse had convinced him to stay on part-time. "Maybe he can help out."

"I'll call him," Molly said. "Don't forget, you're onboarding our new hire today. He'll be here in a few minutes."

"'Onboarding'?" Jesse asked. "Where the hell did you hear that?"

"That's what it's called when you bring someone new into a team, Jesse," she said. "Welcome to twenty-first-century management techniques."

"You're learning how to manage now?"

"Someone in this place has to."

Jesse went into his office and looked at the file of paperwork he still needed to sign for his latest addition, Derek Tate, sitting on his desk.

But first he wanted to think about Phil Burton and his haunted house.

He took his glove and a baseball from his desk. For as long as he could remember, smacking the ball into the glove helped him think. He stood and looked out the window, snapping the ball into the glove with an easy, smooth motion of his wrist. It sounded like someone working the heavy bag in a gym.

What they had was called an orgy of evidence. Too many clues and no way to piece them together into a rational narrative. They were all basically blind men trying to describe an elephant from behind.

Every crime was an explosion in someone's life, tearing things up and leaving debris everywhere. Most people panicked, even if the crime was small, at the violation of it, the way it disrupted everything that was supposed to be normal.

Jesse didn't. There was always some way to uncover

the truth buried underneath the rubble. The size of the mess didn't matter. Though the pile of junk from the Burton house was enormous. Still, there was always a starting point.

He broke it down in his head. It was how he approached every problem, almost instinctively. It's why the LAPD had tapped him for its elite Robbery Homicide Division when he was starting out there. He had a talent for it.

The photos of the bodies and the papers were already piling up in a cleared space inside the house. The crime scene techs wanted to get to those first, naturally. So they'd moved out a bunch of old furniture and garbage in what might have been Burton's dining room years before. Then they began going through the boxes, looking for anything that might help ID the dead people in the pictures.

And there were a lot of them. Lundquist, over the phone, had told Jesse they'd uncovered a hundred more photos of dead people so far. Some were duplicates or multiple angles of the same killing, and some didn't show the victims' faces. There had to be photographic evidence of at least sixty different murders, and there was still more, not counting the ones Jesse still had in the folder in his car.

But not one of them had a name attached. Without more information, there was nothing to connect them to any known killings.

Jesse hadn't expected it to be that easy, to be honest. He'd thanked Lundquist and asked him to keep him informed, and then focused on the part of the puzzle that belonged solely to him: Phil Burton.

Burton had lived in his town for years, but nobody seemed to know him. Even Jesse didn't know him, and Jesse knew a lot of people. Molly knew *everyone*, and she'd never seen Burton, either.

A recluse. A hoarder. A man who died alone in the wreckage of a wasted life, surrounded by memories of death. On a stack of cash bigger than most people ever saw. Like some kind of demented version of an ancient king in a burial mound, his corpse piled on top of all his wealth.

Jesse smacked the ball into his glove.

He began to make a mental list. He had to call Dev and Lundquist again. He should reach out to the Feds, see if the serial numbers on the cash matched anything on their lists. He thought of a dozen other small chores that needed doing.

But most of all, Jesse needed to know who Phil Burton was before something in him went wrong and he retreated from the world.

To do that, he needed to find Matthew Peebles. Burton's only friend, who'd scampered away at the first sign of trouble, but who was concerned enough to alert the police.

Jesse thought about it. Why would a guy in his twenties from New York be friends with an aging hoarder in Paradise? He'd said Burton was a friend of the family, but Jesse didn't buy that, not after what he'd found in the piles of Burton's trash. Peebles had to know more than he'd said.

Jesse realized his hand stung, even with the glove. He was putting a lot of power into his wrist. He was angry.

He knew himself well enough to know that. It wasn't just the lack of sleep. Something about this case was bothering him.

What he couldn't figure out was why.

He shoved it aside. Put the ball and glove back into their spot on the desk. The glove was a custom replica of the one he'd used in the minors, a gift from his son, Cole, who was out in California again. They hadn't talked for a while. Jesse knew he should call. He put that on the list with everything else.

Jesse looked at his notebook and the driver's license information he'd taken down about Peebles. No criminal record in Massachusetts, but maybe NYPD had a line on him. He sat down and reached for the phone to get started.

But before he could lift the phone, Ellis Munroe, the district attorney, walked into his office, pausing only to rap his knuckles lightly on the door.

"Got a minute?"

Jesse stared at him. Ellis labored under the belief that he was Jesse's boss, which he thought gave him the right to enter Jesse's office uninvited.

Jesse looked past Ellis and called to Molly, in the outer office. "Molly, did I have a meeting with Ellis Munroe this morning?"

"Jesse, come on—" Ellis began.

"I told him not to go in there," Molly called back. "He went right past me."

"Sorry, Molly," Ellis said.

"You apologize to her?" Jesse said.

"Yes, I apologize to Molly. I've known her longer than

I've known you. Our kids went to school together. My son took one of her daughters to a dance once. You, on the other hand, are the chief of police, and I can come into your office whenever I damn well please."

He leaned in closer and spoke in a lower voice. "Also, do I look stupid enough to pick a fight with Molly Crane? Give me some credit, Stone."

"Flattery will get you nowhere, Ellis," Molly said.

"Thank you, Molly. I've got it," Jesse said. He sat back in his chair. "Well? What do you want?"

"I see you're in your usual mood this morning," Ellis said. "Okay. Let's get to it. I want to know where you put the two million dollars in cash you found at a crime scene last night."

The money. Of course. That much money was going to attract attention. It already had.

"How'd you hear about that?"

"Jesse. Come on. A dead man on top of a couple million dollars? Everyone in town knows about it. And I shouldn't have had to hear about it from anyone else. Now, where did you put it?"

"It's still with Dev. He'll send it over to the state evidence facility when he's done with it."

"That money belongs to Paradise," Ellis said. "We should have it."

Jesse kept himself from laughing out loud at Ellis. "Really?"

"Money and other valuables gathered in the commission of a crime can be confiscated under both civil and criminal penalties by the responsible jurisdiction," Ellis said, almost making it sound like he was quoting some court decision. "The Town of Paradise should hold on to that money until we determine the proper ownership, and its proper disposal."

"We don't have the facilities to keep it safely," Jesse said. "You want me to lock it in a jail cell? Besides, it's a little sticky."

"It wasn't your call, Jesse. That should have been up to me. I should have been informed."

"I just got in, Ellis," Jesse said. "I would have called you."

"Yeah," Ellis said. "Sure you would have. Eventually."

Jesse shrugged. "Well, you're here now. You want to know what we know?"

"If you could spare the time in your busy schedule," Ellis said.

"Don't be shitty, Ellis," Molly said from her desk.

"Sorry, Molly," Ellis said again.

Jesse wondered how he could scare Ellis as much as Molly did. He wasn't sure it was possible without drawing his gun. Something to consider in the future.

"I don't have a lot to tell you yet, Ellis," Jesse said. "It's why I didn't call. We've got a dead body on top of a lot of money. We've got photos of other dead bodies packed among a couple metric tons of garbage. We're unpacking it as fast as we can."

"Do you think this dead guy—"

"Phil Burton."

"—whatever. You think he was a serial killer?"

Jesse inhaled deeply through his nose. He was trying to keep his temper with Ellis. He really was.

"No," he said.

Ellis waited. Jesse didn't say anything else.

"That's it?"

Jesse nodded. That was all he had to say.

"Then what the hell are the pictures of the bodies doing there? Why did he have all that money?"

"Well, those are very good questions, Ellis. We certainly intend to look into that."

"Don't patronize me, Jesse. I want answers."

Jesse had had enough. "Ellis. You want answers? So do I. Will you please get out of here so I can find them?"

Ellis sat for a second longer, scowling. "I want to be kept informed, Stone," he said.

He tried to glare. Jesse tried to look terrified. Neither of them was very successful.

He got up and left the office.

"Next time, call first," Molly said, as Ellis exited, doing his best not to slam the door.

"You couldn't keep him out of my office?" Jesse said to Molly.

"Deputy chief, not your secretary," Molly said.

Jesse tried to get his thoughts back in order. He had calls to make. A crime to solve. A new hire to onboard, as Molly said.

"Is there anything in that book of management techniques about doing what your boss tells you?" he asked her.

"No, but there is a whole chapter on setting proper boundaries," she said. "You should read it."

SIX

J esse went over the personnel file of Derek Tate. He felt
a little uncomfortable. He hadn't had as much time
with Tate as he'd wanted, and he was, despite what Molly
said, very careful about who he allowed to join his team.
They were a small department, and they had to work
closely together in all kinds of bad situations.

But the mayor, Gary Armistead, had been pushing
Jesse to fill the open spots in the roster. "You've been
bitching about a lack of personnel for as long as you've
been in the job," he said. "Now you're dragging your feet.
Just hire someone already."

Armistead and Jesse did not get along. But, Jesse had
to admit, he had a point. The problem was, there was a
shortage of police officers—and all first responders—
nationally. COVID and the unrest in the cities during the
lockdown had hollowed out a lot of the bigger departments

as veterans took early retirement or simply quit altogether. Now those cities were luring good cops away from small departments with higher salaries and better benefits. Jesse had lost two new recruits to Boston and New York in the last year.

So when Tate's application crossed the mayor's desk, he sent it on to Jesse with a Post-it telling him that this was his next employee.

On paper, Tate looked good. He was young. He'd worked for a couple of bigger departments, starting out in Philadelphia before moving over to the Helton PD.

When Jesse had interviewed him, he'd asked why Tate wanted to leave the bigger cities.

"A couple reasons. I want to have a family someday," Tate had said. "I want my kids to be able to walk to school safely. That's the kind of town where I want to live, and I want to be a cop."

Then he'd taken a deep breath and told Jesse the other reason. "And you're going to find this out eventually, but I screwed up in Philly," he'd said. "I got too rough with a civilian. You know how it is. I was new, I was overwhelmed by everything going down around me. And this guy came up behind me, and I swung—"

"And you ended up hurting him."

"Yeah," Tate had said.

Jesse had, in fact, seen the incident report in Tate's file. But like all of these reports, it was light on details, just in case it ever showed up as evidence in court. No police force ever wanted to look too closely into its officers, just from a liability standpoint.

Tate had not been asked to leave Philly—he'd transferred to Helton on his own. But he'd cracked an unarmed civilian in the head, which was definitely against procedure. The guy had escaped with only a concussion and some bruising, according to the report. Maybe there was a lawsuit. Tate's personnel file didn't say.

"I screwed up," Tate said again. "I know that. I didn't get into this job to hurt people. I want to help them. And I did the wrong thing here. The guy was coming to me for help. He was looking for his kid, a little boy, they'd gotten separated. And I clocked him without thinking about it."

In most departments, that wouldn't be enough to get Tate fired. So Jesse wondered what made this different.

He'd asked Tate that same question in the interview.

When he answered, Tate had looked genuinely ashamed. "It was my fault. I didn't sign up to be a soldier, sir. I did enough of that in the army. I want to look people in the eye. So I chose to go to a smaller PD."

"Helton was still too big for you?"

Tate shrugged. "Honestly, I think I'd like it better here. I could *do* better here. This seems like a place where I could make a fresh start. You know what I mean?"

Jesse did. That's what Paradise had been for him.

Jesse had been a drunk, and it cost him his badge with the LAPD. He'd made mistakes that came back to haunt him. He'd hurt people.

So he could understand wanting to start over.

After the interview, Jesse had decided to take a chance on Tate. Give him a shot at redemption, the same way Paradise had given him one.

He'd changed his life here. He'd made it better. He'd found a family, of sorts, in Molly and Suit and all the other people who'd trusted him. He figured Tate could do the same, if he wanted.

Jesse wanted to give him that chance.

Molly knocked on his door, bringing him out of his thoughts. "The new kid is here. Are they getting younger or are we getting older?"

"Gotta be the first," Jesse said. "Because we're just as young and attractive as we've ever been."

Molly gave him a brilliant smile. "Well, at least one of us is."

"Which one?"

"I think we both know the answer to that."

Jesse felt a little better for the first time that morning. "Send him in," he said. "Let's start onboarding."

Derek Tate came into Jesse's office, his Paradise PD uniform tight and spotless. Jesse wondered if he'd had it tailored. He was a good-looking kid, only a couple of years older than Jesse's own son, Cole. White. Brown-haired, blue-eyed, gym-built muscle.

He wore a tactical vest under the shirt and the full range of gear on his belt. He creaked just while standing there. Jesse didn't usually require his people to wear all the toys and tools while on patrol, but he understood Tate was still young. His back and kidneys wouldn't give him trouble for years.

"Ready to go out and kick ass and take names, Chief," Tate said, smiling.

Jesse didn't comment on that. Tate was young. "It's Jesse," he said. "We're not that formal around here."

"Got it," Tate said, still smiling. Well, at least someone was happy to be at work, Jesse decided.

"I'm going to need you to get over to the Burton house. Gabe and Suit have been there all night. You'll relieve them on the line, keep the neighbors and the lookie-loos away."

Tate frowned for the first time.

"Something wrong?"

"No," he said quickly. "I mean, I'm not a rookie. I was hoping to get out there and work cases. Really do the job, you know."

Jesse looked at him for a moment.

"I mean, I'm not complaining, Chief—" Tate said.

"Jesse," Jesse said. "Always Jesse. And I understand. You want to help. You're ready to go out and fight the bad guys. That's fine. But I'm sure you've already learned this by now: Ninety percent of police work is showing up and waiting around."

"Yessir," Tate said, still looking disappointed.

"Jesse," Jesse said again. "And don't worry, you'll get plenty of chances to do the job. I guarantee it. Because you know what the other ten percent of police work is?"

"What?"

"That's what happens when the bad guys show up, too."

SEVEN

At the Burton house, Suit was dead on his feet by the time Tate pulled up in his Paradise SUV.

"It's the new guy," Gabe Weathers said to him.

Suit yawned. *Thank God.* Elena was going to murder him if he didn't get home sometime soon.

A giant dumpster now sat on the road, already half-way full of things that couldn't be salvaged or couldn't possibly be used as evidence. Newspapers, stacks of them fused into solid blocks by years of mildew. Pizza boxes from restaurants that no longer existed. A sedimentary layer of beer cans crushed flat. Things like that.

The state evidence collection techs had been joined shortly after seven a.m. by a private crew of cleanup people. They also wore head-to-toe Tyvek suits and respirators—the air inside the house had grown steadily more rank as each layer of filth was unearthed—but in different colors. The state evidence people had basic white. The private crew was in a whole rainbow. It reminded Suit of that game he played sometimes on his phone, with the little spacemen in their spacesuits.

The new guy—Tate, Jesse had reminded him in a text—came out of the SUV, all smiles.

"Hey, guys, what's up?" he said, bringing a box of donuts and a tray of coffees.

"Not me, not anymore," Suit said.

Tate put the donuts and coffee down on the hood of the nearest Paradise SUV. He shook hands with Gabe and Suit. They went around with introductions. Tate seemed delighted when he heard Suit's name.

"Call me Slate," Tate said.

That stopped Suit.

"Slate?" he said. "I thought it was Tate."

Slate smiled. "Yeah, well, it's a nickname. Guys gave it to me at my old job."

"Slate," Gabe said, like he was testing the word out in his mouth. He looked at Tate for a long moment.

"Yeah," Tate said.

"Why did they call you that?" Gabe asked.

Tate looked a little uncomfortable. He shrugged. "Dunno," he said.

"You don't know?" Gabe asked, same deadpan expression, same monotone voice. Suit had seen him use both when questioning suspects.

"Well," Tate said, "I guess it was because I was so hard."

"'Hard,'" Suit said.

"Yeah. You know," Tate said. "Like a rock. Granite. Slate."

Gabe and Suit looked at each other, both thinking the same thing: Was this guy trying to give himself a cool nickname?

Suit hadn't given himself his nickname. He didn't even like it at first. He'd never heard of the ballplayer who shared his name. But he was a rookie, so he learned to answer to it. And after a while, it just became part of him.

That was how nicknames worked. You couldn't just tag yourself with one because you thought it was badass. Had no one ever explained that to Tate?

"Isn't slate the stuff they make chalkboards out of?" Gabe asked.

Tate looked uncomfortable. "I guess. Maybe."

"Huh," Gabe said. "I don't think of chalkboards as particularly hard."

Tate looked down, then away, a red flush working its way up from his neck to his forehead.

Suit tried not to grin.

"Suit, did you find chalkboards hard when you were in school?"

"Only in math."

"Look, it's just a nickname," Tate muttered. "Use it or don't."

Whatever, Suit thought. He took a donut. At least Tate got the first part of police work right.

Gabe did the same and they both headed to their cars.

"Uh, hey, wait," Tate said, standing by the yellow tape. "Anything I should know? Any troublemakers?"

Troublemakers? Suit thought. The street was empty.

The techs and the cleaners were doing their work. The local TV station got some video and left. The neighbors got bored hours ago.

"No," Suit said. "No troublemakers."

He turned to leave again.

"But what should I do if someone comes by?" Tate's voice, calling him back again.

Gabe gave Suit a look. He was struggling not to smirk. Not doing a great job of it.

"Just keep people off the property," Suit said. "Keep them on the other side of the tape. Standard crime scene procedure. If you run into anything you can't handle, call Molly, and she'll get some help out here. But you should be fine."

"Molly," Tate said. "She's the one with the great ass, right?"

Gabe stopped smirking. Suit froze in place, staring at Tate.

Even Peter Perkins, on the other side of the rising garbage pile, heard that. He stopped what he was doing, too.

"What?" Suit said, his voice dangerously quiet.

Tate didn't catch the tone. He kept grinning. "I mean, I know she's a mom, but she's definitely a mom I'd like to—"

"Deputy Chief Crane is your superior officer," Suit said, his voice suddenly a full octave deeper and much sharper. "And aside from Jesse, there is no better cop. Understand?"

Tate's eyes went a little wide. "Uh," he said. "I was just—"

"Do you understand?" Suit asked again.

Tate had the good sense to look down, shamefaced.

"Yeah. Sorry. I was just joking around."

Suit and Gabe and Peter all looked at him for a full thirty seconds, the silence growing uncomfortably long. Even some of the techs stopped what they were doing.

"Yeah," Suit said. "All right."

He tossed the donut into the nearby dumpster. Suddenly not hungry at all. He and Gabe walked to their vehicles without looking back at Tate.

"Damn, Suitcase Simpson finally met someone he didn't like," Gabe said quietly. "You worried he's going to replace you as Jesse's favorite son?"

"I didn't like how he talked about Molly," Suit said.

"Come on, we always give Molly crap. She can take it."

"To her face. Never behind her back."

"Just saying, you might have been a little hard on him."

"You think what he said was okay?" Suit said.

Gabe shook his head. "I think he's a new guy. Trying to fit in. I know we all love Molly, but he pulls that with her, she'll stomp his head down between his shoulder blades. He made a mistake."

"Maybe," Suit said, stopping at his car and opening the door. "But who tries to give themselves a nickname?"

Gabe shrugged. "Whatever you say, Suitcase."

Suit looked back at Tate, now handing out the donuts and coffee to everyone who was still at the scene. All smiles again. Not a hint of any embarrassment or anger.

But Suit could have sworn he saw something when he was staring at Tate. Something passing over his face before he looked down.

Not shame. But rage.

"Something about the guy just bugs me," Suit said.

EIGHT

Jesse signed off on Tate's paperwork and finally had a moment to get back to the case. He'd been trying to get NYPD on the line all day, but one thing after another kept cropping up.

"Molly, call NYPD for me," he shouted.

"I'm busy," she shouted back.

"Busy doing what?" he snapped.

"Busy knowing how to dial a phone without anyone helping me," she snapped back.

Jesse sighed. He didn't need this today.

Then Molly came into his office with a stack of papers, fresh from the laser printer, in her hand.

"Matthew Peebles," she said, putting the papers on Jesse's desk. "Resident of New York. Thirty-four years old. Occupation: club manager."

"Where did you get this?" Jesse asked.

"The wonders of the Internet," Molly said. "I could have emailed all this to you, but you're a caveman who hates and fears our modern ways."

Jesse just stared at her.

"I will take that blank stare as praise for my brilliant research," Molly said. "So listen. The address on Peebles's driver's license is out of date. His credit report shows he's moved twice since then. I called NYPD to see if they could do a drop-by to talk to him at his latest place."

"And?"

"The guy who answered told me he'd get on it just as soon as they solved every other crime in New York City."

"Ah, the spirit of cooperation."

"Yeah, he was almost as grumpy as you."

"Funny," Jesse said.

"Wasn't trying to be."

"So all this information and we still don't know anything."

"In fact, I have already taken steps to find Mr. Peebles, which reminds me of a cartoon character, now that I say it out loud."

"Molly, would you please get to the goddamn point."

"You *are* in a mood, aren't you?" Molly said. "I showed some initiative. Called the landlord of his current apartment building, got the manager's name and number. When I talked to him, he was a good citizen. He told me Peebles had been gone for a couple days and hadn't returned. He even went into the apartment and checked for me."

"Huh," Jesse said. He thought for a moment. "So he came here to Paradise and hasn't come home yet."

"All evidence points in that direction."

"Which means he could still be around here, waiting to see what happens at Burton's place."

"And that," Molly said, "is the goddamn point. You're welcome." She turned and left Jesse's office.

"Good work, Molly. Thank you," Jesse said.

"Deputy chief," she said. "Not your secretary, not just a pretty face. I think I've mentioned it."

At that moment, exactly 12.3 miles away from Jesse's office, Matthew Peebles sat on the coverlet of the bed in the motel room and tried to decide exactly how screwed he was.

He watched the morning news on WBZ, looking at the video of the growing pile of debris on the front lawn of Phil's house. He knew this was his fault. What he didn't know was how he could possibly fix it.

This was supposed to be easy. A regular little favor. Barely a chore. He went by the old man's place and made sure he was still alive. Dropped off an envelope sometimes. Most of the time, the old guy barely cracked the front door. Grabbed the envelope with one clawlike hand, like a toy bank Matthew had when he was a kid, a zombie's hand that emerged from a grave whenever you put a coin on it and snatched the coin down into its coffin.

He wondered what happened to that bank.

The reporter on the TV, all tanned, with bright white teeth and slick hair, said something that Matthew felt like a punch in the stomach.

"And now I'm being told by sources close to the investigation, Lisa, that police have found pictures of dead people in the house. There has been no comment from the Paradise PD, but these same sources tell us the hoarder was found sleeping on a mattress made of hundred-dollar bills, totaling possibly millions of dollars, I'm told."

"Wow, Ty, that is really something. A real mystery."

"I guess he didn't want to use the banks, Lisa. Or a maid."

The anchors laughed politely at the not-very-funny joke, and moved on to the weather and sports.

Matthew stayed where he was. Any chance of this going away on its own was long gone now. A hoarder with millions of dollars in his house packed with crap? That was national news right there. And pictures of bodies? That couldn't be good.

When his phone buzzed on the bed next to him, Matthew knew who it was. Of course he'd be watching the news. Matthew's luck just kept getting better.

Matthew took a deep breath and answered, because dodging the call was only delaying the inevitable.

"Hello?" he said.

"Well," a dry, raspy voice said to him. "You have well and truly fucked the dog on this one, haven't you?"

This wasn't his fault, Matthew wanted to say.

But he knew there was no way he could say it. He was, he had to admit, too chickenshit to ever talk back.

The man on the phone was more frightening than any zombie or ghoul or horror movie.

"I didn't know—"

"Shut up. I don't want to hear any more about how

you screwed this up. Now we're going to talk about how you make it right."

Matthew listened. He even found a pen and a pad on the hotel desk and took notes. He was very committed to doing as he was told.

And when he hung up, he looked at his new set of instructions, and he wondered how he could have ever, in his life, thought it was cool to be a gangster.

NINE

Daisy heard about the trouble over at Phil Burton's house. She was a friend to Jesse and his officers. She knew that they didn't always take the time to take care of themselves. So even though she gave them all a lot of crap when they came into her café, she always took care of them.

She told her latest hire, a completely dim-witted kid named Jordyn who was baffled by everything from the cash register to the coffee maker, to watch the place for a while. The breakfast rush was down to only a few people lingering over their coffees. She hoped Jordyn could handle that. Daisy loaded up her car with muffins and pastries and big catering jugs of coffee and drove out to the Burton house.

She saw the police tape and the state crime scene crew filing in and out of the house carrying junk. One of the techs was pushing a wheelbarrow with a half-deflated tire. She wondered if that was part of their equipment or if it had been buried in the house with all the other stuff piling up on the lawn.

Daisy stared at all the junk, wide-eyed. She had no idea how that mountain of trash had fit inside Burton's place. She saw Peter Perkins disappear around a stack of cardboard boxes, and she stepped onto the lawn, prepared to call out to him.

But someone shouted at her first.

"What the fuck do you think you're doing? Don't move!"

Daisy froze. In one arm she had three boxes of muffins. In her other hand she had a jug of coffee.

The crime scene techs were frozen, too. Everyone turned to look at her.

She turned to look in the direction of the voice.

And saw a cop in a Paradise PD uniform charging at her, face red, hand on his holster.

"I said don't fucking move!" he shouted again. "Drop what's in your hands! Do it! Now!"

Daisy looked at him, confused. Surely he couldn't be talking to her. She looked behind her—nobody there—and back at him again. It would have been comical if the cop didn't stomp to the edge of the tape and shout in her face.

"Are you deaf? I said drop it! Now!"

Daisy was not about to dump three dozen muffins and a pot of perfectly good coffee onto the ground. She never liked to waste food.

"Now, hold on—" she began, trying to smile.

She didn't get any further. The cop cut her off. "Is this funny to you? I gave you an order. Put the goddamn stuff down and let me see your goddamn hands."

And then he unsnapped the holster on his gun and put his hand on it, like he was prepared to take it out right there.

It took only a second, but the moment stretched for what seemed like forever as Daisy tried to process what was happening.

Daisy had been in Paradise for so long, she had gone from pain-in-the-ass troublemaker to beloved institutional figure. She once had to be prepared to fight anyone—sometimes literally—who made bigoted comments about her sexuality or her rainbow flag over her business. Now she was more or less accepted. Although over the last few years, she had seen more of the bigots mouthing off, like they'd suddenly been given a hall pass out of detention and were running all over the place.

But all the time Jesse had been chief of the Paradise PD, she'd known the cops had her back. Jesse wouldn't have it any other way. He treated people like people. Everyone. Didn't matter who. She loved him a little for that.

And now there was this kid, *this kid she'd never even seen before*, screaming at her and putting a hand on his gun.

She was, for once in her life, speechless.

Peter Perkins rushed over to see what all the shouting was about.

"Hey," he said. "Hey. New guy."

The young cop turned and glared at Peter as if he might draw down on him, too.

Daisy was suddenly aware of how old and frail Peter looked. He was supposed to retire a while ago. His face was lined and his hair was gray. The kid looked like he ate fifty-pound weights like pancakes.

"Sorry," Peter said, smiling. "Don't know your name yet."

The young cop snorted. "It's Tate."

"First or last?"

His eyes narrowed. "What?"

"Is that your first or last name?" Peter said, still quiet and gentle.

"Uh. Last." The young cop finally seemed to realize that all work had stopped on the crime scene. Everyone was staring.

"Right. Okay. Officer Tate. This is Daisy. She's a local business owner here in Paradise. Daisy's café. You been?"

"What?"

"Have you been?"

"No," Tate said, eyes still locked on Daisy.

"Really? You're missing out. Best food in town," Peter said. "I'm sure the chief would have taken you to Daisy's and introduced you if he'd had time. Anyway, she's a friend. She makes a point of bringing us coffee and snacks when we're working a big case."

The young cop—*Tate,* Daisy thought, *his name is Tate,* and she repeated it to herself so she wouldn't forget—scowled again. "She shouldn't approach an active crime scene with stuff in her hands. Or cross the line."

"Did she cross the line?" Peter asked, still very gentle. He looked pointedly at the crime scene tape.

Daisy was a couple of feet away, on the other side.

Tate went red in the face again. "She approached a crime scene. I was doing my job."

"She's bringing coffee and muffins," Peter said. "She does it all the time. You didn't know."

"I was doing my job," Tate said again, but his voice was smaller now. He looked deeply uncomfortable.

Peter lifted the crime scene tape.

"Daisy," he said. "Thank you for bringing the food. It's really nice of you and we always appreciate it. And I can see you've met our newest recruit."

He was trying to laugh it off. Tate still glared at her like she belonged in cuffs.

If Jesse had been here, Daisy might have said something funny and sharp. Like, "Did you think I was smuggling a bomb in the blueberry muffins?" Something to make it funny, to defuse the tension.

But inside, Daisy still felt cold. He'd gone for his gun. *He'd gone for his gun.*

So she didn't feel like making jokes.

"I wasn't the one who crossed a line here, Peter," she said, her voice still shaking a little despite her best efforts.

Peter threw Tate a significant look. Tate caught it. "Sorry," he mumbled, glancing away from her. "I didn't know."

Daisy didn't say anything to him. The adrenaline washed out of her now, leaving her legs a little rubbery and her arms weak.

She passed the boxes and the coffee to Peter.

Then she turned and walked away without another word.

She could feel everyone's eyes on her as she went to her

48

car. She still had another three boxes of pastries and a couple more jugs of coffee in the back.

She left them there, started her car, and carefully drove away, headed to her café.

They all watched her go. She didn't care.

For the first time ever, she felt like a criminal in Paradise.

And she had no idea what to do about it.

TEN

Daisy went to Jesse. Because of course she did. She drove right from the Burton house to the station, because Jesse was her friend, and he'd want to know. He'd want to know, and he'd listen to her, and he'd help.

He always did.

She entered the station and walked directly back toward Jesse's office. She didn't bother to stop or say hello to Molly, but Molly stood and looked in her direction anyway.

"Daisy?" she said, her voice tentative, like she was afraid of spooking a wild animal. "Are you okay?"

"I need to see Jesse."

"It's not a great time."

"I need to see him, Molly," she said, and kept going.

Molly didn't stop her.

She entered Jesse's office. He had his back to her,

staring into nothing, slapping that stupid ball into his stupid mitt.

And then it came pouring out of her, the anger and the fear. She never wanted to look scared. She was tough. She'd made a life out of being tough, because that's what you had to be when she was growing up. An openly gay woman had to be tough to hear all the insults and the veiled threats and the not-so-veiled ones and keep going forward. It was either that or hide from the world, and Daisy was damned if she'd hide.

"Your fucking new officer is a goddamn lunatic," she said.

Jesse turned, his face pulled into a deeper frown than usual. If he'd come into the café like this, Daisy might have noticed. She might have seen that something was bothering him, deep down, working its way to the surface. But she'd just been frightened half out of her mind, and this wasn't the café, so she'd missed it completely.

Instead, all she heard was his heavy sigh and his bored tone. "Come on in, Daisy. Nice to see you, too."

"Don't give me that, Jesse. That kid is a menace. He is dangerous, and I cannot believe you put him on the force."

He put the ball and the mitt down and sat in his chair. "What happened?" He sounded tired. Or bored.

Which only made Daisy angrier. "He pulled a gun on me when I tried to bring muffins and coffee! Muffins, Jesse!"

Jesse sat up. That got his attention. "He pulled a gun on you?"

"Well," Daisy said, thinking back. It didn't happen

exactly that way. "No. Not all the way out of its holster. He put his hand on it. And he screamed at me. And he—"

"What were you doing?"

"I was bringing muffins! Jesus!"

"I'm sorry. I meant to say, what did he say you were doing? Why did he react like that?"

Daisy didn't like this. It wasn't going like she thought it would. "He said I crossed the crime scene tape—"

"Did you?"

"No!" Daisy was shouting again. "Jesus Christ, Jesse, even if I had, would that be a reason to shoot me?"

Jesse put both hands up as if in surrender. "I'm sorry. He's new. I'm sure he was just a little overanxious. The training says to keep a hand near your weapon when confronting a suspect—"

"I am not a suspect, Jesse!"

"Of course you're not. But he didn't know you. And it was an active crime scene—"

Daisy could not quite believe what she was hearing. "Are you saying what he did was right?"

"No. I'm sure it was just a mistake. I'll speak to him."

His mouth was a hard line. He seemed to think that was the end of it. But Daisy was not about to leave it there.

She made one last try to explain. "Jesse, you know me. You know I would not come to you if it was just about my feelings getting hurt. This was not normal. It was pure rage. I really thought he was going to shoot me."

"I'm sure you did. But sometimes a police officer has to make a quick decision—"

That was about all Daisy could stand. "Oh, bullshit. If your cop can't tell the difference between a middle-aged woman carrying muffins and a hardened criminal, then you need to take away his gun before he hurts someone. What do you think will happen next?"

Now Jesse's eyes went dark. Daisy had seen it before. Everyone in town knew that Jesse Stone was a dangerous man. He'd proven it a dozen times or more. But Daisy had always thought that his anger was reserved for people who deserved it. Criminals. People who would hurt people like her.

At this moment, she saw it aimed at her.

"What I think is that I am working a case, Daisy. People are dead. And there's more important things going on here than your muffins, okay?"

Daisy stepped back. She realized they were both facing off like boxers.

"You cannot think this is okay, Jesse. I have supported and helped you and your cops for years. I am your friend."

"Daisy. I can't play favorites."

"I'm not asking you to. I'm asking you to listen."

"I have. I'll listen to Tate, and then maybe you can come in and the two of you can talk it over."

"No," Daisy said, shuddering at the thought of being in the room with that man again, looking at the pure anger in his eyes. "No. We're past that."

Jesse stepped back, too. He rubbed his face with his hands. Tried to smile at her. For a second, she thought they were about to sit down and start over. Talk it out calmly. Then she could make him understand.

Instead, Jesse said, "Daisy, do you think maybe you're just overreacting a little? Police work isn't like baking muffins."

Daisy stood for a moment, making sure she'd actually heard him properly, that he really had just said that to her.

"Goddamn it, Jesse," Daisy said. "How dare you."

She turned on her heel and walked out of his office, not looking back.

ELEVEN

Derek, can you come in here a second?" Tate heard Jesse call as soon as he stepped inside the door from his shift.

Tate took a deep breath and tried to remember everything Bill Fawcett, the Helton chief, had told him before he left that department.

"Stone is a big believer in second chances, because he was a drunk when he came to Paradise," Fawcett had said. So Tate had laid it on thick in the interview. He thought he'd said all the right things.

But now he knew he was in trouble again. He'd lost it with that Daisy Dyke woman. He saw someone disrespecting him, disrespecting the uniform, and the red mist came down like it always did.

Truth be told, it had happened to Tate for a long time before he ever wore a badge. Any time someone got in his way, got in his face, or told him what to do, he felt the rage well up inside, inflating him, making him ten times stronger than normal.

And then, a few minutes later, he saw the wreckage as if it hadn't been him who'd done any of it.

He felt like he could do anything at moments like that. It was one reason he became a cop. He figured if he was telling people what to do, then there was less of a chance they'd piss him off. Disobey a cop, Tate thought, and you deserved whatever you got.

But he had to be careful. He knew this was his last chance, here in Paradise. Stone held his career in his hands.

So he plastered an idiot grin on his face and walked into Jesse's office.

"Hey, Chief, what's up?"

Tate thought he sounded normal. Stone looked at him for a second that felt like it stretched out much longer. He was so still behind the desk. Like he didn't want to waste a single motion. Frankly, it creeped Tate out.

But he kept smiling.

"It's Jesse," Stone said. "Not 'Chief.' Always Jesse."

"Sorry. I guess I'm kind of a stickler for chain of command."

Stone seemed to like that. He smiled a little. Then he asked the question Tate had been dreading.

"What happened at the Burton house today?" he asked.

Your dyke friend got too close to a crime scene, Tate wanted to snap, but didn't. Instead, he played dumb. "What do you mean?"

"I heard you had a run-in with my friend Daisy?"

"Oh, that? She's a friend of yours? Yeah, I mean, I got a little loud. I was worried about her approaching all the evidence. It's a lot of stuff and, you know, it's all part of the case."

"Is that it?"

"I mean, yeah," Tate said. "It was nice of her to drop off the food and coffee. Everyone sure liked it."

Tate wondered if this was possibly playing it too dumb.

"Maybe I was a little overzealous," he said. "It's my first day. I might have been trying to make a good impression."

"Okay," Stone said.

Tate let that sit there, trying to look pleasant and harmless.

"Tell you what, Derek," Stone said, after another pause. "I want you to spend some time on foot on your next shift. Just walk around Paradise. Get out of your car and get to know people."

Tate did his best to look confused. "Okay. I guess."

"Is that a problem?"

Immediately suspicious. *Crap.* Tate tried to backtrack. "Well, no, Chief—"

"Jesse."

"Right, sorry, Jesse. It's just that I won't really be able to cover much ground that way."

"I'm not worried about that. We'll call you if there's a problem."

Tate shrugged. "You're the boss."

"I want you to talk to people. Learn who they are," Stone said. "And they'll learn who you are, too. In Paradise, that's important. People need to trust you."

Tate was doing his best to show his belly and look submissive, but damn, Stone was making it hard. *Foot patrol?* Like he was some goddamn rookie? He saw red at the edges of his vision again.

"I didn't do anything wrong," he said. It just slipped out.

"I didn't say you did."

Tate muttered something under his breath.

"Pardon?" Stone asked, a little more edge in his voice than Tate would have liked.

Again, he couldn't stop himself. "I said, you're kinda acting like it."

Stone stared at him.

Tate knew all the coded words in the cop world. He knew how to make the right noises for *civilian oversight* and *community engagement* and *proper use of force* so he could avoid a lawsuit. But Stone really seemed to take this crap *seriously.*

"You need to know people in this town if they're going to trust your judgment. And I need to trust it, too. This is the job."

Tate clenched his jaw tight and shoved the anger away. He shrugged. Nodded.

"I get it. I do."

"Good. Have a good day."

Jesse looked back down at his desk. Tate got out of the office as fast as he could.

TWELVE

At two-fifty-six a.m., Jesse sat in his Explorer, looking at the Burton house. The pile of trash and debris sat in the front yard, behind the evidence tape.

He thought maybe if he just kept staring at the pile of garbage, something might come to him.

He couldn't sleep. It happened a lot. So he got up, got dressed, and drove over to the Burton house. He'd sent Gabe home and told him he'd watch until Suit showed up in the morning. Gabe hadn't argued; he wanted the rest.

Jesse was just glad it wasn't raining. They needed to move all this evidence inside somewhere, but there hadn't been any time yet. Lundquist promised they'd begin trucking it all to a state evidence collection facility in the morning, but they'd needed to clear out enough space.

One night couldn't hurt, he and Jesse had decided.

Two million dollars and change, and Burton had been

sleeping on it. Files filled with pictures of dead people. Jesse still had the papers and Polaroids he'd grabbed back at the office, but there could be dozens, even hundreds, more hidden in the warrens of junk and piles of rotting trash.

The state crime scene people hadn't even finished going through the file boxes piled up around Burton on the couch. But they had found a deposit of margarine from what appeared to be the 1990s in a restaurant-sized case blocking the stairs.

Jesse rubbed his eyes and reached over for his thermos of coffee, wishing there was something stronger in it. The thirst was bad right now. Nothing he couldn't handle. But bad.

He thought about Daisy and Tate and their little altercation at the police line, then his own disastrous conversation with her in the office.

Jesse knew he had not handled that well. He was sleepless and tired and had been thinking about Burton and the case. He'd been impatient. Had just wanted Daisy out of his office, to be honest.

But he also found it hard to believe Daisy's dire warnings about Tate. So the kid had been a little overzealous. Every new cop had an adjustment period. He remembered his first days with the LAPD.

Well, he remembered most of them. He'd been drinking pretty hard then.

Jesse figured a little time on foot would give Tate a chance to see that Paradise wasn't Philadelphia, or even Helton. He could tell when someone wasn't thrilled about their assignment. Also, Tate wasn't doing much to hide it.

He seemed to withdraw into himself, like a turtle into its shell.

But he was new, Jesse reminded himself. He was used to bigger departments, bigger towns.

Still. It bothered him. Because Daisy was his friend—at least, she was before this morning—and she wasn't the kind of person to make things up. He'd meant to talk to Peter Perkins about it, but Peter went home directly from the scene, so Jesse didn't get a chance. They'd catch up tomorrow. Maybe that would shed some more light on the whole thing.

Maybe Tate could apologize and that would be the end of it.

He took a sip of the coffee, but it no longer tasted good. It wasn't what he wanted.

Goddamn it, he wanted a drink.

Then Jesse looked up. Headlights, coming down the street. He couldn't quite make out the car behind them—the residential neighborhoods in Paradise had opted for cute little streetlamps on the corners instead of high-intensity lights on overhead poles.

The car braked hard, then swung around in the street.

Jesse could see it better now. A Toyota, relatively new. The rear license plate was missing.

Maybe someone who'd just bought a new car. Maybe a drunk tourist who'd gotten lost on the way back to their hotel.

Maybe not.

Jesse reached for the dash, about to hit the siren, when the car door popped open and Peebles, the witness who'd skedaddled, stepped out quickly. He took two steps away from the car, winding up like a kid trying to chuck a stone across a pond.

Jesse saw what Peebles had in his right hand.

A glass bottle with a burning rag.

Catching a glimpse of Peebles's face in the flickering light, Jesse saw a mask of fear and sweat and panic.

He hit the siren, hoping to stop Peebles, distract him.

Too late.

The bottle flew through the air.

It hit the front of the house square under the eaves and exploded in a fireball. Molotov cocktail.

The dry old wood and peeling paint caught instantly.

THIRTEEN

J esse was out of the door, hand on his gun. "Peebles!"
he shouted.

Peebles was already back inside the car. The Toyota
peeled away, tires screeching, engine a high whine as Peebles floored it.

Jesse didn't want to fire after him, shooting blindly
into the dark. No telling where the bullet could end up.

He looked back at the house. The fire was already
spreading rapidly, years of accumulated scrap going up
like dry kindling.

Any chance of finding an answer could still be buried
under there. And the neighboring houses were at risk.

Jesse saw the Toyota's lights disappear around the
bend in the street.

He had a choice. But it was no choice at all, really.

He turned back to his Explorer and grabbed the mike from his dash. "This is Chief Stone. We've got a fire at the Burton place. Someone tossed a gasoline bomb into the house. We need all units and fire response immediately."

Then he ignored the sudden squawking of questions and alarm from the radio and ran toward the burning house.

The neat piles the crime scene techs had made were smoking. The heat from the fire was intense. He leaped over a stack of curtain rods and old draperies and charged up the front steps of the house. The door was already burning.

He kicked it open, pulling his leg back quickly as though he were trying to avoid being bitten. He turned just in time to avoid having his eyebrows singed off by the sudden burst of fire that roared out of the open door, fed by the fresh oxygen.

Jesse checked the entryway. Mostly tile, mostly clear. The ceiling obscured by rolling smoke.

Good enough.

He ran inside, T-shirt over his mouth, eyes watering, throat already closing up.

From memory, he turned left, into the room where Burton's body was.

Jesse remembered there were cases of motor oil. Stacks of newspapers and phone books.

Perfect fuel for a fire. He really hoped the techs had gotten that stuff out.

He could barely see a foot in front of him now. He bumped into a stack of boxes that went over in a shower of sparks.

He reached out and grabbed whatever he could. He brought a file box up to his chest.

The rest of the room was going up. He turned, began to run out the way he'd come, but bounced off a wall.

He'd gotten turned around.

The box in his hands was burning. Everything was burning.

He couldn't believe how fast it was all going.

Jesse took a moment to be still. Tamped down the instinctive panic of an animal trapped by heat and flame.

Looked for the smoke. Jesse saw it rolling in big clouds, tumbling in the direction of the fresh oxygen feeding the fire.

He heard something crack like a gunshot deeper in the house. He felt, more than heard, the ceiling shift above him.

Jesse ran in the direction of the smoke, hoping he was right.

He bounced off another wall. Tripped. Got back up.

Nothing but smoke on all sides of him now. Red-and-gold flames the only light he could see. Each breath into his lungs like inhaling broken glass. The pain in his hands reached his brain now. He had to get out now. Or he wasn't getting out at all.

He moved forward, pushing against the smoke like it was a solid thing.

And stumbled again, tripping, trying to stay upright.

He hit the ground, realizing he was under the night sky. He'd made it onto the lawn, which was now burning, too, the piles of trash and carefully collected evidence all going up at the same time.

Jesse managed to get to his feet again, made it farther down the lawn, the box still in his hands, smoldering but not aflame.

He dropped it and rolled, hoping that he wasn't on fire, either.

He finally stopped and rested on his back, wet enough from the dew on the lawn that he figured he must not be burning anymore. His lungs felt like they were medium rare. His hands were blistered and red.

He glanced over at the smoking, crumpled cardboard box a few feet away. It was an empty husk, the bottom burned out, whatever was inside it lost to the flames.

Jesse looked up at the stars, which seemed distant and peaceful, as sirens wailed in the distance.

FOURTEEN

D o you have a death wish, Stone?" Robbie Williams said, his face only inches from Jesse's. "Because there are easier ways to go, and none of them involve my guys risking their asses to save yours."

Jesse didn't respond. He was still sucking down oxygen through the mask the paramedics had given him. He was seated on the bumper of their ambulance, feeling a little crisp around the edges. He'd turned the mask down at first, but once they'd strapped it onto his head, he had to admit it made his lungs feel better and the spots stop dancing in front of his eyes.

Probably a coincidence, he decided.

Robbie was the fire chief of Paradise, and he'd never liked Jesse. He resembled a fire hydrant, short and squat, except that he spewed insults and abuse instead of water. His one saving grace was that he was good at his job, which is why Jesse had never punched him.

Robbie probably had similar thoughts about Jesse, actually.

Ordinarily they gave each other enough space to do their work. Robbie was violating that space right now, almost nose-to-nose with Jesse. Although, to be fair, Jesse had run into a burning building, which was technically Robbie's area.

"You want to explain to me what the flying fuck you were doing, Stone?"

"Ease up, Robbie," Suit said. Suit stood over Jesse as well, looking concerned.

Everyone from both departments was there, surrounding the ruins of the house, now just smoldering timbers. Robbie's guys were good—they'd kept the fire from spreading.

But everything inside the house, and most of the stuff on the lawn, was charcoal. A crowd had gathered. Now the TV crews from Boston were here. A potential murderer, a burning building, an injured cop. Everything they loved. Jesse could see the cameramen trying to get a shot of him.

"Fire doesn't make you deaf or mute, Stone," Robbie said. "Believe me, I would know. Now, you got an answer for me or what?"

Jesse took the mask off his face and looked at Robbie for a long beat. Even seated, he was almost as tall as Robbie. Robbie stepped back without seeming to realize it.

"That house was filled with evidence of dozens—

maybe hundreds—of murders," Jesse said. "I had to try to get what I could."

"Moron," Robbie said. "You think anything in that place was worth your life?"

"Guess we'll never know."

Robbie threw up his hands, turned, and stalked away.

Jesse flexed his fingers. They were still tender and blistered from where he'd grabbed the burning file box. The paramedics had wrapped them loosely in gauze.

Jesse looked at Suit. "Anything salvageable?"

Suit shook his head. "We had a few things down at the station, but most of it was still being tagged and excavated out here."

"I should have put it all into a warehouse."

"Jesse, we were working on it," Suit said. "You didn't know."

"It was just sitting out here."

"Come on, Jesse. Let's get you to the hospital."

"I'm fine."

"No, you're not," Suit said.

Jesse stood and looked at the burned house of Phil Burton again.

He felt sick and guilty and angry. So many people died, and they were all connected in some way to this man in his town.

He had a chance to find answers.

And he'd blown it. Literally. He'd screwed it up.

Suit put a hand on his shoulder.

Together, they walked to Suit's car and headed to the hospital.

The doctor who swept into the exam room was dark-eyed, slim and pale, her black hair pulled back in a messy bun. She kept her eyes on Jesse's chart until she was almost right on top of him.

"Chief Stone," she said, with a half-smile. "Figured I'd get to meet you in here sooner or later."

"It's Jesse."

"Jesse," she said. "Rachel Lowenthal. I'd offer to shake hands, but . . ."

"A funny ER doctor. You must leave your patients in stitches."

She rolled her eyes. "My kid learned the same joke last year, but in his defense, he's only six."

She put the chart down and examined Jesse's hands and arms carefully but quickly. She listened to his chest with her stethoscope. Then she got a scope and began looking down his throat and up his nose, which was less comfortable. Her movements were practiced and assured.

"So you thought it was a good idea to run into a house on fire?" she asked.

"Seemed like the right thing to do at the time."

"You're lucky," she said. "No blistering in the nose or throat, no damage to your sinuses. Some irritation, but that should pass. I'm going to bandage your hands with some burn pads and gauze. You'll need to come back in a couple days to change the dressings, or do it yourself. From your chart, I see you have plenty of experience getting hurt, so you're probably good with bandages."

She tossed the plastic cover from the tip of the scope into a nearby wastebasket. Quick and efficient. She told him to hold out his hands.

"You're new in town?" Jesse asked, as she gingerly cleaned his blistered skin.

"Not really," she said. "Been here about six months."

"I'm surprised we haven't met."

She smiled. "I'm surprised you've managed not to show up in the ER all this time. I've heard about you."

"What have you heard?"

"That you get shot so often I should probably be treating you for lead poisoning."

Jesse laughed. "I wouldn't say it's that often."

"I would. I saw your chart." Rachel finished cleaning the skin and placed thin, gel-like bandages on the palms and fingers of Jesse's hands, where the burns were worst. They made his skin look like steak under plastic wrap. "Tell me, have you ever considered ducking? Or getting behind things?"

Jesse laughed again.

"Hold still," she said.

"Sorry."

"These will cover the burns, but they breathe," she said. "Try not to put too much pressure or weight on them. You want something for the pain?"

"I'm good."

"Right. Tough guy. I almost forgot." She snapped off her gloves, tossed those into the wastebasket, too. "Okay, then. You're free to go."

Jesse figured, *What the hell.*

"Hey, Doc."

"Don't call me Doc," she said. "Really cannot stand that."

"Okay. Rachel."

"Dr. Lowenthal is fine." But she was still smiling, so he plowed ahead.

"Can I see you again?"

Her smile grew broader. "I am sure you'll manage to get hurt again. You'll be back in my ER before you know it."

"No, I meant coffee. Or dinner."

She looked tempted. Jesse was sure of it.

"No," she said after a moment. "I appreciate the offer. But no, I don't think so."

"Why not?" Jesse asked.

"Like I said, I've heard about you," Rachel said, as she headed for the door. "I'm not ready to join the Jesse Stone Lonely Hearts Club."

Then she was out and in the hallway.

"See you around," Jesse called after her.

"Drop by anytime," she called back.

Shot down hard, Jesse thought. That about fit with the way everything else was going in his life right now.

FIFTEEN

The pain in Jesse's hands wouldn't let him sleep, even though he'd been up all night at the scene, then at the hospital. At six a.m., he gave up trying. He showered and got dressed and headed to the station.

He'd barely gotten behind his desk when he received a call on his cell. It took him too long to get it out of his pocket with his clumsy hands, which felt like they were the size of catcher's mitts. Without looking at the screen, he answered.

"Hey, Chief, this is Ty Bentley at WBZ," the voice on the other end said.

Jesse spent a moment trying to remember Ty Bentley. He was new and young, like they all seemed to be these days. He finally placed him from a stand-up he'd done in front of a crime scene last year. Lots of makeup to make himself look tan. Product in his hair. Teeth unnaturally white.

There were only a couple of reporters Jesse trusted. One had recently left him for a job in New York. The other was not Ty Bentley.

"What's up, Ty?"

"I was doing the stand-up in front of the Burton place about the dead hoarder, and I happened to run downtown. That's when I found out you and your department have been banned from a local restaurant that has some kind of beef against cops," he said.

"What?"

"The restaurant owner has a sign in the window. NO COPS ALLOWED. I've already got photos if you want me to shoot them to you."

"No, thanks, Ty. Listen, I'm in the middle of something—"

"Right, the dead hoarder. Like I said, I'm covering that, too. Any updates there?"

"No comment."

Ty hesitated. "On which story?"

"Either one. Both. Take your pick."

"What?"

"No comment, Ty."

"Oh, come on, Jesse. This is good for you. Let me be on your side for once. I was thinking I'd come down there and we'd get you on camera, see if we can get your story out there."

"No," Jesse said.

Ty was struck silent for a beat. "But—isn't this discrimination against cops? Don't you want to let people know about that?"

"No comment, Ty."

"Chief, come on. I bet your officers would have something to say. And I bet Daisy would think twice about that little sign in her window if she got a little taste of the spotlight, if you know what I mean."

"What? Daisy?"

"Yeah. Daisy's café. I thought you guys were friends."

Jesse hung up. He breathed in deeply through his nose and exhaled through his mouth. His psychiatrist, Dix, had suggested it as a way to help him contain his temper sometimes. It didn't really help.

He got up and left the station, walking down the street toward Daisy's.

Jesse didn't quite believe Ty about Daisy. Ty had been known to stretch the facts to fit a story before. No outright lies, but definitely some bending and framing.

It was entirely possible, he thought, that he had been a little dismissive of Daisy and her complaint about Tate. Maybe they could talk. He was pretty sure everything could be smoothed over.

But when he got to Daisy's, he stopped dead in his tracks.

There was a sign, handmade, written with Day-Glo markers, taped to the front window.

It said: **NO PARADISE COPS ALLOWED.**

Four words. Simple and direct.

And yet he still had trouble understanding what they meant.

He opened the door.

And because he understood the intent of the sign if

not the reason it was suddenly staring him in the face, he stayed on the threshold of the café without stepping over it.

Everyone inside the café looked up from their breakfasts. Some looked away quickly, as if embarrassed. Others glared, as if daring Jesse to walk in. It was particularly disturbing to see Emmy Knox, the ninety-three-year-old volunteer head of the Friends of the Paradise Library Book Sale, clench her fists like she was prepared to throw down if Jesse put so much as a toe on the floor.

So. People were choosing sides. Jesse had seen it a lot in his time here, and that was never a good thing in a town as small as Paradise.

"Uh, Jesse," Jordyn, behind the counter, Daisy's latest assistant, said to him. "I'm sorry, man, but you can't come in."

"I'm not," Jesse said. "Can I speak with Daisy, please?"

"Um. She's in the back. Baking. I don't think she wants me to bother her."

Jordyn's eyes pleaded with Jesse, *Don't do this to me,* but Jesse didn't feel like letting him off the hook. He waited.

Jordyn took a deep breath and went into the kitchen.

Everyone could hear the tone of their conversation, if not the words. It didn't sound good.

Jesse tried to smile at Daisy's customers. There was a couple sitting at his table. The one where he always sat. They stared down into their coffees. Emmy Knox glared even harder at him.

Daisy emerged from the back. Face a blank slate, arms crossed.

"What?"

"No cops allowed?"

"I have the right to refuse service to anyone, as long as it's not based on race, creed, ethnicity, gender, or sexual orientation," Daisy said. "Believe me, I ran into plenty of people who tried to keep me out of places. I know the rules. You and your department are no longer welcome here."

"Don't you think you're taking this a little far, Daisy?"

"I need at least one place I feel safe in this town," she said. "And I don't want to take the chance your new hire will pull a gun on me or my customers."

"Daisy."

"What?"

Jesse shook his head. "You're really telling me I can't come in?"

"Does Derek Tate still have a job?"

"Yes."

"Then no."

"Can we talk about this?"

"I tried to talk to you, Jesse. You told me to stick to baking muffins. So that's what I'm doing. You stay on your side of the line. I'll stay on mine."

Jesse took a deep breath. Tried to count to ten. Got to five before Daisy spoke again.

"It's cold out, Chief," she said. "Please close the door."

"Fair enough," Jesse said, and turned on his heel and walked away.

SIXTEEN

Molly was at the station by the time he walked back inside. She handed him a fresh cup of coffee. He took it gratefully, even though the heat irritated the burns on his hands. It had been a long day already, and it was only eight-forty-five a.m.

"Wait," he said. "Since when do you get me coffee?"

"Don't shoot the messenger," she said. "The mayor is here."

Jesse rolled his eyes. Gary Armistead was not going to improve his day or his mood in any way.

"Remember, I only escorted them in," she said.

Jesse sighed heavily. "'Them'?"

"Ellis is with him, too," Molly said, and then, more quietly, "And I know you've had a terrible day already, but you can't punch them."

"Why not?"

"Because they'll probably fire you. And I don't want your job. So play nice."

Jesse grimaced. "I'm always nice."

That made Molly laugh. "Sure."

Jesse walked into his office, where Armistead and Ellis Munroe were already seated in front of his desk. They sat up straight, chests out, jaws set like they were going into a bar fight, or a tennis match, or whatever these two did on the weekends. Jesse didn't really know or care.

"Stone," Armistead said.

"Gary," Jesse said. "Ellis. Make yourself at home."

"Don't worry, Jesse. We won't be staying that long," Ellis said, and, with a flourish, slapped down a piece of paper on Jesse's desk.

Jesse read it.

Then looked up at both men, who sat there, proud of themselves.

"You can't be this stupid," he said.

Armistead's face went deep red.

"Jesse!" Molly shouted.

"Stop eavesdropping, Molly," Jesse called back. He picked up the paper. It was an order, signed by Ellis in his capacity as DA, claiming the $2 million in cash found in the Burton house as evidence and demanding it be turned over to the City of Paradise.

"This is a terrible idea," Jesse said. "I am still trying to find the suspect in this arson. I haven't identified a motive or any of the victims involved. And you want to get into a pissing match over the money."

"You haven't surrendered the case to the State Police," Ellis said. "The money is evidence in the case. We have every right to keep custody of it until the case is con-cluded."

Armistead finished for him: "And if there are no legal claimants to Burton's estate, that money belongs to the town."

"Finders keepers. Is that the legal standard?"

Ellis frowned at him. "Civil forfeiture, Jesse. You know that as well as I do. Any assets that are suspected to be the proceeds of a crime are subject to confiscation and sale or use by the government. In this case, that's us."

"That's usually for drug cases. This is not a drug case."

Ellis shrugged. "This much cash, who's to say? Drug dealers leave a lot of small bills lying around."

"It's not a drug case," Jesse said again.

"Well, the courts are pretty lenient on that standard," Ellis said. "And we still have a claim to the money as ille-gal proceeds of a crime."

"That money could do a lot of good here in town," Armistead said. "We still have a hole in the budget from the pandemic. Tax receipts are down, tourism is still re-covering. We've got roads that need fixing, maintenance for city buildings . . ."

A mayor's office that needs redecorating, Jesse thought but didn't say.

". . . and new equipment for you and the fire depart-ment," Armistead continued.

"I get all that," Jesse said. "What I don't understand is why you want to keep it here in Paradise instead of at the state evidence facility."

Ellis looked uncomfortable. Armistead didn't. He plowed

right ahead. "We don't want the state to get any ideas about claiming it."

"Are you serious?"

"It's a lotta money. People get greedy."

"Yeah, they do," Jesse said.

"Pardon?"

"Nothing." Jesse looked at Ellis. "You really think the state is going to try to steal the money from Paradise on the off-chance we get to claim it."

Ellis shrugged. "They could make an argument that they're entitled to part or all of it. The state evidence team collected and bagged it. And they've got a hole in their budget, too. Don't tell me you think they wouldn't jump at the cash."

Jesse didn't reply. He couldn't say that Ellis was wrong.

"Look. If this is our case, then it's our money. We should hang on to it," Ellis said. "It's that simple."

Jesse looked at Armistead. "And you clearly feel the same way."

"I would feel better knowing we have the cash under our direct supervision," Armistead said.

"Well. As long as you feel better about it."

"Excuse me, Stone?"

Jesse could see Armistead was dug in on this, no matter how dumb it was. He tried another approach. "Where are we going to keep it?"

That stumped Armistead for a moment. "Don't you have an evidence locker?"

"We have a closet. It's secured with a padlock. And it's mostly full. Does this look like Fort Knox to you?"

"So empty it out."

"This is more than two million dollars in small bills. They carried it out in two big duffel bags. It won't fit."

"What about a safe?"

Jesse pointed to the safe bolted to the floor in a corner of his office. It was smaller than a mini-fridge. "This is our safe."

"That's it?"

"I've been asking for a better one for years."

"Don't try to blame this on me, Stone. I'm trying to get more money here, and all you're doing is—"

Ellis jumped in before Armistead could finish his sentence. "You could take the guns out of the weapons locker. Pack it in there," he suggested.

"We're not leaving our guns lying in the hallway, Ellis."

"I'll call the bank," Armistead said. "They'll put it in their safe and—"

Ellis cut him off before Jesse could. "That would break the chain of custody. Too many people going in and out. It's not an official facility. We have to maintain control over it or any halfway decent defense attorney could keep it out of any trial."

"Well, I'm sure you could still win the case without the money," Armistead said, not willing to let go of his inspiration.

"But you wouldn't get to claim the money, either," Jesse told him. "If it's not part of any criminal case, then we can't seize it under the civil forfeiture statutes. It would go to Burton's heirs, if he had any."

Armistead looked at Ellis.

"Hate to say it, but he's probably right," Ellis said.

"Oh."

They both went quiet. Jesse waited. This was their plan. Let them try to save it.

Ellis looked like he had a cartoon lightbulb go on over his head. "Jesse, didn't you say something about locking it in a jail cell?"

They both smiled at Jesse like this was the most brilliant idea they'd ever heard.

He flexed his fingers. The burns still hurt like hell.

Despite his promise to Molly, that was pretty much all that kept Jesse from punching them both in the face.

SEVENTEEN

As soon as the mayor and the DA left, Jesse rubbed his eyes, then drank more coffee. Then he picked up the phone and dialed Suit's house. All Paradise cops were required to have a landline in case of emergencies. Power outages could take out cell towers, mobile phones had batteries that could run down, and, most important, mobiles could be turned off, like now, when Suit was probably out cold.

Elena, Suit's wife, answered.

"Luther is sleeping, Jesse. You kept him out two nights in a row."

Only Elena and Suit's mother regularly called Suit by his given name.

"I'm sorry, Elena. It's not like we were out gambling."

"You need to let him sleep. He's no good to you dead."

"I know that, Elena. If there were anyone else who could do this, I'd ask. I promise."

"Fine," she said, in a tone that indicated it absolutely was not. The phone went silent as she got her husband.

Elena loved Suit more than anyone in the world, and Jesse was on her list somewhere in the top ten for the times Jesse had saved Suit's life. But Jesse also put Suit in danger simply by continuing to employ him, which complicated things.

There was a clunking noise on the line as Suit picked up his phone. "What?"

"Rise and shine. I have a job for you."

"Isn't it enough I pulled you out of a burning building?"

"Pretty sure I made my own way out."

"Well, at least I was there," Suit said.

"Listen. The mayor and Ellis have decided we're keeping the money from the Burton house in our station."

There was a long pause on the line.

"You've got to be kidding me."

"There's a piece of paper and everything."

"Jesse, where would we even keep it?"

"The cells."

"They want us to lock up two million dollars in cash in the same cells where we put drunk drivers every weekend?"

"That's their plan. They want someone to go pick up the money ASAP."

"Jesse. Come on. Surely you can find someone else to do this."

"Actually," Jesse said. "I can't."

Heavy sigh. "Why not?"

Jesse explained what Armistead and Ellis wanted, then he explained what he needed. Then he said, "I need someone I can trust, Suit."

Another long pause.

"Okay," Suit said. "I'll get dressed. But don't blame me if I take the cash and Elena and run away from all of this."

"Honestly, Suit," Jesse said. "If Elena says yes, I'd give you a head start."

Daisy sent Jordyn home after the lunch rush. The kid was learning. Sort of. He'd spilled a couple of drinks on customers. But he hadn't squirted the soap into anyone's food while washing dishes in the back. Definitely an improvement over last week.

She cleaned the counter, scrubbing at a spot Jordyn had missed, when she felt someone's eyes on her.

Daisy was a woman and she was gay and she had learned the hard way to be aware of her surroundings. She'd been jumped once in a parking lot in her twenties, after a long night of dancing with her friends. A group of men had waited outside, hiding behind the cars, and rushed them when the club closed. She'd been punched in the head and kicked when she was down, and had managed to get up and throw a punch herself before one of her friends pulled her away. She didn't even realize she was missing a tooth until she was home and the shock and adrenaline wore off. She felt the crown with her tongue all the time, as a reminder.

When she looked up, she was surprised, but not shocked, to see Derek Tate standing at the front door, looking at her sign from the other side.

He made a show of reading it, moving his lips and his whole face, so she could see him sounding out the words.

Then he opened the door. Slowly.

Daisy held on to the edge of the counter so her hands wouldn't shake.

When the door was all the way open, she said, "That's far enough."

He held up his hands. He smiled. He didn't step inside.

He looked friendly. She didn't buy it.

"I just came over to see if I could get some lunch. Maybe as a way to clear the air."

"No," she said flatly. "You are not allowed in here."

His eyes went cold, but he tried to keep the smile on his face. "Come on. Let's talk it out. It was a misunderstanding. We can end this."

"This only ends when Jesse finally gets smart and fires you."

That might have been a mistake. The skin on Tate's neck flushed red. His mouth set into a scowl. He wasn't trying to look friendly anymore.

"I didn't know you were a friend of the chief's—"

"That shouldn't *matter*," Daisy said. "You should treat everyone in this town with respect. No matter who they know."

"Sure." He didn't sound convinced. "I'll just say 'please' and 'thank you' to every fucking scumbag who might pull a gun on me."

"Jesus Christ. Do I look like I have a gun?"

"No," Tate said. "No, you don't. But you might. Anyone might. How am I supposed to know? Sometimes you have to draw first and take the consequences."

Daisy didn't like the way he said it. He stood at the threshold of the café. Like he was waiting for something.

"Well, I don't have a gun. I don't like them."

"Maybe you should get one. If you're going to be crapping on the police. Maybe there won't be anyone to protect you."

Daisy's mouth went dry.

"Like, this is a cute little sign." He flicked it with one finger. "But I don't think it's going to stop anyone from coming inside your place."

He put his foot over the threshold. Kept it right above the floor, holding it there.

"You stop," Daisy said, and was proud her voice didn't quiver at all. "You are not allowed in here."

Tate smiled at her again. It was not a nice smile this time.

"Really? Who's going to stop me? What are you going to do about it, Daisy?" he asked. "Call a cop?"

Then, smiling, he turned and walked away.

Tate strolled happily down the street, feeling pretty good about the start of his first day on patrol. He'd done just what Stone had asked: gotten out into the community. Introduced himself to the people. Told them what they could expect. He'd managed to keep the red mist in check.

Hell, he'd even obeyed the stupid sign.

He'd never set foot in Daisy's café.

EIGHTEEN

Matthew Peebles didn't strike Jesse as a master criminal, which meant he probably wasn't any good at running from the police. If he wasn't in New York, he was still close by, as Molly said. He wouldn't be hard to find.

Suit was busy running Jesse's errand with the money, so Jesse called in Gabe Weathers, who was happy to go along.

They started working their way down the highway, hitting the cheapest motels as they went south from Paradise. These were the places that took cash and didn't check IDs. There weren't many of them. Real estate around Paradise was too valuable to waste on anything cheap, and almost nobody took cash anymore.

They got lucky at the third place they tried, the Beachside, outside Saugus. It was a beat-up collection of buildings left like old dog turds around a cracked parking lot. If there was a beach anywhere nearby, Jesse couldn't see it.

The clerk, an older Asian man tapping away on a laptop behind the counter, looked at their badges. He sighed and stood up from a high-tech office chair that was probably the most expensive piece of furniture in the place.

"Let me guess," he said. "You're looking for the guy who checked in early this morning and smelled like gasoline."

Jesse smiled. "We are, in fact, looking for an arsonist."

Gabe showed the clerk a headshot of Peebles, taken from his Facebook page and printed to letter size. People who took a lot of selfies were much easier to identify.

The man nodded. "Room Fourteen. Ground floor, right corner."

"Anyone in the rooms next to him?" Jesse asked.

"No," the clerk said. "Too early in the season. Not many people desperate enough to stay here until the other places fill up."

"You got a master key?"

"Absolutely," the clerk said. "I don't want you kicking in the door."

"Is this your place?" Gabe asked, while the man got the key from a lockbox behind the desk.

"Thought I'd retire someplace near the ocean," the clerk said. "Have a nice little second career making people happy on their vacations."

"How's that working out?" Jesse said.

The clerk stared at him, dead-eyed, as he handed over the key. "People on their vacations are the most miserable bastards you'll ever meet."

"Sorry to hear that," Gabe said.

The clerk shrugged. "I'll sell the place eventually. Maybe I'll do better on my second retirement."

Jesse took the key and he and Gabe drew their side-arms as they left the office.

"Wait," the clerk called. "Take this with you."

He handed Jesse a tool with a handle on a thin piece of steel with a forked end.

"It's an emergency-release tool. You can use it to flip the privacy latch if he's got it engaged."

Jesse looked at the tool. "You really don't want us to break the door down, do you?"

"And try not to shoot him if you can avoid it, please," the clerk said. "I just patched the walls in that room."

"We'll do our best," Jesse said.

They moved fast down the walkway toward Room 14, Jesse taking the lead.

They stopped at the door. Jesse eased the key into the lock and pushed the door open slowly and quietly. It stopped a couple of inches into the room. Peebles had thrown the security latch.

Jesse handed the clerk's tool to Gabe. His hands were too clumsy with the bandages. Gabe pushed the tool through the gap, and the latch flipped back easily.

Jesse stepped forward. He always went through the door first.

They rushed into the room, Gabe right behind Jesse, guns up and out, shouting, "POLICE! FREEZE!" Maximum noise, maximum impact, hoping to shock-and-awe

Peebles and whoever else might be inside into a quick surrender.

Matthew Peebles, asleep on the bed, looked up blearily, squinting in the sunlight from the open door.

He said, "Oh." Like he'd been waiting to see them. The look on his face was one of the saddest things Jesse had ever seen. He looked like this was the last thing he needed in the world, and the first thing he'd expected this morning.

Jesse didn't waste a lot of time feeling sorry for him, though. "On the floor. Now," he said, keeping his gun aimed at Peebles's head, just in case there was a weapon hidden under the pillow or the sheets.

Peebles slowly got out of the bed and slid down onto the beat-up old carpeting.

Gabe holstered his weapon while Jesse kept Peebles covered. He put a knee on Peebles's back, grabbed his hands, and cuffed him.

"Matthew Peebles, you are under arrest," Gabe said, and began to read him his rights.

"Yeah," Peebles said, face down on the carpet, his voice muffled. "I figured."

NINETEEN

J esse put Peebles in the cells in the back of the station. They'd been remodeled during the pandemic, when almost no one was using them and they'd received an unexpected grant for law enforcement from the federal government. Armistead wanted Jesse to buy an army-surplus armored vehicle, but Jesse overruled him.

Instead, they modernized the holding cells. Now they had new doors, controlled by keypads, with remote entry and lockout, so a single officer could control the cells without ever entering the room. They also had slots for meal trays, so they could feed someone if they kept him overnight without opening the entire cell door. It was a big step-up from a small-town drunk tank. It looked more like Gitmo than Mayberry.

Jesse put Peebles into the nearest cell, then took his shoes and his phone, along with his wallet and his jacket.

Jesse stood outside the cell and asked him if he wanted some coffee. Peebles just stared at him.

"You want something to eat?"

The same empty look.

"You want a lawyer?"

Peebles shook his head.

"You want to tell me why you burned down Burton's house after you asked me to check on him?"

Peebles leaned forward, his arms resting on his knees.

"Why'd you do it?" Jesse asked.

For a moment, Jesse thought Peebles was about to speak. But he just put his head in his hands. Shame and desperation came off him in waves like the fumes of gasoline still stuck to his clothing.

"See, this is what I don't understand," Jesse said. "Why call the police to look in on your friend if you didn't want us to find what was there? You had to know there was a chance he was dead. You had to know we'd go inside."

Peebles remained silent. It was the one smart thing Jesse had seen him do so far.

"My only guess is you didn't know what we'd find. I'm willing to bet you didn't really know anything about Phil Burton. Not really."

Still nothing.

"I am still willing to believe you don't have anything to do with the dead people or the money, Matthew."

Peebles smiled sadly. "It doesn't matter," he said, his voice very quiet.

"I think it does," Jesse said. "Right now, you're the only person we've got connected to the house and what was inside. You could answer some questions for us. Fill in the blanks. But if you don't, well . . ."

Jesse let it hang there for a moment, left the consequences to Peebles's imagination.

But Peebles only snorted.

"Something funny?"

"You. Trying to scare me."

"I'm not trying to scare you, Matthew. I'm trying to help you."

"You can't help me."

"Give me a chance. I'm pretty good at it sometimes."

Peebles looked at the floor again. Then at the wall, then at the ceiling. Anywhere but at Jesse. He bounced his leg up and down, anxiety spilling out of him.

"Talk to me, Matthew. Tell me what you were doing at the house. Tell me about Phil Burton."

"Like you said: I don't know anything about him," Peebles said. "Not really."

"Then tell me who does."

Peebles opened his mouth to say something, then closed it again, and looked away.

When he looked back at Jesse, Jesse could see the moment had passed. Peebles's face was blank again, his mouth drawn into a thin line.

"I am exercising my right to remain silent," he said.

"Matthew. Whoever you're scared of, we can protect you."

Peebles snorted again. "You can't protect me," he said. "I'm already dead."

"Why do you say that? Who's going to kill you?"

"Never mind," Peebles said. "Just leave me alone."

Jesse shrugged. "All right," he said. "But I want you to remember this moment, Matthew."

Peebles glared at him. "What moment is that?"

"The one where you made the wrong choice. Again."

As promised, Peebles remained silent. Jesse took his things and left him alone in the cell.

A million dollars is not as much cash as people think, Jesse knew. In hundreds, it would just about fill an oversized briefcase or a five-gallon paint bucket.

But in small bills—twenties, tens, even fives and ones—cash becomes considerably more bulky. Drug dealers end up with more of it than they know how to handle. You can't just walk into a bank with a pallet of cash. Jesse didn't know why Burton had converted so much of his worldly wealth into small denominations. Maybe it went along with the hoarding. Maybe he was just paranoid and waiting for the end of the world. Whatever his reasons, the state evidence techs had to count and document each bill—including the ones stained by body fluids and decomposition—before they packed them neatly into two giant duffels. They looked like big black bricks, weighing a little less than a hundred pounds each.

That's why Jesse sent Suit to the state evidence facility. The former football player was big enough to handle both oversized bags, haul them into the station. But even he looked smaller carrying the duffels, his face flushed as he walked through the door and down the hall to the cells.

As Jesse watched Suit go by, he understood why

Armistead and Munroe wanted the cash so bad. That amount of money could tempt anyone.

Except Suit, who carried them as if they were nothing more than bags of laundry he'd brought home for his mom to do. Suit was incorruptible.

Which was one of the other reasons Jesse had asked him to do the job.

"Any problems?" Jesse asked.

"Piece of cake," Suit said, as he came back from the cells, wiping a little sweat from his forehead.

"Maybe a little too much cake lately, Suit."

Suit looked wounded. "Like to see you carry that weight, old man."

"That's why I pay you the big bucks," Jesse said. "Did you put the money in the cells?"

"Yup. I see you found Mr. Peebles," Suit said. "Molly is right. That does sound like a cartoon character."

"How *is* our guest? Did Mr. Peebles say anything?"

"Oh, yeah," Suit said. "We sat down and had a good long talk about the New Wave Surrealists."

"You have thoughts on the New Wave Surrealists?"

"No, but Elena's reading a book on them, and she has many thoughts on them. Something for one of her classes."

Elena was a teacher. She never stopped learning. Jesse admired that about her.

"So Peebles did not take the opportunity to unburden himself to you."

"He did not. The guy looks catatonic, Jesse. It's like he's given up."

Tate suddenly appeared from the hallway outside Jesse's door, popping in uninvited.

"Maybe you could give me a few minutes alone with him," he said. "I could persuade him, if you know what I mean."

It was a small station, Jesse knew. People overheard conversations all the time. But Jesse didn't like that Tate was eavesdropping on them.

Suit didn't appear to care for it, either. "Maybe it's not the best time for you to be joking about police brutality," he said to Tate.

Tate smiled broadly. "Lighten up, Suit. I'm just saying, you want this guy to start snitching, I bet I could make that happen. Anybody you want him to name?"

Suit stared at Tate until the smile faded. Jesse knew he didn't like Tate. Which was worth noticing. Suit liked everybody.

"Just a joke," Tate said. He cleared his throat.

"Thanks, Suit," Jesse said, intervening before the tension between them escalated.

"Yeah," Suit said. "No problem, Jesse."

He left, purposely not giving Tate any room as he cleared the door. Tate was broad and muscular, but Suit towered over him. Tate had to shrink against the frame to make room for Suit to slip by.

When Suit was gone, Jesse asked Tate how the day went.

"Easy," Tate said.

"Really? No problems."

"Nope," Tate said. "You were right, Jesse. It's good to get to know the people here a little."

TWENTY

The next morning, Jesse sat with Molly and Suit in the conference room. He wanted to think out loud on the case, and Molly and Suit almost always saw something he didn't. If Jesse was a TV detective, he'd have a big bulletin board with pictures and red string connecting a bunch of different pieces of evidence.

But he didn't have that. He had Molly and he had Suit and he had donuts. He stuck with what had always worked before.

The hot cup of coffee still hurt Jesse's burned hands, even through the bandages. But then again, no pain, no gain.

He'd gone for Dunkin' after Molly and Suit both complained about being hungry. Jesse felt he owed them something.

He lifted one of the donuts from the box and took a bite. Not as good as Daisy's fresh-baked turnovers, sadly. He knew he'd have to talk to her again, but in the meantime, he could live with donuts. He didn't like the thought of losing Daisy as a friend. Or, for that matter, never having one of Daisy's pastries again.

Right now, however, he couldn't think about it. He needed to focus on the case. He needed ideas.

"Okay," he said. "What the hell is going on here?"

Suit yawned, exhausted.

"Why didn't you get turnovers?" Molly asked.

Jesse sighed. "You know damn well why. Can we focus on the case, please?"

"Don't snap at me."

"I didn't snap."

Molly gave him a look. Jesse thought he might have snapped. He put a donut on a napkin and put it in front of her as a peace offering. Or at least a distraction.

It worked. Molly glared at the donut instead of glaring at Jesse.

"So we've lost most of our evidence," Jesse said. "The crime scene techs still had the file boxes with the papers and photos in a stack inside the house. They all went up in the fire."

"How much was there?" Suit asked, fighting a yawn. He hadn't had any trouble sleeping. Jesse had to call Elena to wake him up and get him to the station.

"The count was at sixty-four different bodies and crime scenes," Jesse said.

"Jesus," Suit said.

"And there were still dozens of boxes to go. All gone now."

"Didn't they take pictures?" Molly asked. "I thought that's what they were supposed to do."

"They did," Jesse said. "But they didn't have time to get everything. They thought they'd be able to go through the files later."

"And then Peebles came and threw his Molotov cocktail."

"Right," Jesse said. "I tried to grab one of the boxes, but we see how that turned out."

He held up his bandaged hands.

"Does it hurt?" Molly asked.

"Yes."

"Serves you right for running into a burning building," she said. "You dumbass."

"Now you sound like Robbie."

"We don't agree often, but on this one, he's right."

Suit, bless him, tried to get them back on track. "Do we have anything left?"

"Just the papers and pictures I grabbed on my first trip into the house. I didn't get around to handing them off to the state's people, so they're still on my desk."

"There's one thing I don't get," Suit said.

"Just the one?" Jesse said.

Suit looked hurt but covered it quickly. Jesse was not winning any friends this morning. "I don't understand why Peebles came to us about Burton if he wanted to hide what was inside the house," Suit said. "Why call the police if you're trying to cover up a crime?"

"He didn't know what was inside," Jesse said. "He told me he was checking on Burton because he was an old family friend. Thanks to Molly, we know that's mostly crap. There are no apparent connections between him and Burton. So why keep tabs on him?"

"Well, Burton was sleeping on a couple million bucks," Suit said. "So someone was paying him to do something."

"Right," Jesse said, and Suit looked happy again, like he'd pleased the teacher.

"Any chance he was framed?" Molly said.

"I don't see how," Jesse said. "You'd have to go back years to accumulate all that evidence, and then cram it in among his junk without Burton saying or doing anything. Also, he died of natural causes. Dev is sure of it. Weird way to frame a guy."

"I know. I just find it hard to believe he killed all those people himself," Molly said. "None of these murders were local, or we would have noticed. The photos go back years."

"Maybe he traveled," Suit said.

"That would make him a serial killer or a hit man," Jesse said. "And nobody pays a serial killer. Nobody has to. They do it for themselves."

"So a hit man," Suit said.

"He wasn't a hit man," Molly said. "He barely left his home in the last ten years, his neighbors said. And look at him." She rummaged for the coroner's report. "Five-eight, one-fifty. He wasn't a big guy. Not strong, not imposing."

"Killers don't always look like killers," Jesse said.

"But they do need some way to kill people," Molly

shot back. "And what's the one thing they didn't find in all that junk piled up in his house?"

"No gun," Jesse said.

"Right. Not even one."

"Huh," Suit said. "I mean, there could have been one buried deeper."

"People who use guns like to keep them close," Molly said. "Where's yours? Your backup, I mean?"

"Taped to the headboard," Suit said with a sheepish grin. "Don't tell Elena. She hates it. She wants me to keep it in a lockbox."

"Nightstand drawer," Jesse said.

"But we've all had people try to kill us," Molly said. "So of course we keep a gun close. If Burton was a hit man, you think he'd bury his gun under a pile of crap where he couldn't get to it?"

"No," Jesse said. "You've convinced me."

"Because I'm right."

"And because you know hit men so well."

Molly rolled her eyes. "Good you're letting that go."

Suit ignored the hints about Molly and the gun-for-hire, Crow, who sometimes still came around Paradise. He wasn't so dumb that he'd missed all the subtext over the years. He just pretended not to notice, as if his mom and dad were fighting.

"Well, if he wasn't a hit man and he's not a serial killer, then what was he?" Suit asked. "Who was this guy? Why was he connected to these murders? What was he being paid for?"

Suit had, in his usual blunt-instrument way, pointed out all the holes in their case. They didn't know anything.

They all went quiet again. Suit looked glum. Molly lost her staring match with the donut and began to eat.

Jesse flexed his fingers to keep them from stiffening. He could feel the skin breaking under the bandages. It wasn't quite like the pain from throwing the ball into his glove, but it wasn't completely unlike it, either.

Maybe it was close enough to get his brain working again, because he thought of something. The money.

"Someone had to pay Burton all these years, right?"

"Sure," Molly said, around a mouthful of donut and powdered sugar.

"What if that's why Peebles was here? He said he came by about once a month. Just to keep tabs. He was checking on Burton for whoever paid him."

"Sure. Makes sense."

"And they didn't trust Peebles to know what he was doing. They just used him for the check-ins."

Suit and Molly nodded.

"But when we went inside . . ." Suit began.

"We found the tip of the iceberg," Molly said. "Whoever was behind Peebles and Burton got nervous."

"Not just nervous," Jesse said. "Furious. Assuming they were paying Burton. They'd be pretty unhappy to learn Burton kept all those records."

"Well, yeah, obviously," Suit said, not getting it yet.

But Molly did. "And they'd be even unhappier to know that the police had those records."

"Exactly," Jesse said. "They'd probably even send someone out to destroy the evidence."

"Peebles," Suit said, getting the idea now. "That's why he threw the firebomb. He was told to clean up his mess."

"Now. Just imagine how angry those people will be when they find out he didn't get all of it," Jesse said.

He cracked a smile. He had an idea now.

"Let's tell everyone we've still got it here," Jesse said. "Let's see who comes looking for it."

Molly and Suit looked at each other. "And then what happens?" Molly asked.

"What do you mean?"

"The media has already reported we've found a couple million bucks. Now you want to tell the world that we're sitting on evidence connected to multiple murders," she said. "And someone has already burned down a house to get rid of it. What do you think is going to happen when those killers hear about this?"

"That's the idea," Jesse said. "We're going to draw them out."

"Maybe it's not the best idea to have a bunch of murderers coming to town," Molly said. "I know you, Jesse. You're painting a target on your own back."

"No," Jesse said. "I'm putting it on my front. So I can see them coming."

Molly and Suit just looked at him. "Not funny," Molly said.

"Either of you got any better ideas?"

Neither of them said anything.

"Then we're doing it," Jesse said flatly. "I've got just the reporter we can use."

"Anything for an excuse to call your ex-girlfriend," Molly muttered.

Jesse frowned at her. "Now who's not letting things go?"

———

Jesse did not, in fact, call his ex where she worked at *The New York Times*. This story was local, and he didn't really want to try to get through a conversation with Nellie anyway. Ty Bentley was happy to rush back over to Paradise for a stand-up interview in front of the station. Nobody else had anything on the fire, and Jesse promised him an exclusive on the pictures of the dead bodies.

His cameraman shot Jesse with the mic in his face as Bentley asked the questions.

"Chief Stone, are you saying these murders could be Mob-related?"

"It's too soon to speculate," Jesse said. "But we are investigating every connection. Someone out there knows who these people are. Someone did this. And we want to find them."

Bentley nodded, then turned to the camera, looking solemn. "Chilling photos, unsolved mysteries, and an unknown killer. From Paradise, this is Ty Bentley, WBZ."

His grim expression vanished as soon as the cameraman turned away, replaced with a huge grin. "This is so great, Chief," he said. "We are going to go national on this one, I can feel it. CNN, the networks, everybody's going to want a piece."

"You sure about that?"

"Are you kidding?" Ty laughed. "It's got everything. Dead bodies, money, a weird old guy in a haunted house, and a killer on the loose. People eat that shit up with a spoon."

"Terrific," Jesse said. "Maybe you can use this instead of the piece on the sign in Daisy's café."

Bentley looked confused. "Oh, I already did that piece. Ran at noon and again at five. I put you down as 'no comment.'"

"Thanks for that."

Bentley didn't catch Jesse's tone at all.

"Yeah, that one's going to go national, too. Every other station in Boston has already jumped on it. 'Culture war comes to small seaside town. Are the police out of control?' You know the drill."

Jesse didn't say anything. Ty shifted uncomfortably.

"You should really think about saying something next time," Ty said. "It makes you look terrible when you just let that stuff go out there without any pushback."

"I'll keep that in mind," Jesse said, and walked back into the station.

TWENTY-ONE

The man now going by David Elliott came into his house after stowing his golf bag in the garage. It was a perfect day on the greens, still cool in the morning, early enough in the spring that the course wasn't clogged with too many idiots. He never thought he'd be a golfer, but since his retirement he'd really leaned in to the clichés: moving to the desert, buying a house by a golf course, taking up the sport, eating early, going to bed after the late news.

Kate, his wife, sat at the breakfast bar, a cup of coffee going cold by her elbow while she looked at her phone. Elliott glanced at the screen when he kissed her cheek. She said hello but kept staring at the pictures of her sister's grandkids.

"Do you see how big Taylor is getting?" she said.

He made a noncommittal noise and got himself a cup

from the pot. She'd always wanted children. He'd told her he was sterile and never wanted to adopt. In fact, he'd gotten a vasectomy at an early age. He'd never wanted the liability of kids hanging around his neck. He'd seen that weakness exploited all too often.

After a couple of dead-end conversations on adoption, she went along with him, like she did on most things. Still, it was a real source of pain to her, he knew, like a splinter buried way down deep in the skin, mostly forgotten except when she picked at it.

He didn't like to hurt her. But there were worse kinds of pain, and many other little lies in their marriage he'd used to spare her from them.

Kate believed they were living comfortably off his Social Security and the investments made after a long career as a sales rep for an electronics company, which explained his many absences and irregular schedule. Elliott had never paid taxes in his life, instead using a crooked accountant to launder his income so it came to him in the form of checks from a company that didn't exist.

He thought that part of his life was over now, though. He'd survived. He'd beaten the odds, and now he looked forward to becoming a boring old man, sinking putts, taking occasional trips to Hawaii with Kate, building birdhouses or something equally useless on the tool bench in his garage.

Then his cell phone buzzed in his pocket.

He didn't recognize the number and was almost retired enough to let it go to voicemail.

Instead, he stepped into the living room and answered.

"Turn on CNN," someone told him.

He didn't recognize the voice, but he knew the tone. Elliott found the remote and turned on the TV.

There was a report of a house filled with garbage, and buried among the garbage were pictures of dead people. Lots and lots of dead people.

They even showed a few of them on TV, their eyes blanked out, the worst parts blurred, but Elliott recognized them.

He knew his own work.

The police were clueless, as usual. That's not what the pretty anchorwoman on CNN said, but it was what she meant. That was why they'd released these photos and talked to the media. They were hoping to shake something loose, hoping to find someone who knew the identities of the dead men.

Elliott did. And so did the people who'd paid him.

Other people would, too, given enough time. Nothing ever really stayed buried.

"You see the problem?" the voice asked.

He didn't know how they'd found him again, but he wasn't surprised. The outfit had enough resources to find anyone. He had done his job faithfully and well for years, and he'd been considered loyal enough to be allowed to go away and find himself a new life. But even though he was done with them, they were not done with him.

"I'll handle it," he said.

"Good man," the voice said, and then hung up without another word.

They didn't have to tell him what to do. He was still professional enough to know that all by himself.

Elliott felt a familiar coldness in his chest, along with something he didn't expect: regret.

He had enjoyed retirement. He'd liked being a normal guy.

"What's on the news, dear?" Kate asked from the kitchen, not really interested, just asking with the usual politeness of marriage.

"The same old garbage. Blood and disaster. I was just checking the market." He switched the TV off.

Elliott turned and walked back into the kitchen, forced a cheerfulness into his tone that he didn't feel, crafting another lie easily. "That was Frank on the phone, from the firm. He asked if I could come out for a few days, show the new kids a thing or two. Would that be okay with you?"

She looked up at him and shrugged. "If that's what you want," she said. She'd never fought him on anything. He'd always ask, and she always went along with whatever he decided. "I mean, if they can't manage without you."

He put his arms around her.

"It seems like they can't," he said.

Raney wasn't his real name, but it was the one he used now. His parents named him Bailey, one of the many things they got wrong. So when he got out of the service after four long tours in Iraq and Afghanistan, he left that name behind along with everything else, not once looking back.

He was not a big guy. He was young and looked younger. His hair flopped down over his forehead, and his face was unlined and looked soft. He sometimes still got carded in bars.

Most days it didn't bother him. He liked it when people underestimated him.

But he did wonder why so many big guys assumed that their size alone made them scarier than anyone else they met.

Case in point, this guy at the pawnshop, trying to screw him.

Raney had been hired by the pawnshop's manager, a guy named Poole, to recover some stolen goods. His shop had been robbed, which Raney thought was a little funny, considering most of the stuff inside was stolen to begin with.

It wasn't like he had to track down the thieves. Poole saw them on the security video, knew exactly who they were: a couple of meth addicts who sold stuff to him all the time. He'd turned down some of their offerings and they broke in to get what they thought they were owed. They didn't even wear masks. Not smart, but meth addicts aren't known for making good choices.

Poole didn't really care about the junk. It was mostly stuff he kept in the front of the store, which he used as a cover for the high-quality merch that went out of the back. But he didn't want people to think he'd let something like this pass. That would be blood in the water, and every junkie, crackhead, and dipshit in town would start hitting his place, looking for an easy score.

So Poole called around and found Raney and named a price, and Raney agreed to the job. Simple.

It was far below Raney's skill set, but he was lying low in Portland after a couple of hits in Florida, and he needed the cash.

In the service, Raney discovered he didn't mind killing people. He was, in fact, pretty good at it. So he learned every possible way to do it that he could. He hung out with the Explosive Ordnance Disposal guys and learned about bombs. He talked to the Special Forces guys and learned about knives and guns. He took instruction in advanced combat classes when he could.

And when he got back to the States, he found people who needed someone killed, and he offered them a service at a reasonable price.

Raney found the addicts exactly where Poole said they'd be, in a tent in an encampment near the overpass five blocks from the pawnshop. They still had the stuff, including the locked gun case that Poole desperately wanted back.

Raney tossed a foil packet of meth laced with enough fentanyl to drop a rhino in their tent. They didn't even question their good fortune. Again, meth addicts don't make the best choices. Their bodies were going cold a couple of hours later as Raney entered the tent and took back everything they'd stolen, loading it into the same cart they'd used to carry it away.

One of the other homeless guys said, "Hey, what are you doing?" to Raney, but backed away quickly when Raney gave him a hard look. Wasn't any of his business. He knew Raney was more dangerous than he looked.

Which made him much smarter than Poole.

Poole barely glanced at Raney as he sat behind the bulletproof glass that separated the counter from the rest of the store. He was watching CNN.

Which Raney never understood. There was enough bad news in most people's lives. You didn't have to watch any more of it on TV. Raney liked sitcoms.

Poole put a stack of bills in the little drawer on his side and shoved it through toward Raney.

Raney knew just by looking that it wasn't enough.

Raney waited. Poole kept staring at the TV.

"You planning on doing this in installments?" Raney asked.

Poole looked at him. He was not your usual sleazy pawnshop guy. He wore a crisp flannel shirt, had a neatly trimmed beard. He was fit and healthy. He wouldn't have looked out of place in an ad for camping equipment.

"That's all there is," Poole said.

"That's not what we agreed."

Poole shrugged. "Didn't even take you twenty-four hours. I told you where to find them. That's plenty for the effort you had to put in."

Raney let out a very small sigh of irritation.

"It's not what we agreed."

Poole shrugged again. "Sue me."

Raney rolled his head on his shoulders. He didn't need this. He didn't get into this line of work for more stress.

"Look," he said. "Can we agree that this could go badly from here? We don't have to do it this way. You just pay me what you owe me. And I'm gone. We both get on with our lives. It doesn't have to be some big drama."

"You're right. It doesn't," Poole said. "All you have to

do is walk out that door. With the money I gave you. Or you can try to get through four inches of bulletproof glass and then somehow dodge this." He lifted a sawed-off shotgun, double-barreled, from under the counter.

"Cops come, I tell them you tried to rob me. Had to defend myself. No drama at all."

Raney smirked. "Wow. You've thought of everything."

Poole grinned. "Sure did."

"I was being sarcastic, you asshole."

Raney reached into his jacket pocket and took out a can of lighter fluid. The nozzle fit easily into the slot of the drawer, and when he squeezed it, the liquid sprayed Poole from his beard to his crotch, soaking his nice flannel shirt.

Poole spat and sputtered, wiping his face. "You son of a bitch—"

Raney turned around and looked through the aisles of the pawnshop. He was sure he saw one before. There it was.

A long-handled crowbar sat in a barrel with a bunch of other heavy tools, all probably lifted from construction sites by thieves like the addicts. Raney took the crowbar from the bin and walked to the door into the back room.

Poole was still yelling at him from behind the glass, in his little cage. Probably still thought he was safe in the back room. And it was true that Raney could hammer at that bulletproof plastic all day without doing much more than scratching it.

But the door was another matter entirely.

Sure, it was steel. But the lock popped right off with just a little pressure from the long crowbar. It didn't take that much strength at all.

You don't have to be big if you have the right tools for the job, Raney thought, not for the first time.

He took out his gun, an S&W .45 that was mainly good for intimidation, pulled open the door, and walked into the back with Poole.

Poole wasn't a complete idiot. He held the shotgun in front of him, but he didn't pull the trigger. He was soaked in flammable liquid and afraid of a spark from the muzzle flash. He sat on his stool, glaring at Raney.

"Last chance," Raney said. "The rest of my money?"

"Fuck you," Poole said.

Raney flicked open a matchbook. It was getting harder and harder to find these. People didn't smoke as much. He usually had to buy them in bulk at the supermarket now.

He lit it with one hand. A trick he'd learned in the army.

Poole's eyes went wide with fear, right before Raney shot him in the forehead.

Poole dropped to the floor. Raney wasn't about to risk being burned in the sudden explosion of fumes and flames. The gun worked fine.

He blew out the matchbook, then put two more in Poole's chest, because he was thorough and he was a professional, not because it was necessary. The back of the pawnshop owner's head was all over the wall.

Raney spent thirty-four minutes finding all the security cameras, removing the hard drive from the system, and making sure there was no cloud backup. He figured that someone who did so much illegal business wouldn't want too much incriminating evidence out there on the Internet where anyone could find it, and he was right.

Then he took all the cash from the register and the safe. There were some gemstones removed from pawned jewelry in there, too, but he left them. Probably couldn't be traced, but better safe than sorry.

He also left the gun case. Whoever had wanted that would probably come looking for it, another headache he didn't need.

He used the rest of the lighter fluid to douse everything inside the office, then lit another match.

He was about to drop it when he looked up and saw the story on the TV, still stuck on CNN.

It was about a little town in Massachusetts and another dead man there.

Raney saw the photos arrayed across the screen.

"Son of a bitch," he said.

He had another mess to clean up.

He dropped the matches and the empty container and left as the fire started burning.

Then Raney got into his car and began the long drive to Paradise.

TWENTY-TWO

Molly intercepted Jesse as soon as he came back into the station.

"It's Ellis Munroe on the line," she said. "He wants to know why you didn't tell him you caught the arsonist."

"I'll take it in my office."

"Have fun."

"Wouldn't be the word I'd use," Jesse said. He went back behind his desk and hit the button on his phone to pick up Ellis.

"You got him?" Ellis said.

"And hello to you, too, Ellis."

"Don't be a dick, Jesse. I heard you broke into a hotel room yesterday and caught the arsonist."

"Maybe," Jesse said.

"I can have him in front of a judge this afternoon and arraigned—wait, what?"

"I said 'maybe.'"

"*'Maybe'*?" Ellis's voice was doing that thing where it increased in volume, sounding shrill. Couldn't be a good trait for a lawyer who had to appear in court all the time. "What do you mean, *'maybe'*? Is this the guy you saw throw a gasoline bomb at the Burton place or not?"

"I'm not sure that's the most important piece of the puzzle here."

"It's a pretty big goddamn part of the crime of arson, Jesse!"

There were a couple of ways Jesse could play this. He could snap back, slam the phone down, or he could ignore Ellis and do what he wanted to do. He'd done all of those in the past.

But he knew Ellis pretty well by now. So he tried something new.

"Ellis, I know this is the guy who did it. But I think I could find out why. I think I can find out who's behind it. And it might be an important lead on identifying those people in the photos."

"I know you love playing cops and robbers, but in my office, we like to put criminals in jail once we've caught them."

Jesse held his tongue for a second. "I'm not suggesting we let him go. I am sure he knows what we need to know. If we arrest him, he gets a lawyer. He gets bail. We could lose our only lead."

Ellis grunted. "And this is your alternative. Keeping him in your jail."

"He could be a key witness. If you give me the chance, I can talk him around. I've got seventy-two hours I can hold him."

"Forty-eight, actually," Ellis said.

"Seventy-two with the right judge and a smart lawyer making the case," Jesse said. "We hold him as a material witness for questioning."

"Don't try to bullshit me. Are you going to do this whether I sign off on it or not?"

"I'm hoping we don't have to find out."

A deep sigh came over the phone.

"You think he knows who those people in the photos are?"

"I can guarantee he knows who told him to burn the house."

Another deep sigh.

"Go play cops and robbers. I hope it works."

"You and me both," Jesse said. "Thanks, Ellis."

"Why, Jesse. I believe that's the first time you've ever thanked me for anything."

"Don't worry," Jesse said. "I won't get in the habit."

TWENTY-THREE

As soon as Jesse hung up, he heard arguing in the main bullpen outside his door.

Tate and Molly and Suit were all standing there. It didn't quite look like it was about to become a fight.

But it didn't look friendly.

"So let him go hungry. Jesus, you guys want to coddle the guy after he tried to kill the chief?"

"That's not exactly what happened—" Molly said.

"We still have to feed him—" Suit said.

Tate began to argue back with both of them. Then they all shut up when they saw Jesse looming nearby.

"What's going on?"

"Uh, Jesse, we've got a problem here," Suit said.

"What?" Jesse did not want to hear about problems.

"Well, usually we feed whoever's in the holding cells with takeout from Daisy's . . ."

"And Daisy won't let cops into her diner anymore."

"Just Paradise cops," Molly reminded Jesse. "I assume police officers from departments where you aren't the chief are welcome."

"Thank you, Molly."

"It's why I'm here."

"So what?" Tate said. "Screw her. I'll buy some dog food. Better than the asshole in the cell deserves anyway."

Jesse, Molly, and Suit all looked at Tate.

"Thanks for your input, Derek," Jesse said. "But we can't just feed him dog food."

"How about McDonald's?" Suit said.

"Cruel and unusual punishment," Molly said.

"Hey, I like McDonald's," Suit said.

"You like anything that gives you a toy with your Happy Meal," Molly shot back.

"Tell me you've ever eaten anything better than a McDonald's french fry. I dare you."

"Enough," Jesse said. He got a pen and a piece of paper and scribbled a quick note. "Suit, please take this to Daisy. Don't go inside. Have someone pass it to her. Peebles isn't a cop. I'm sure she doesn't want him to go hungry. See if that loophole works for both of us."

Suit left with the note.

Tate shook his head, watching Suit go. "I don't know why you're bending over backward for either of them," he said.

"Derek, you're on patrol, right?" Jesse said.

"Yeah."

"Then why are you still here?"

Tate muttered something and left. Jesse didn't feel like pursuing it.

Molly gave him a long look.

"What?"

"You're going to have to deal with Daisy and Tate sooner or later."

"I'm working on it," Jesse said.

In the meantime, he'd had an idea.

"I'm going to go speak to our guest about the problems we're having with room service."

"I'm starving," Peebles said as soon as Jesse appeared in the cell corridor.

"We're working on it," Jesse said. "You got anyone you want us to call? Anyone worrying about you?"

"I told you. I don't want to talk."

"I don't want you to talk to me," Jesse said. "I want you to tell your people where you are. So they don't worry. If you won't call a lawyer, at least call your mother."

That got him. Peebles suddenly looked nervous. Even hardened criminals choked up when Jesse mentioned their mothers, and Peebles was not a hardened criminal.

"You'd do that? You'd give me my phone?"

"Give me a minute," Jesse said. "The reception in here is terrible, but I can give you our cordless phone. We'd just need your mom's number."

"It's on my cell."

Of course it was, because nobody remembered numbers anymore.

"I can't give you your cell," Jesse said. "Not allowed."

"I'll just use it to look up the number," Peebles said.

Jesse pretended to think about it for a second, then nodded. He went out and came back with both Peebles's cell and the station's cordless phone. Peebles looked up the number, and Jesse dialed it into the cordless. Then he took back Peebles's cell phone.

He walked to the entry door and gave the phone to Suit, who'd returned from Daisy's.

By the time Jesse got back to the cell, Peebles was on the line with his mom. Jesse couldn't make out the words on the other end, but she didn't sound happy. She promised to call his uncle. Jesse could hear that much. In fact, Jesse could hear everything loud enough to hurt his ears, and he was six feet away.

"Mom, please, don't—" Peebles said.

But she'd already hung up.

"Why don't you want her to call your uncle?"

Peebles handed him back the station phone. "It doesn't matter," he said. "He was going to hear about it anyway."

Jesse walked away slowly. It wasn't a long hall, but he wanted to give Peebles every chance to change his mind.

If Peebles had second thoughts, he didn't voice them. He didn't say a word as Jesse left the cells, the door shutting behind him with a final, quiet click of the lock.

"Well?" Suit and Molly were waiting for Jesse in the conference room.

"It worked," Suit said. "He opened the phone when he called his mom."

"And then we got into the settings and kept it open so we could look at everything he has inside it," Molly said.

"Smart," Jesse said.

"It was my idea," Suit said.

"It was not," Molly said. "I said we should unlock his phone."

"And I was the one who knew how to do it."

"We'll call it a team victory," Jesse said.

"My idea," Suit said.

"Mine," Molly shot back.

Jesse ignored them. "So what's on the phone?"

Suit took it out of his pocket and began scrolling through it. "Nothing incriminating so far," he said, "unless you count some dick pics he's been sending to a bunch of different women he seems to have met at the club where he works."

"Ugh," Molly said. "Who the hell thinks that works?"

"Well, he does, apparently," Suit said.

"Do any of the girls?"

"None yet, but he keeps on sending them."

"Hope springs eternal."

"And he sends the same pic every time. Doesn't even take a new one. I mean, come on, dude. Get creative. Be a little original."

"Suit," Jesse said.

"Pure laziness," Molly said. "I tell you, I weep for this generation."

"Right?" Suit said. "Whatever happened to the days when you would put a little thought and effort into your nudes?"

Jesse rubbed his eyes. "Amateur porn aside, is there

anything we can use? Any phone calls before he decided to torch the house?"

"Yes," Suit said. "One incoming call from a number in Boston. It says Uncle Charlie."

"Well," Molly said, "that does not exactly break the case wide open."

"His mom mentioned an uncle, too. Peebles seemed pretty upset by the idea. Maybe we should look a little deeper," Jesse said.

He took the number and went to his office, where he made a call to Lundquist.

"Got a lead on our arsonist," he said when Lundquist finally came on the line.

"Terrific. Why are you calling?"

"You said you wanted to stay in the loop. Here's the loop. You're in it."

"You said you'd handle it. I assume that means you'll call when your bad guy is dead on the street somewhere."

"You know me so well."

"I speak from experience. So what's the lead?"

Jesse told him about the phone number and Uncle Charlie. He did not tell him he had Matthew Peebles in the cell just a few yards away. He trusted Lundquist, but he didn't want anyone else knowing Peebles was in custody yet. Something about how he'd seemed both scared and resigned set off alarm bells for Jesse. He needed more answers before he declared the arson solved.

"Don't you have anyone who can look up a number?" Lundquist asked.

"We're a twelve-person department. I have people who'd call your people. This saves time."

Lundquist grumbled and yelled at someone else to look up the number. Jesse waited. Within a few seconds, he had an address and a name.

"Charlie Mulvaney. No way. This can't be the *actual* Charlie Mulvaney."

"Who's that?"

"You don't know?"

"No," Jesse said. "You know who he is?"

"I shouldn't be surprised. He was before your time. A real greatest-hits, back-in-the-day, original gangster. Damn."

"What did he do?"

"What hasn't he done is the real question."

"If you're having trouble with the details," Jesse said, "I can just look up his record. It might save time."

"You won't find anything. Not the real story, anyway. Mulvaney was always too slick. Nothing ever stuck to him is the way I heard it."

"So why don't you tell me?"

"Well, like I said, I have other things to do, and this is your case. But you should get in touch with Healy and ask him. He'll love it."

"Healy's retired. He tells me so every time I talk to him."

"Yeah, but for this, he'll cancel his golf game. Trust me."

TWENTY-FOUR

Jesse and Healy pulled up outside the grand house in Beacon Hill and parked at a hydrant. Jesse hoped the cherry lights and the big PARADISE POLICE DEPARTMENT markings on the car would keep it from being towed, but you never knew with Boston parking enforcement. Sometimes he thought they'd tow the president's limo if it was parked in the wrong spot.

The house was two stories, nestled between a couple townhomes just like it, and was probably worth ten or twelve million dollars. It was impressive what even a small-time mobster could afford.

Healy got out of the car and looked at the house, checking the address. "Long way from Southie," he said. "Why don't cops ever retire in places like this?"

He and Jesse had been friends since Jesse came to Paradise. Healy used to be the head of the State Homicide Division before Lundquist, and they'd worked cases together for a long time. Healy had worked even more cases before that, a lot of them dealing with organized crime. He'd seen bodies pile up in the wars between the remnants of the Irish gangs and the Italians. He knew most of the people responsible for the deaths, even if he couldn't necessarily prove it.

He said he didn't miss the job, that he never wanted to be pulled out of bed at three in the morning again to fish a floating corpse out of a river.

But when Jesse called, Healy almost always put down what he was doing and showed up to help.

This time, Lundquist had been right: All Jesse had to do was say the name *Mulvaney* and Healy started laughing. "Oh, yeah," he said. "I want in on this one."

So now they were at Mulvaney's very nice townhome.

Jesse and Healy walked up the steps. Jesse knocked on the door.

A woman in a nurse's uniform answered. She was younger than Jesse expected, and she filled the uniform very well. Especially the top.

"Yes?" she said, looking blankly between Healy and Jesse.

"Police," Jesse said, showing his shield. "We were hoping to speak to Charles Mulvaney."

It was like shutters went down behind her eyes. Her slight smile turned into a scowl. "I'm not sure he'll want to see you," she said.

Healy smiled as if she'd invited them in for coffee.

"Oh, I think Mr. Mulvaney will want to talk to us," he said. "Tell him we're here about his nephew."

Her scowl deepened, which Jesse didn't think was possible. She closed the door and left them waiting there.

After five minutes, the door opened again. This time, a squat man in a tracksuit stood in front of them.

"You the cops?"

Healy looked at Jesse in his hat and jacket, both with the official seal and PARADISE PD on them. Then he looked back at the Explorer, clearly visible from where they were standing, with its lights and markings. "I swear, Jesse, I dealt with a smarter breed of criminal, I really did."

The squat man in the tracksuit didn't appear to take offense or, really, even understand what Healy was saying. He just stared back at them.

"Yes," Jesse said. "We're the cops."

He nodded, and turned and walked into the house, waving for them to follow.

Jesse and Healy walked after him.

The inside of the house was not as nice as the neighborhood's real estate prices would suggest. The floor was scuffed and in need of a good cleaning, and the furniture seemed like it had been shipped direct from the 1980s. There were family photos on a hallway table with a thick layer of dust.

But everything inside the place had once cost a lot of money. If nothing was old enough to qualify as an antique yet, it still wasn't thrift-store material, either.

The nurse still glared at them from a couch in the living room. The man in the tracksuit walked past her without a word. Jesse and Healy followed, though Jesse wasn't entirely sure he wanted to turn his back on her.

Tracksuit escorted them into a room that could have been a den or an office once, but now appeared to be a part-time hospital room. There was an adjustable bed, a bank of equipment, a set of plastic drawers filled with medical supplies.

In a wheelchair, staring at them, sat an old man. White hair, paper-thin skin laced with blue veins, an oxygen tube hooked into his nose.

But he sat up ramrod straight. He grinned when they entered the room, showing a row of bright white teeth.

Tracksuit took a position by the door.

"Charles Mulvaney?" Jesse asked.

"The fuck did you expect?" the old man said. "You came to see me, didn't you?"

Jesse flipped out his badge and credentials again. "Jesse Stone. Paradise PD. We wanted to ask you a couple questions about your nephew."

Mulvaney didn't look at Jesse or his badge.

"I don't know you," he said, turning to Jesse. "But I know Paradise. The fuck is a meter maid like you doing bothering me?"

"As I said, we want to talk to you about your nephew. Matthew Peebles."

Mulvaney made a face. "He's not my nephew. He's my sister's grandkid. Fucking useless. What did he do now?"

"He burned down a house in Paradise."

"On purpose?"

"He threw a bottle full of gasoline at it, so, yeah, I'd say so," Jesse said.

"Well, with that kid, you never know. Wouldn't be surprised if he torched a place by accident. What's it got to do with me?"

"He says he went out to Paradise to check on a friend of yours. Phil Burton. He said you ask him to look in on Burton every few weeks."

"Phil Burton? Doesn't ring any bells. But I'm an old man, like your pal here said. I forget things."

"Weird," Healy said. "You called your nephew a few hours before it happened."

A little tic of irritation moved across Mulvaney's face. Then he shrugged. "Did I?"

"Says so right on his phone. You might not be up on the technology these days, but it keeps all the calls on a list."

"Oh, yeah," Mulvaney said, not putting much effort into pretending to remember. "He'd called me for money. I was calling him to tell him to fuck off."

"You're not a close family, then?" Jesse said.

"Wait, wait, something's coming back to me," he said, rubbing his chin. He stared intently at Healy. "I know you, don't I? Healy, wasn't it?"

"Good memory for a guy your age," Healy said.

"You were Boston PD—no, wait, you were State Police."

"That's right."

"Can't believe you're still working. Didn't you put anything away for retirement?"

"I did," Healy said. "Sometimes I like to visit elderly crooks as a public service."

Mulvaney laughed at that. It sounded like the last gasp of a drowning man.

"I'm no crook. Just a sad old man with an idiot nephew. Hope you put him away for a while. Getting ass-raped in prison might help him build a little character."

Healy laughed like that was hilarious. Then he unleashed a smile as sharp as a knife as he said to Mulvaney, "Did that work for you?"

Mulvaney froze. Jesse watched him carefully, wondering how he'd react.

For a split second, the doddering old man dropped away. He glared at Healy, and someone else—someone colder, more lethal—looked out from behind his eyes.

"You musta been a terrible cop," he said after a long moment.

Healy kept grinning, not even slightly offended. "Why would you say that?"

"'Cause if you were any good at your job you probably would've been put in a ditch somewhere."

"Maybe I was good enough to avoid that."

Mulvaney smiled, showing those pearly white dentures again. "You think you still are?"

Jesse kept his eyes on Mulvaney carefully during the whole exchange. Taking notes inside his head. Measuring the man.

Mulvaney turned, as if he felt the weight of Jesse's stare on him. He shrank a little in his chair. His hands shook. He yawned, a harmless old crank again, barely capable of gumming his mush at breakfast.

"Look. I'm tired. I'm sick. And if you were gonna bust me for anything, it would've been back when I was actually doing something. Now I'm gonna get back in bed. And the two of you are gonna get the hell out of my house."

He pressed a button on a lanyard around his neck. The door opened and the nurse came in and began pulling down the sheets on the hospital bed, while Mulvaney buzzed his electric wheelchair into position beside it.

"It's time for you to leave," the nurse said to Jesse and Healy in the same tone you'd use to tell someone you hoped they'd die of cancer.

"We were just going," Jesse said.

The nurse didn't respond, busy helping Mulvaney into the bed. He looked like a stack of dried kindling wrapped in silk pajamas. He settled back onto thousand-thread-count sheets and nodded at Jesse and Healy.

"Thanks for dropping by, gentlemen," he said. "Sure livened up my morning."

Jesse didn't move. "What did Phil Burton do for you, Mr. Mulvaney?" he asked. "You don't seem like the type to do favors for anyone out of the goodness of your heart. So why did you send your nephew to keep tabs on him?"

Mulvaney leaned his head back on the pillow.

"You'll die wondering, cop," he said, and smiled, and closed his eyes.

TWENTY-FIVE

Jesse went to the bowling alley in Cambridge where Vinnie Morris held court. They were close enough that he could have called first. They were probably even friends.

But this wasn't likely to be a friendly visit, and Jesse didn't want to give him the heads-up.

It was Healy's idea, actually, but it wasn't offered with much grace. "Well, that scumbag wasn't helpful," he said, when they parted outside Mulvaney's townhome. "But you know another scumbag, don't you? Maybe you can ask him."

Healy had never liked Vinnie, because Vinnie was a gangster—an old-school gangster who still followed a code of conduct you saw only in movies. But Vinnie was still a criminal, and for Healy, that put him on the other side of the line. He'd never liked Jesse's relationship with him, and was never shy about saying so.

For Jesse, Vinnie was more complicated. Vinnie Morris was one of the best shooters Jesse had ever seen, or even heard about. For years, he'd used his talents for a mobster named Gino Fish. Then, when Fish was killed, Vinnie went out on his own. He and Jesse had helped each other over the years. Jesse didn't ask what kind of activities funded the empty bowling alley or what Vinnie's crew did when Jesse wasn't around. They were bound by old debts and secrets and some genuine regard for each other, though neither of them would have ever said it out loud. They were on opposite sides of the law, but they shared a belief in a stricter kind of morality, a need to do the right thing despite the rules of their different worlds.

Or at least Jesse thought they did. Sometimes he wondered if Healy was right, and he was just kidding himself.

The bowling alley was quiet, as it always was. There were places where people still bowled, Jesse knew. They had kids' parties and loud music and neon lighting. Slightly older kids went to those places to get drunk and hook up and occasionally toss a ball down a lane.

Vinnie's was not one of those places. It was a relic, frozen in a time when men owned their own balls and joined leagues and left the house every Tuesday night to have a few beers away from the wife and kids. You could put the entire building in a museum. Nobody came around to bowl. Which was how Vinnie liked it.

Jesse walked past the lobby and into the bar. The bartender, a new kid in Vinnie's crew, scowled at Jesse. "We're closed, Officer."

At least the kid could spot a cop. Of course, Jesse wasn't making it that hard. He still wore his Paradise PD gear.

"Tell Vinnie I want to see him."

The kid, all testosterone and not enough smarts, came out from behind the bar. "I said we're closed."

Jesse smiled. He had to admit his mood might be improved by a fight. But then Vinnie came out from his office in the back.

"Mikey, the hell you doing?" he said. "Go back behind the bar."

"Vinnie, this guy—"

Mikey went silent as Vinnie looked at him. There was something cold in Vinnie's stare, and nobody argued with him for long when he turned it on them.

"Sorry, Vinnie," Mikey said, and went back behind the bar.

Vinnie was, as always, immaculately dressed, as if he were in Milan instead of a grimy bowling alley. He wore a perfectly cut navy blazer today made of a linen that would probably wrinkle if you breathed on it wrong, complemented by gray wool slacks with a knife crease down the front and a shirt of robin's-egg blue. He wore no tie, which made Jesse wonder if this was casual Friday.

He shook Jesse's hand, but he didn't look much friendlier than Mikey had. Jesse suspected that Vinnie knew what this visit was about.

"Come on," he said. "Take a seat."

They went to one of the vinyl booths and sat down. "You want something to drink?" Vinnie asked.

Jesse did. He'd looked at the bottles behind Mikey

with a little too much nostalgia. But he had Dix to deal with that. For now, he shoved the desire down and focused on Vinnie.

"This isn't a social call," Jesse said.

"Yeah. I thought as much. I saw the news."

"Then you know why I'm here," Jesse said. He took out his folder of photos and papers from the Burton house and opened it on the table.

Vinnie only glanced down, then looked back at Jesse.

"No" was all he said.

"No?" Jesse repeated. "No, you don't recognize these guys, or no, you don't know what I'm talking about, or—"

"No, as in we're not going to talk about this, Jesse."

"Why not?"

Vinnie sighed. "You don't want a drink? I could use one." He signaled to Mikey, and the kid started pouring something.

Jesse refused to be distracted.

"What is this, Vinnie?"

"I'm getting to it," Vinnie said. He and Jesse waited for Mikey to deliver the whiskey to the table, then walk away.

Jesse looked at the brown liquid in Vinnie's glass and then looked away quickly.

Vinnie noticed. He noticed everything. It was how he stayed alive. "You okay?"

"I told you this wasn't a social call," Jesse said.

Vinnie shrugged and took a drink.

"Fine," he said. "You want to know what this is. I can give you the general shape of it. There are people, sometimes, who need to be dead. You know this."

Jesse nodded. He would argue about who the people were, but that was one thing he and Vinnie had always agreed on: The world was better off without some people in it. Vinnie had helped Jesse with one of them, a while ago. He didn't have to bring that up. They both knew it, and it was always between them.

"So, in some organizations, you have people who do this work for you. You've got the talent in-house."

"Like you and Joe Broz, and then Gino Fish."

Vinnie smiled a little. "You wearing a wire, Jesse?"

Jesse didn't reply.

"Like I said, sometimes your organization has that talent. But a lot of times, you don't. It's not an easy thing to do well, and not a lot of people have the skills or the opportunity to practice."

"Right," Jesse said.

"And guys who can do this work, well, they don't always get along well with others. They might not fit into a group that asks you to follow a bunch of rules. They might be more comfortable in a less structured environment."

Jesse wondered for a moment if Vinnie had been reading Molly's business books.

"Sure," Jesse said. "Freelancers."

Vinnie made a little gun with his thumb and forefinger and pointed it at Jesse. "Bingo. But how do you know a freelancer can do what he says? How do you choose to trust that guy? Most of the time, you can't. You need someone to vouch for him. You need an honest broker."

Jesse looked down at the pictures.

"You need an agent," he said. "Someone who finds the talent and provides it."

"Exactly," Vinnie said.

"Did you know Burton?"

Vinnie took another drink.

"I'm not asking you to give anyone up, Vinnie."

"I'm sure you think that."

Jesse made a noise in the back of his throat. Then he tried another tack. "Let me guess, then. You never worked for him. But you knew people who did. Or who used his services."

Vinnie said nothing, his eyes cold and still.

"So let's talk hypothetically."

"Hypothetically. Sure."

"Hypothetically," Jesse said, "a guy like Burton would find a hit man—"

"Contractor," Vinnie interrupted.

"—a contractor," Jesse said, "for a client. But because the client didn't have your kind of organization, your kind of trust, they'd want some proof of the results."

Vinnie nodded.

"And so the broker would provide it. Like these pictures."

"If he and the contractor wanted to get paid, yes," Vinnie said.

"Verification. Proof that the target didn't just run off to South America or something. That the job was actually done."

"Right," Vinnie said. "But then both parties were supposed to destroy the materials. So there was nothing left."

"And, clearly, that didn't happen here."

Vinnie shrugged again. "Sure looks like it."

"I'm going to ask you again, Vinnie. Do you know anyone in these photos?"

Vinnie looked away, then back at Jesse. "I think you know me well enough to know I don't leave fingerprints behind, Chief."

"I didn't think you did any of this," Jesse said. "I thought you might know who did."

"Sure," Vinnie said, the word dropping like a stone into a well.

"Did you know Burton was working out of Paradise?"

"I think what you mean is, if I did, why didn't I tell you about him?"

"Did you?"

"No," Vinnie said. "I knew there was a broker around Boston, but there are a few guys like that. They don't generally get caught. One day they're taking contracts, the next they don't answer the phone. They either retire or die, but either way, nobody ever hears from them again."

"You think someone would have killed Burton for this?"

"If he was keeping photos like this? Definitely." Vinnie tapped the folder and looked Jesse in the eyes, just to make sure he got the message. "Anyone holding this kind of stuff, he's got a target on his back. There are people who will do whatever it takes to make sure it stays buried. If I were to find something like this, I'd burn it and bury the ashes under a landfill."

Then Vinnie took another drink. Something shut down behind his eyes. Jesse could tell that was as much as he would get today.

Jesse closed the folder. "You know I can't do that."

"I know," Vinnie said. "When do you ever do the smart thing?"

Jesse appreciated the warning. He imagined it cost Vinnie something to give him even that. It was possible he'd damaged what passed for their friendship by coming here today.

But he didn't have a choice.

"Good to see you, Vinnie," he said, and stood up.

"Sure," Vinnie said again.

Jesse was halfway to the door when Vinnie spoke up one more time.

"Jesse," he said. "There are some people I owe more than you. Even if they're not around anymore. I can't watch your back on this one."

There might have been something like regret in his voice.

"I didn't ask," Jesse said, and left.

TWENTY-SIX

J esse gathered his officers the next day for an all-hands meeting in the conference room. He brought donuts.

He looked around. Gabe Weathers sat at the table next to Jimmy Alonso and Barry Stanton. Stanton and Alonso had become friends, since they came on the job at about the same time. Molly had a spot closest to the donuts. She hadn't chosen it. Jesse had put the box by her on purpose. Her look said she'd make him pay for it. Peter Perkins was late, so there was no room for him at the conference table. He stood, leaning on the doorframe. Tate wore sweats, since he was technically off-duty today. He managed to sit apart from everyone even when he was right next to the others.

Suit was uncharacteristically late. Probably sleeping. Jesse decided to start anyway.

"We have trouble coming our way," Jesse said.

"This about Daisy?" Jimmy asked.

"I can't go on without her potpie, Jesse," Barry said. "Just do whatever she tells you."

Everyone laughed. Except Tate.

"It is not about that," Jesse said. "Daisy has a difference of opinion with me about something. I'm sorry it's spilled over to affect all of you, but as far as I'm concerned, it is between me and her. It is not official department business. Until it gets settled, I want you to respect Daisy's wishes, but continue to respond to any calls to her address like you would anyone else's."

Jesse tried to get them back on track.

"This is about the Burton house. I've been told that there are people who are still interested in the evidence we managed to gather from the house. We will have bad men coming to town."

"How reliable is this information?" Tate asked.

All the other cops at the table looked at him. It wasn't that Jesse didn't allow questions. It was that the others had already learned that Jesse didn't say anything if he wasn't sure.

"As far as I'm concerned, it's one hundred percent," Jesse said. "There are people who want the secrets in that house to stay buried. Our job is to dig them up. That's going to make them angry. So on patrol, I want you on point. You are the first line. You see something, you call it in immediately. If you're worried you're wasting my time, don't. I want to know about it."

"At last, a little action," Tate said.

"No, Derek," Jesse said. "This isn't good news. This means people could get hurt. I want to avoid that at all costs. Your job is not to fight these guys. Your job is to watch and monitor and report back. Please do not take this the wrong way, but you are not qualified to take these guys on. These are serious people. And I do not want to go to any of your funerals. Keep your heads on a swivel, starting now. You see something, you keep your distance, you call for backup. That is an order. Understand?"

They all looked at Tate again. They couldn't help it. He flushed red. His jaw clenched.

"Right. Understood. Sorry, Chief."

"I keep telling you, it's Jesse—"

Suit rushed into the conference room then.

"Jesse, you should probably come see this."

Over the years, Jesse had learned to recognize the different degrees of worry on Suit's face. He was a terrible poker player because he could not help broadcasting exactly what he felt. Right now, this looked like a four on a scale of one to ten—nobody was bleeding, but something bad was going down. More than anything, Suit loved to keep the peace, and his face said this was something public and messy.

Jesse followed Suit out the front door after putting on his ball cap and attaching his holster to his belt. The rest of the crew trailed after them.

He didn't bother to ask what was happening. He'd see it soon enough.

Actually, he heard it first.

As he and Suit walked down the street toward Daisy's, Jesse heard shouts and chants—not too loud, but shrill and angry, like a small murder of crows fighting over a discarded bag of fast food.

When they rounded the corner, he saw the source.

A mob of people screaming at each other were on opposite sides of Daisy's front door.

"What the hell?" was all Jesse could think to say.

"They both showed up at about the same time," Suit said, head down, as if he was apologizing. "They're fighting over the sign."

"Well, yeah, Suit, I got that."

"I tried talking to them, to keep them apart."

"How'd that go?"

"Apparently I'm both a fascist and a liberal cuck."

"That's a neat trick."

"My mom always said I was versatile."

Jesse took a deep breath and walked across the street to take a position just in front of the door.

There were, of course, two opposing groups, each lined up on either side of the entrance to Daisy's. One was in front of the window with the sign, and seemed to be broadly in favor of it and its message. Jesse saw several people he knew, including Margaret Pye, Paradise's head librarian, and a few of Daisy's friends. There were also a couple of strangers who seemed to be there for the protest alone.

They were trying to get a chant going, but it's tough to chant with barely more than a half-dozen people, Jesse noticed. "ONE TWO THREE FOUR . . ." they began, and then trailed off in search of a rhyme that worked for the occasion. Paradise wasn't really a town for people who made a lot of noise, anyway. Jesse nodded to a couple he knew. They looked vaguely embarrassed, but didn't flinch from his gaze.

On the other side of the door, crowding the sidewalk, was a group that was louder and angrier. Jesse saw only a couple of familiar faces among them. They were yelling. Well, mostly *one* guy was yelling. A heavy, middle-aged man in a SWAT ball cap and what looked like a bullet-proof vest riding up on his gut stood at the front of the group. Jesse had never seen him before. He didn't live in Paradise.

Jesse just stood there, still and silent.

It took them a moment, but eventually everyone noticed him, standing there with his badge and gun, waiting patiently.

The chanting and shouting stopped. They quieted down and turned to him, waiting for him to say something.

"Hi," he said, smiling at all of them.

"Hi," a few of the protesters on both sides said back, looking confused, as if they were expecting more yelling.

"I'm Jesse. I'm the police chief here," he said.

"You can't arrest all of us," someone in the pro-sign crowd said.

"Why aren't you arresting those dirty—" the man in the black tactical vest began.

Jesse put up his hand, and the man shut up.

"I am not here to arrest anyone," Jesse said. "We support the right to protest here in Paradise. A couple of you seem to be new to our town, so I just wanted to let you know that despite what you may have seen on the news, you can say pretty much whatever you want. Just keep the sidewalk clear and let people get in and out of Daisy's so they can get their coffee and breakfast, okay?"

Jesse looked at both sides. They stared back, uncertain of what to say.

"And do not threaten or try to hurt each other. I'm sure none of you need to be reminded of that, right?"

All the protesters stared at him.

"Thanks," Jesse said. "Appreciate you listening."

He turned to go.

"Wait, that's it?" someone yelled.

Jesse turned. It was the middle-aged man in tactical gear. He held his sign like a club. His face was beet-red under the cap.

"Don't you have anything else to say?" he said.

"Yeah," Jesse said. "You should try the turnovers if you go in. They're great."

He turned again, but Tactical Dude was already shouting.

"You're really not going to arrest anyone?"

"Not unless you give me a reason," Jesse said.

"They're the ones who hate cops," Tactical Dude muttered.

"No, we don't!" Margaret shouted back at him. For a librarian, she had quite a set of lungs. "We know what that guy did!" she said, pointing across the narrow street at Tate, who stood there scowling. "And, Jesse," she said, wheeling on him, "you ought to be ashamed! Daisy is your friend! That you would let that animal work for you—"

"See! They hate you!" Tactical Dude shouted.

"Daisy has the right to keep anyone she wants out of her place!" Margaret shot back.

"Fascists!" Tactical Dude screamed.

"You're the fascist!" a gray-haired woman on the opposite side screamed back at him. She looked like someone's grandmother, wrapped in tie-dye.

Jesse felt a headache coming on. He stepped forward again, trying to project calm.

"You see! You see!" Tactical Dude said. "They're violent and dangerous! They threatened me! Arrest them!" Little flecks of spit formed at the corners of the man's mouth.

"Oh, you want to see violent?" Margaret began, taking a step forward, fists clenched.

Jesse took a step closer. "Whoa, whoa, whoa," he said, warning Margaret to stay put.

That's as far as he got when the front door opened and Daisy stepped out.

"Jesus Christ," she said. "Don't any of you have anything better to do?"

"Oh, there she is," Tactical Dude said. "The agitator herself."

"Hey," Jesse said sharply. "Watch your mouth."

Daisy rolled her eyes. "'Agitator'? That's a new one."

She turned her back on him and addressed the pro-sign crowd. "Will you all just go home? Please? I didn't ask any of you to do this. Can you just let my customers get some goddamn breakfast without all this shouting?"

Tactical Dude shoved his way closer to Daisy.

"You should've thought of that"—here Tactical Dude

pointed at the sign—"before you put that bullshit in your window!"

Jesse took another step closer. "Sir," he said. "Please step back."

"I can handle this, Jesse," Daisy snapped.

Jesse didn't care. He moved directly in front of Tactical Dude, blocking Daisy.

Tactical Dude did not recognize danger when it was staring him in the face. Everyone else on the sidewalk did, including Molly, Suit, and Gabe. They were all looking at Jesse. He could feel their eyes on him.

Daisy was still in the doorway, trying to hold it open so her customers could get out. Barry, Jimmy, Tate, and Suit all stood to one side. Peter stood a little farther back. They looked torn.

Jesse opened his mouth to tell Tactical Dude to step back again, to give everyone a little space. He was sure this didn't have to get worse.

Then three things happened.

First, Tactical Dude pivoted from Jesse to face Daisy. His mouth opened and he began screaming another slur. It began with the letter *c* and he seemed to be aiming it at both Daisy and Margaret. Or maybe the grandmother. Or maybe everyone within earshot.

As he turned, he swung his sign around.

Daisy ducked to avoid it. The crowd pushed forward and into her. She lost her balance, stumbled into Tactical Dude.

And that's when Tactical Dude dropped his sign and went for something underneath his jacket, stuck in his utility belt, screaming, "I FEEL THREATENED!"

Something in Jesse snapped. He threw the punch without thinking. Pure reflex. His right fist knocked the man off his feet and put him flat on his back.

Everyone on the street went silent, like someone had suddenly turned the volume way down.

Jesse was already on top of Tactical Dude, turning him over, pulling the black object from his hand.

It was a can of bear spray. Tear gas.

Not a gun.

Jesse felt the tension flood out of him. He got up off the man, who was now cuffed, face down on the sidewalk.

But at that point, Jesse became the new focus of everyone's rage. Some of the pro-sign protesters were aghast. "Jesus *Christ*, Jesse," Margaret said. "You didn't have to kill him!"

Meanwhile, the anti-sign protesters began shouting about lawsuits and lawyers.

Tactical Dude was still struggling to stay awake. "What jush happen?" he slurred. His jaw was not quite aligned with his skull anymore. His cap had been lost somewhere along the way on his short trip to the sidewalk.

Jesse looked at Daisy, who'd regained her feet. She looked like she wanted to take a swing at him herself.

"Damn it, Jesse," she said. "Do you think that *helped*?"

"I am trying to do my job," he said, maybe a little angrier than he intended.

"Are you?" she said, and moved past him, toward the fallen man.

She kneeled down and helped Tactical Dude into the recovery position. His eyes were still unfocused and a long string of drool dripped from his mouth. "That really *hurt*," he said slowly, in the voice of a toddler who'd stepped on something sharp.

"I'm sure it did," Daisy said. "Just take it easy. We'll get you to a doctor." She helped him to his feet. He took her hand gratefully.

Molly and Suit and Gabe gently moved Daisy aside to take the man into custody. Daisy stepped away, still looking daggers at Jesse.

All the protesters had gone quiet, glaring at Jesse, taking videos with their phones.

Well, Jesse thought. *At least I brought everyone together.*

It absolutely did not help that Tate chose that moment to let out a war whoop of victory and shout, "Damn, Chief, you kicked that guy's *ass*!"

TWENTY-SEVEN

Ellis Munroe was spending far too much time in Jesse's office lately. From the look on the DA's face, Jesse could see that he thought so, too.

"Goddamn it, Stone, what the hell were you thinking?"

Jesse stared hard at him. "Not today, Ellis. Not in my office. Have a seat and I'll get you some coffee and we can discuss this like civilized people."

Ellis fumed for a second, but he picked up on Jesse's tone. He was a lot of things, but stupid was not one of them. He looked at Molly, who leaned against the wall, like a referee watching over a boxing match. She gestured to the chair.

Ellis sat down heavily.

"Isn't that better?" Jesse said. "You want some coffee?"

"No, thank you," Ellis said. "Now can we talk about the turd you just handed me?"

"I arrested a guy for assault. Surely you can handle that."

"You dislocated the guy's jaw," Ellis said. "He's in the ER right now having it reset."

"He was going for a weapon."

"A nonlethal self-defense device that is sold over the counter to women who walk their dogs in the park."

"A little misogynistic there, Ellis," Molly said.

"Sorry, Molly," Ellis said. "Not my intention."

"Bear spray," Jesse said. "Two percent capsaicin. Made for bears. It says so right in the name. It causes temporary blindness, vomiting, and respiratory distress. We use that stuff on crowds. And he was swinging a sign like a club."

Ellis waved a hand as if this was irrelevant. "He didn't hit anyone."

"He shouted, 'I feel threatened,' which is one of those idiot phrases they teach people to use to justify their actions before they shoot someone. So they can call it self-defense later."

"Jesse's right," Molly said. "There are YouTube videos made just for guys like that. How to create a legal pretext for deadly force."

"Yeah," Ellis said grudgingly. "I've seen them."

"That's why I thought he was going for a gun. I didn't know it was bear spray."

Ellis sighed heavily, the front of his white button-down riding up his gut.

"Well, you got fast hands, I'll give you that. He never had a chance," Ellis said. "Would have been better if he'd actually had a gun."

"Maybe I should have let him shoot someone, Ellis," Jesse said. "Would that have helped?"

Molly gave him a look. Jesse ignored it.

"His pals already have a lawyer at my office," Ellis said. "I will talk to him. Maybe drop the charges in exchange for a release of liability."

"You're going to let him go?" Jesse asked.

"You have nothing, Jesse," Ellis said. "You don't even have resisting arrest, because you nearly took his head off his shoulders and it's all on video. He's not going to look very dangerous, sitting on his ass on the pavement. I take this in front of a judge, I'm getting laughed out of the arraignment."

Jesse stared at Ellis for a moment. He realized the DA was probably right. It didn't help.

"Fine, Ellis."

"We'll be lucky to avoid a lawsuit."

"I said *fine*."

Ellis opened his mouth to say something else, but Molly shook her head quickly. Ellis got the message. He stood up.

"How's Mr. Peebles holding up?" he asked.

"He's still not talking," Jesse said. "You want to let him go, too?"

"He's the guy I want to charge, but you won't let me, remember?"

"Let me do my job, and you do yours, okay?"

Ellis made a noise. "I'm not your enemy, Jesse. I am trying to work with you on all of this. Maybe stop and think before you sucker-punch someone next time."

He walked out of the office, muttering to himself.

Molly went to the door and closed it, then turned back to Jesse.

"Okay," she said. "What the hell?"

Jesse picked up his ball and glove and then remembered the burns on his hands. He flung them back to the desk, hard. "Not you, too, Crane."

"Don't you snarl at me," Molly said. "I have known you too long for that shit, and I am pretty sure the bear spray is still around here somewhere."

Jesse almost smiled at that, but clamped down on it. He knew he was angry, and he wanted to hang on to it for some reason.

"I am trying to figure out what's wrong with you," Molly said. "You've been angry and dismissive since you found Burton's body."

"I'd be fine if people let me do my goddamn job," Jesse said.

"Really? Is that what you told Daisy?"

"Maybe Daisy needs to recognize that sometimes she doesn't know what the hell she's talking about," he said. "And neither do you."

Molly looked at him. "Now, where did that come from? Why are you pushing me, Jesse?"

Jesse didn't respond.

"The silent treatment, huh? Not going to work this time. You need to tell me what's going on. Why are you so angry?"

Jesse took a deep breath, counted back from ten. "I am not angry."

Molly snorted. "Well, that was convincing."

"You want to talk about Tate? Okay. Here's what

happened. He's new here. He overreacted a little. But Daisy shouldn't get special treatment just because she's my friend."

Molly rolled her eyes. "Some friend."

"Excuse me?"

"Oh, is something wrong with your hearing? Is that the problem?"

"Look—"

"No, Jesse, you look. You know Daisy has the thickest skin of anyone in this town. She's not a complainer. If she told you about this, she's concerned. And you should listen to her. Because she loves this town and she doesn't want to see anything hurt it."

Jesse sighed and rubbed his face with both hands. He was rapidly losing patience. "Jesus, Molly. It was a misunderstanding."

"You really think after all her time dealing with you and us that she would misread a situation so badly?"

"She's a civilian."

Molly stopped cold. Blinked at Jesse.

"'A civilian'?" she said. "Are we at war, Jesse? Are we soldiers now? Is that why you cold-cocked that nitwit out there?"

"You know what I mean."

"Yeah, I think I do. And that's the problem."

Jesse sat back. "Then enlighten me. Because I don't see it."

"You were the one who told me: As soon as we start seeing our job as us versus them, something has gone badly wrong. We're all supposed to be on the same side here, Jesse."

"It doesn't always work like that and you know it."

"Maybe not in other places. But this is Paradise," Molly said. "What kind of message do you think that sends the new guy? Is that how we do things here? We're supposed to be better than that. You were the one who told me that, too."

"Is this still about Tate?"

"I don't know," Molly said. "Is it? Are you cutting him slack because of your own history?"

Cheap shot, Jesse thought. *Accurate, maybe, but cheap.*

"I don't need a shrink, Molly."

"I think you do," she said. "Because if you won't talk to me, you better talk to somebody before it eats you up again."

She turned her back on him, opened the door, and walked through, very pointedly not slamming it shut.

He had to admit, that was a perfect strikeout pitch. Way to close down the side.

Jesse turned in his chair and tried to calm down. He did the breathing exercises he'd been taught a long time ago. They didn't work. He spun back around toward his desk.

And without thinking, he reached for the bottom desk drawer.

Opened it. Nothing there.

He stared. He didn't know if he was relieved or disappointed.

Molly's voice broke into his thoughts.

"What are you looking for, Jesse?"

He looked up and saw her standing at the door. She'd turned back and saw what he'd done.

Jesse withdrew his hand like the drawer was scalding hot. "I'm not sure."

"Really?" Molly gave him a look like he was a teenager caught sneaking in after curfew. It annoyed Jesse. Mainly because he knew he'd just lied to her.

Jesse took a deep breath. Let it out. *Honesty,* he reminded himself. *Drunks lie. Honesty is an alcoholic's kryptonite.*

"I was about to reach for the bottle," he said.

"I know."

"It's not there. And I reached for it anyway."

"I know that, too."

Molly came into the office and closed the door behind her again.

She sat down.

"Jesse," she said, looking directly into his eyes. "You worked really hard to let go of that bottle. I know what it cost you. I was there. So if you're reaching for it again . . ."

She didn't finish. She didn't have to.

Jesse took a deep breath, tried to stay calm. Even. She was acting as his friend here.

"This shouldn't be a big deal," he said.

"You think?" Molly asked. "I told you what Suit and I would do if you started drinking again. Seems pretty big to me."

"Not what I meant," he said. "I thought it was under control. Hell, Molly, I've been in worse situations than this and I never once felt the need."

"Not once?"

"You know what I mean. I've been under more pressure. I don't know why this is different."

Now he could admit it, at least to himself. This whole thing—the dead body, Daisy, Tate—it was piling on him. He could see the Scotch and the soda over ice in the glass. He could feel the burn in his throat as he pulled straight from the bottle.

He really wanted nothing more than a drink.

And he didn't know why.

That bothered him.

"You don't get to decide how much some things affect you," Molly said. "Sometimes you have to just take the punch. You taught me that."

"Yeah, but—"

Molly smirked a little and cut him off. "Yeah, but you're different? The great Jesse Stone is above all that? You can do it yourself? Bullshit. We're not doing this again. So maybe instead of carrying this around and acting like an asshole to everyone, you start dealing with whatever's bothering you."

Jesse nodded. He'd given his word. He said he'd never put Molly, or Suit, or Paradise through his problems again.

"You're right," he said.

"I'm always right."

Molly reached across the desk and briefly put her hand on his.

"Now call Dix," she said. "He gets paid for this and I've been giving it away for free."

"Yeah, that's what—"

"Don't," Molly warned.

She got up to go.

"Sure you don't want to place the call for me?" he asked.

"You know how the phone works," Molly said, and closed the door behind her.

Right. She trusted him to do it himself.

Jesse picked up the phone and dialed.

He'd given his word. Sometimes he'd rather get shot again, but he had to admit it.

Whatever was going on inside his head, he needed some help.

TWENTY-EIGHT

Elliott drove through the streets of Paradise. It didn't take long.

He'd flown up the night before and got a rental car and a motel room outside Boston. Now he was glad he'd kept a little distance. He had a feeling it would be easy to get stuck here.

Everything in Paradise was too nice, too clean for him. The high school could have been edited out of a movie and plunked right down on its lot. Even the town's police station looked like it belonged in a kid's play set.

But it seemed like a place that was used to tourists, so a stranger in town wouldn't rouse too much suspicion, at least not right away.

He had a little trouble believing this was where Burton had lived, a man who'd been responsible for hundreds of deaths in his life. Elliott had used Burton's services many times, when he wasn't working for the organization. Elliott was a freelancer, so he took contracts when he wanted to, and Burton had been an honest broker. They'd put a lot of bodies in the ground together, made quite a bit of money along the way.

Elliott couldn't quite picture it, Burton squatting in this clean little town among all these good citizens, like a tumor in an otherwise healthy body.

But you could probably say the same thing about him. He looked harmless. He knew that. He worked at it. When he saw himself in the mirror, he saw an aging white guy, a gray-haired retiree in a Tommy Bahama shirt and slacks. So that's what other people saw. As long as they didn't look too closely at his eyes.

The eyes gave Elliott away. They were cold and flat, always searching. Looking for angles, looking for weaknesses, looking for an escape.

But 99 percent of the world didn't pay attention to things like that. They barely paid attention at all.

Time to check in. He pulled into a parking spot on Paradise Road and picked up his burner phone. It had only one number programmed into it, and only one person had its number.

"Yeah?"

"The fuck is going on there," the old man rasped at him. "You waiting for this prick to die of old age?"

At one point in his life, Mulvaney snarling at him like this would have filled him with dread. Or at least worry. Now he knew he was likely to outlive Mulvaney or anyone Mulvaney could send. Things had changed. He was doing the job because he was a professional, and he was also at risk from Burton's files. But he was not about to jump because Mulvaney was impatient.

"I'm gathering information," he said. "Putting it together. He's a cop. That's a little trickier."

"Christ, he's a mall cop. He came into my home. I should've just popped him then myself if I'd known you were so scared of him."

Elliott bit back his first reply, which was to tell Mulvaney that he'd never done his own wet work ever, so he didn't know shit about how long it took. Instead, he said, "Lot of people thought Stone was a speed-trap cop. They're in the ground now."

"Where'd you hear that bullshit?"

Elliott sighed. "Read the papers sometime, Charlie. Stone has a body count. And I've asked around. Heavy hitter out in Vegas named Cromartie told a guy I know—"

"I could give two shits," Mulvaney said. "Every day he's aboveground is another day my goddamn useless nephew could decide to talk. You gotta take care of that, too."

Elliott sighed. "Your nephew?"

"Stone popped him for the arson."

"Jesus Christ."

"Yeah, well, that's why you shouldn't be waiting around. He's in the station. Along with the money."

"This just gets better and better," Elliott said. "You want me to go into a police station, do the job, and steal two million dollars on top of it?"

"Hey. Watch your mouth. We're on an open line."

"Fuck your open line, Charlie. This is suicide."

"Is he better than you?"

Elliott paused. He honestly didn't know. Back in the

day? Probably not. He was cold and solid and perfect in those days. Nobody could touch him. Nobody even came close.

Today? Today he was an old man. Sure, he still nailed everything inside the rings at the shooting range. He could still throw a punch and take one, and he could run a marathon if he had to.

Even so, his eyes were weaker and his hands shook sometimes. So he didn't know. Was he better than Stone?

"I'm not sure," he said.

"Well, you better figure it out fast," Mulvaney said. "You and I both know we weren't the only ones who used Burton's services."

"What's that supposed to mean?"

"Nobody knows how much Stone and the cops managed to save from the fire. There have to be at least a half-dozen more hitters who have to be worried now. You think they're just gonna wait around for someone else to clean this up?"

Shit. Elliott hadn't thought of that. There would be other contractors who would hear about this. They'd be on their way. If they weren't here already.

"You better get Stone quick," Mulvaney said, his voice mocking, "or someone else is going to. And they'll probably get that two million dollars, too. Clock's ticking, buddy."

He hung up. Elliott put the phone away.

He didn't want to admit it, but Mulvaney was right.

The small town of Paradise was about to get very crowded with people who killed people, and who were very good at it.

TWENTY-NINE

Jesse sat in the chair facing the desk, like he had many times. Dix, as always, looked impeccable. Crisp white shirt. Shaved head gleaming and clean. The only decoration on the wall of his office was his Harvard diploma. No records from the years he'd spent as a cop before he became a psychiatrist. For that matter, no personal photos, or any sign of the years he'd spent as a drunk. Just like Jesse.

Dix looked at the Rolex watch under the cuff of his immaculate shirt. "You going to just sit there, or are you going to say something?"

"Have someplace else to be?"

"I bumped people to see you today. I've got other clients, you know."

"Do you?"

"You sound skeptical."

"Just surprised anyone puts up with you."

It always started a little confrontational. Like an interrogation. Probably a hangover from Dix's cop days. Or just because Jesse, despite all the years he'd been going, still resented the idea of needing therapy.

Dix waited. Jesse still didn't speak. So Dix asked the question that always got them started.

"Why are you here, Jesse?"

Jesse thought about it for another second and did his best to answer honestly. "I don't know," he said. "I'm angry. Taking it out on the people around me. It's going to affect my work—it's going to affect my case—if I don't figure out why."

"And you want a drink."

"And I want a drink," Jesse admitted. "You could look a little more shocked."

"Jesse, you were a dry drunk for years. You know what that means?"

Jesse nodded. A dry drunk was an alcoholic who didn't stop being an alcoholic just because they quit drinking. He'd done that for a long time, as Dix said. It didn't work.

"And how did it feel?" Dix asked.

"Like I was hanging on by my fingernails every day. Like I was about to explode."

"You were angry all the time, right?" Dix said. "You were looking for an excuse to take it out on someone."

"Not all the time," Jesse said.

"But a lot."

"Yeah. A lot."

"That's because you couldn't do the one thing you wanted to do: get drunk."

"I know all this."

"And yet, here you are."

Good point, Jesse thought. "I went to rehab. I'm doing the meetings."

"But you're still angry."

"I've got it under control."

"You sure?"

"I'm being polite to you, aren't I?"

That made Dix smile. "Jesse, you're an alcoholic. You know we don't get over that. It's not the flu. We are going to carry that with us until we die. But we can be aware of the things we're doing that give us the excuse to drink."

"You think I'm looking for an excuse?"

"Are you?"

"No," Jesse said. Then he said something that was hard for him to admit. "I feel worried. And I don't know why."

"That bothers you."

Jesse nodded.

"You worry about things all the time," Dix said. "You worry about Suit, about Molly, about Cole. You worry about the town and your department, even people you barely know. Why should it bother you so much to worry about yourself for a change?"

Jesse was usually pretty good at keeping his emotions off his face, but he couldn't help scowling.

"Oh, you're angry now? Well, that's new and unexpected. Why do you think that is?"

"Maybe I'm a little insulted at the idea that I need someone worrying about me. I can take care of myself."

"I know you can. You're one of the most competent cops I've ever seen."

"Just not very good at being a regular guy," Jesse said.

"You said it, I didn't."

"You were thinking it."

"Let's keep this on what you're thinking, Jesse. Why is it hard to worry about yourself? Why does it bother you so much? And why *right now*?"

Jesse shrugged. He felt a deep twinge in his bad shoulder. "I don't know," he said. "Why don't you tell me? That's what I'm paying for, right?"

"Doesn't work that way and you know it. Wouldn't mean anything if I just told you."

"You know, sometimes I wonder what the hell I need you for."

Dix smiled at him. "Me, too."

"What?"

"You're a pretty smart guy, Jesse. You're a step ahead of almost everyone. It's why you're a great cop. Except in one area."

"What's that?"

"Nobody sees their own problems clearly. Not even a smart guy like you."

Dix looked at the clock. "That's our time. Why don't you think it over and come back with an answer."

"That's it?"

"Next time, start talking when you get here. We can get more done."

"I need to figure this out, Dix," Jesse said. "I don't have time for the usual games."

"I agree," Dix said.

"What?"

"Something's really bothering you. You're on edge. You want a drink. So you and I should talk every day."

Jesse stood. "Well. I've got this case. I don't know if I'll be able to come in every day."

"I figured," Dix said. "I think you should call me. Every day."

"What?"

"I don't have time for you to come in every day, Jesse. But it's clearly what you need. You just told me you can't play the usual games. Me, either. So call me, every day, when you're done with your shift. We'll talk."

Jesse stood there, trying to think of a reason he couldn't do this. Dix saw his wheels spinning and headed him off.

"Your phone still works, right?"

Jesse felt his anger suddenly turn on Dix, at his clean white shirt, at his immaculate desk, at his smug insistence that he knew all the answers.

"You're really giving me homework? You're making me check in? Like some kind of . . . I don't know, child with a curfew?"

He took a deep breath, trying to calm down.

"What's wrong, Jesse?" Dix asked.

Jesse didn't answer. Just kept glaring.

"What do you want to tell me?" Dix asked.

"I wish," Jesse said, teeth clenched, "that for once you would just stop playing around and tell me what you mean."

"Okay," Dix said.

"What?" Jesse was caught flat-footed by that.

For maybe the first time ever, Dix looked tired. He sat back and rubbed his eyes, then looked up at Jesse again.

"You found a dead guy alone in his own house," Dix said. "Surrounded by the wreckage of his own life. Nobody came looking for him for weeks. And nobody cared. Any reason that might have triggered you?"

"I hate that word. 'Triggered.'"

"Yeah, well, clichés get to be clichés for a reason. You wanted to know what it means? Here's what it means: You thought you were looking at your future. Dead on a floor and nobody gives a shit. It scares the hell out of you, Jesse. That's why you're snapping at everyone and ready to throw hands. You're in full fight-or-flight right now. Because you're scared you're going to end up just like that guy in that house. Forgotten. Abandoned. Alone."

Jesse sat there for a moment. He felt stunned.

"Does that do it for you? You feel cured? Alakazam, all your problems are gone?"

"No," Jesse said.

"Of course not. Because you need to learn it yourself. Knowing is only half the battle. You have to figure it out on your own. Just like solving a case."

"Then why tell me?"

Dix laughed a little at that. Then looked more grim than ever.

"I've lost two patients in the last six months. Guys your age. Single. Professionals. Don't need nobody, got it all handled, too tough to cry, all the same crap. One went out with a drug overdose, the other bought a gun and put it in his mouth. Everyone I know in my profession is seeing more of it. Men dying because they're angry and lonely. Guys like you are actually bringing down the life expectancy of men overall in the whole country. That's quite an accomplishment."

"You think I'm a suicide risk?"

"Not immediately, no," Dix said. "Like I said, you're the strongest man I've ever met. But you're a single, middle-aged guy in a high-stress position. You've got a history of alcoholism and bad relationships. You've already been through more trauma than anyone should have to bear. You've got no family outside of a son you barely talk to. Damn few friends. Loneliness is a killer, Jesse. I'd be an idiot not to consider the risk."

"I'm not lonely—" Jesse began to say.

"Stop it." Dix pointed at him. "You said you wanted to hear it. So here it is: You've been repeating the same patterns for a long damn time. Aren't you tired of it? Aren't you *finally getting tired* of making the same stupid mistakes over and over? I know I'm tired of seeing you do it."

Jesse didn't respond. He hadn't felt like this since their first days working together.

"Everyone in this life has only one real choice: change or die," Dix said. "Which is it going to be? I don't want you to die. I don't think you really *want* to die, despite everything you do. So let's stop screwing around. Let's actually work on the goddamn problem. You can't make it in? Pick up the phone and call me. You think you can handle that?"

Jesse managed to nod.

"Good," Dix said. "Now go do your job. We'll talk later."

Jesse got up and left. He tried his best not to slam the door on his way out.

He didn't quite manage it.

THIRTY

That night, Jesse stood in his condo and looked at his poster of Ozzie Smith. Ozzie was his hero growing up. The man seemed to have superhuman abilities on the ballfield. Jesse had moved house a couple of times since coming to Paradise, but the poster of Ozzie—vintage now, worth a couple hundred bucks on eBay at least—always came with him, and always had pride of place in the living room.

He used to toast the photo with a Scotch and soda when he was still drinking. Now he just looked at it.

There were days when he thought he'd be just as good as Ozzie, if he got on the field, if he made it to the majors. Now there were days when he wondered if he'd ever be as good at anything as Ozzie Smith was at baseball.

Jesse's only witness was in the cells, still reeking of the gasoline he'd used to torch most of the evidence in Jesse's big case. His newest hire had an even worse temper than he did, and it might have cost Jesse one of his only close friends. And his shrink seemed to think he was the human equivalent of a six-car pileup.

Moments like this, he really wanted a drink.

Jesse thought about something else Dix had said that actually landed: "a son you barely talk to."

He hadn't known his son, Cole, for most of his life. He'd never been told by Cole's mother that Cole even existed. Cole had shown up in Paradise as an adult with a lot of anger. He got that much from Jesse, at least.

But the two of them had made their way to a relationship, Jesse thought. Though Dix was right—they didn't talk much. Cole had left for California a few years back, then London, following a woman, which hadn't worked out. Got that from his father, too. Now he was back in Los Angeles again, using his law degree as an assistant United States attorney.

He'd followed Jesse into law enforcement, but they never seemed to have much to say anymore.

Jesse picked up his phone and tapped the button for his son.

The phone barely had time to ring. "What's wrong, Jesse? Are you okay?"

Jesse chuckled. "I'm fine. Just wanted to say hello."

"Jesus. Nobody calls anyone to say hello anymore. I thought you'd been shot or something. Send me a text next time."

Jesse wanted to say that texting was for teenage girls, but he was struck by something else. "Am I back to Jesse now?" he said. "What happened to 'Dad'?"

There was a heavy sigh over the line. "Sorry. It just sort of slipped out."

"No, I didn't mean anything by it. You can call me whatever you want. I just . . ."

Cole didn't say anything, and the silence lingered.

". . . I just like being your dad," Jesse finished.

Another sigh. "Look, I'm about to go on a date. Was there something you needed?"

"No," Jesse said. "I just realized we hadn't spoken for a while. How's the job?"

"Fine."

Jesse waited. That was it. "Fine." Nothing else.

"You still thinking about getting a job with the SEC? Do more finance work."

"Not really."

And, again, nothing else. It was like Cole thought he'd be billed by the word.

"So maybe you heard about this thing with Daisy," Jesse said.

"She gave me a call."

Ah, there it was. Jesse sometimes forgot that Cole had worked for Daisy. She'd given him a place to stay and a job when he'd first shown up in Paradise, broke and practically homeless.

"Oh. She's not speaking to me right now."

"Yeah, well, sounds like she's got good reason."

"Come on. You know that it's never that simple."

"You were the one who taught me that it was."

Jesse hesitated. "Are you angry with me, Cole?"

A longer sigh this time. "No, Jesse. I'm just busy. I've

got a lot going on right now, okay? I don't have a lot of time to chat."

"I know that. I just want to know what's going on with you. I want us to do better," Jesse said.

Cole laughed. "Jesus Christ. Are you drinking again?"

"I'm serious."

"Jesse. I really don't have time right now. Whatever this is. But between you and me, I'm not the guy who needs to do better."

That hurt. Jesse felt it under his ribs.

"You're right," Jesse said. "I'm sorry. That's not what I meant."

"Me, too. Don't worry about it," Cole said, his voice suddenly much kinder. "I really do have to get going. We'll catch up this weekend, okay? I'll give you a call."

"Yeah," Jesse said, feeling like an idiot. "Sounds good."

"All right. Later."

He hung up.

"Later," Jesse said into the dead phone, alone in the room, as the house grew dark around him.

THIRTY-ONE

Peter Perkins waited outside Jesse's door. "Got a minute?" he asked.

"Of course," Jesse said, and they went into his office.

Peter was out of uniform, but he was part-time at best these days. He'd been trying to retire, but the hiring crunch had forced Jesse to keep him on. The department badly needed someone else to do the training as a crime scene officer, but Jesse couldn't spare Molly or Suit or Gabe for the time it would take for the course.

In the meantime, they had Peter. And Jesse was grateful. So he tried to give Peter every courtesy.

Peter sat down and looked at his hands and the floor before speaking. He was never a very forceful guy. Jesse thought he liked doing the forensics work because it took place after everyone else had left and the scene was quiet.

But he was still a decent cop. Peter had been a part of

the Paradise department longer than Jesse had; he'd been there when Jesse showed up, and he'd stood by Jesse when the previous members of the town selectmen had tried to overthrow the Paradise PD by force. That wasn't easy, and Jesse would not forget it.

"I think you might be a little hard on the new kid," Peter said.

"How do you mean?"

"Look, he's young, he's not used to how we do things in a smaller town like Paradise," Peter said. "I know Daisy is a friend of yours, but I think the kid just got over-excited. He was trained in a big city. He looks at everyone as a potential threat."

"That's not how we do things here," Jesse said.

"That's it," Peter said. "That's my point. His reflexes are wrong. But he needs a chance to learn how to do it another way. He's got to learn."

"You keep talking about him as if he's a fourth-grader. He's a grown man, Peter."

Peter ducked his head. "No argument from me. But he listened when I talked to him. I think he can do better."

Jesse thought about that. "What do you suggest?"

"Show him the ropes. Give him a little time. Let him figure out what it's like here. You know, the way you did."

"I'm not sure I'm the best role model for him in this case," Jesse said. "What about you?"

"What about me?"

"Would you partner up with him?"

Peter's eyebrows went up. "You think I could do that?"

"Like you said, he listened to you."

"Yeah, but . . . you think I'm the guy for the job?"

"Peter," Jesse said, "I'd be happy if Tate were half the cop you've been in my time here."

Peter looked down, but Jesse saw the smile before he stifled it. "Well, yeah, sure. If you want. I'd be glad to take him around a bit."

"Okay," Jesse said. "Next time he's on shift, I'll have you ride with him. Thanks, Peter."

Jesse stood up. Peter did the same. He put out his hand. It felt strangely formal to Jesse, but he shook it.

"I won't let you down," Peter said.

"You never have."

Jesse went into the cells to check on Peebles. He had about forty-eight hours left before a judge would find that Jesse was violating Peebles's rights. Give or take, anyway. Then it was either charge him or release him.

If he had Ellis Munroe charge Peebles, he'd go into the county holding facility. If he let him go, Mulvaney would find him. Either way, shortly after that, Peebles would be dead. There was no question in Jesse's mind.

Not that Peebles had demanded a lawyer. He hadn't done much of anything, in fact, except sit and look at the walls.

Jesse wanted to take one more shot at trying to get him to talk.

He stood in front of the cell. Peebles blinked at him like a lizard, then looked away. Peebles acted like he was already dead. It would be hard to save his life with that attitude.

"I'm running out of time, Matthew. So I'm going to be

blunt. Why are you protecting a guy who wants you dead?"

"You think I'm protecting him?" Peebles laughed. "You're kidding, right? I'm doing everything I can to protect myself."

"I know you don't want to believe me, but I'm keeping you here for the same reason. I am determined to keep you safe, Matthew."

"You can't. Nobody can."

"Look, I've met your uncle."

"Great-uncle, actually."

"Right. What makes him so much scarier than every other aging mobster out there?"

Peebles finally seemed to see Jesse, actually focus his eyes on him as a real person.

"I'm not telling you anything that you can use in court," he said. "I mean, let's just say I'm speaking hypothetically here."

"Okay. Hypothetically," Jesse said.

"Let's say there's this kid. He's been raised by a single mom. His dad left a long time ago, and he's only had a series of her increasingly disappointing boyfriends and one-night stands to serve as his piss-poor examples of manhood."

"Sounds familiar."

"Yeah. Lot of that going around, I know. But let's also say this hypothetical kid's mom has a mother who comes around, too. And she's old-school Irish. I mean, tough. Hard as nails. But this kid, she thinks he's special. Thinks he has potential, even though she's the only one. For good reason, I mean. The kid is a complete waste of space, but he doesn't see it yet. He thinks the sun shines out his own ass."

"Maybe the kid just needs someone to look after him."

"Yeah, you'd think so. But you'd be wrong. Because, see, eventually, the grandma takes the kid to meet her brother. His great-uncle. And as tough as she is, he's a goddamn battleship. He's made of plate steel and pure hatred. The kid is terrified of him, and at the same time, he thinks the guy is the greatest man to walk the earth. Eventually, with his grandmother's help, he convinces the guy to let him do some jobs. Run errands. Hang around. That sort of stuff."

"Okay," Jesse said. He noticed Peebles was sweating now, staring into space, like he was someplace else entirely.

"The kid thinks he's a real gangster now. He doesn't see how everything is falling apart, how everyone is paranoid as hell, and how there are guys killing each other right and left for whatever they can grab. He's too young, too stupid. He just knows he's got money for the first time in his life, he's got cool shoes and weed and the kids at school are scared of him and he's even got girlfriends."

"Sounds like he's got it all."

"Yeah, but he's an idiot, remember. Because he doesn't know where it comes from. Not really. But one day he's at his great-uncle's place. He was supposed to deliver some papers from a lawyer, and he forgot—actually, no, he was getting a hand job from an older girl in the back seat of a car. He thought he was a king. Not even old enough to drive yet. She had to drop him off at his uncle's. Because he was late. And because he was late, his uncle was conducting some other business. The kid went to find him in the garage, around the back. His uncle had a big place back then. Lots of room. Thick walls. Cinder-block. Sound-proofed."

Peebles gulped some air. Then he went on.

"So this hypothetical kid, he didn't even hear anything until he opened the door to the garage. And that's when he saw the guy hanging from the ceiling on a hook. While his uncle watched these other guys beat him to death. The kid didn't understand what he was seeing. Not at first. But once he figured it out, he knew he'd never be able to unsee it again. He pissed himself. And he ran away as fast as he could."

Jesse sat quietly. He didn't think anything he had to say would help.

Peebles seemed to snap out of his memories. "So. That kid was never asked by his uncle to come around anymore. He stopped getting money, stopped getting jobs. Because he was weak. See, the uncle had seen the kid, just before he ran away. And that was the thing: The kid didn't run or piss himself because of the guy being murdered. He ran because his uncle looked him in the eye. And the kid was terrified of what he saw there."

"So why does this kid still hang out with this uncle now?"

"Hypothetically speaking?" Peebles said, a weak smile on his face. "He tries not to. He took some money to invest in a club a few years ago, so he could be cool again. But there were odd jobs attached."

"And Burton was one of them."

Peebles shook his head, as if he'd realized how much

had spilled from his lips. "Don't know what you mean, Officer. I was talking about someone else. Just telling you a story."

Jesse sat for a moment. Peebles wouldn't look at him.

"He's not the devil, Matthew. He's just an old man."

Peebles laughed softly. "You sure about that?"

THIRTY-TWO

Jesse was walking through the front of the station on his way back from the cells when he noticed the guy standing inside the front door.

He was young, Jesse thought, but it was hard to tell. He wore a Dodgers baseball cap, sunglasses, and a KN95. Jesse still saw older people wearing those, but not many young people.

Jesse turned to him. "Can I help you?"

The guy tilted his head, as if considering the question.

"I don't know," he said. "Maybe. You Chief Jesse Stone?"

Jesse put his coffee cup on the nearest desk. Something in the guy's tone, his stance, pinged his radar. Made him want to have both hands free. Jesse was no quick draw, but he could clear his gun fast and still shoot accurately.

Once again, he wished the town had let him put

bulletproof glass between the entrance of the station and the desks. But Armistead hated the idea. It sent the wrong message, he said. "We're a friendly little town, Jesse," he'd said. "Try not to treat everyone who comes into the station like a goddamn terrorist."

"I'm Chief Stone," Jesse said. "What can I do for you?"

The guy nodded, like he'd just been proven right about something. "Doesn't seem like much of a police station. More like a cute little dollhouse. You get a lot of crime here, Chief?"

"Not much," Jesse said, putting his right hand on his belt, near his gun. "Paradise is usually a nice place."

"Yeah, it looks nice here. Pretty. Quiet."

"It is. Most of the time."

"What happens when it isn't?"

"Then we handle it," Jesse said.

They stood for a moment, facing each other.

Then Suit walked in from the back. "Hey, Jesse," he said. He stopped short. Looked at the guy and at Jesse. Immediately picked up on the tension in the room.

The two of them faced the man in the mask.

The guy seemed to make a decision.

"Well, I'm sure that's a great comfort to the people who live here," he said. "Nice little town."

"You looking to move here?" Jesse asked. "You give me your name, I can probably have a realtor get in touch with you."

"Aw, that's really nice, Chief," the guy said, already backing away, toward the doors. "But I'm just passing through. Thanks for your time."

He turned and exited.

Suit turned to Jesse. "What the hell was that about?"

Jesse didn't respond. He went around the desk and out the door, looking down the street.

The guy was gone.

Suit was right behind Jesse, his hand on his gun, ready for anything.

"Jesse, what's going on? Who was that?"

Jesse looked both ways again. The guy must have run, ducked down an alley. No way to tell where he was now. And Jesse didn't want to go chasing him around a bunch of blind corners.

"Those bad guys I said were coming?" Jesse said. "First one's here. And he wants us to know it."

Raney took off the ball cap and the KN95. He'd gotten his first look at the station and the cop. Neither one seemed all that impressive.

Raney couldn't believe his contact, Burton, had lived in this upscale little place. It was like the whole town was a yacht club. Everything looked like it cost more than you could afford; if you had to ask, it was too expensive.

Burton had hooked Raney up with some of his first jobs. The photos were from one. A Honduran immigrant who'd seen something he wasn't supposed to or was agitating for more money at his sweatshop. Raney couldn't recall the details now; he tended to forget them as soon as he was done with a job, like he was clearing space on a hard drive.

Maybe there was something to that news report about the money Burton left behind.

Maybe there was a way to get paid after all.

Seeing how rich this town looked, he was sure the chief of police wasn't going to be a problem. A town like Paradise, he was probably more like a butler than a cop.

THIRTY-THREE

Tate came into Jesse's office after his shift, wearing his tailored uniform.

"Molly said you wanted to see me, Jesse?"

Jesse closed the door. He didn't want to embarrass Tate.

"Derek, I have a question for you. It's important."

Tate looked back at him, his face blank.

"Why do you want to be a cop?" Jesse asked.

Tate began to smile. "Didn't we already go over this? In my first interview?"

"Let's say I forgot. Tell me again: Why do you want to do this?"

Tate smirked. "Because I can help people."

"Really?" Jesse said. "Who did you help today?"

"What?"

"On patrol. Who did you help today?"

"I don't . . . Are you asking for what I did with my time? You think I'm slacking?"

"No," Jesse said. "I really want to know. Who did you help?"

"I don't understand. I answered my calls, I did my time out there like you told me—"

"Who did you help?" Jesse asked again. "Did you talk to Tish at Moxie's about the graffiti that's been popping up in the alley behind her store? Did you park by the middle school and keep people from speeding down Village Street when the kids are coming out of class? Did you stop at the Gray Gull for lunch and listen to the regulars complain?"

Tate turned away from Jesse and shook his head, his cheeks flushing. "Look, I don't know everyone in this little town the same way you do."

"Did you give a tourist directions? Did you help an old lady cross the street or get a little girl's cat out of a tree? Anything at all like that?"

"That's not what real cops do."

Jesse sat back in his chair.

"It's not? Because I've done it. I've done all that. And I write budgets and I talk to the mayor and I go to council meetings. Being a cop isn't all running and gunning. Even when I was with LAPD—"

"Yeah, I've heard what you did with LAPD," Tate muttered.

Jesse chose not to hear him. "There were days when all I did was the regular stuff. Taking reports. Writing citations. Knocking on doors and asking the same question over and over again."

"You mean like how you handled that guy yesterday?"

"That was a mistake."

Tate scoffed. Then he saw that Jesse was serious.

"What?"

"I let it go too far."

"The guy got in your face, what else were you supposed to do?"

Jesse looked at Tate while he searched for the right words. "That's the point," he said. "That guy was an idiot. A bully and a loudmouth. If I can't outwit someone like him, I'm not trying hard enough. I should have found another way."

"Are you serious?"

"Look. Usually, if someone's meeting up with us, something has gone wrong in their lives. We're probably seeing them at their worst moment. And we have a choice. We can be the ones who help them out of it, or we can be the ones who make it even worse. It's a split-second decision sometimes. But you have to live with the consequences forever."

"Oh, bullshit, Jesse," Tate said. "It's not that simple. And you know it. What happens when you run into the other guy? The one who pulls his gun?"

"Actually, that's when it gets really simple. What I worry about is a cop who tries to make every situation that simple."

"What? What does that even mean?"

"It's easy when it's bad guys versus good guys, Derek. The job is hard when it's just you and some people out there. When there's noise and screaming and rage and pointing fingers and nobody has any idea what's going on. You have to walk into those situations and find out what happens next. You have to rely on your instincts and you have to rely on people you don't know and you have to listen and wait and see. That's the hard part. That's where we show what kind of cops we are."

Tate laughed. It wasn't a happy sound. "That sounds like the kind of cop who gets shot to me."

"Sometimes," Jesse admitted. "Sometimes there is a guy with a gun. But there's a kind of cop who's ready to meet him. And then there's the kind of cop who's *hoping* to meet him."

"I don't understand," Tate said.

"I think you do, Derek," Jesse said. "The question is, what kind of cop do you want to be?"

Tate had an expression on his face like a kid being sent to detention. "What do you want from me?"

"I'd like you to ride with Peter Perkins. Peter's a veteran. He's been here longer than I have. He knows everyone. I want him to show you the ropes."

"You're giving me a babysitter?"

"That's not what I said. Peter knows more about Paradise than anyone else in the department, except Molly Crane. He can be an expert resource for you. And since he's retiring, I want some of that institutional knowledge to get passed down."

Tate looked like he was struggling to control himself. His jaw set.

"What's the problem, Derek? Talk to me."

Tate crossed his arms. "Still sounds like you're punishing me for what that Daisy . . ."

Jesse sensed Tate was reaching for a particular word. "Don't say it," he warned.

Tate looked offended. "She says it all the time."

"She can. You can't."

Tate rolled his eyes like that was the dumbest thing he'd ever heard. But he complied. "Well. It sounds like you're still punishing me for what that Daisy . . . *person* told you."

"I'm not going to lie, Derek. That concerns me. But it's not punishment. Think of it as having a partner. I don't have time to do it, or I'd ride with you myself."

Tate took a deep breath. Then tried to plaster on another version of his smile. "You're the boss, Jesse. Whatever you say."

"You're okay with this?"

"Absolutely," Tate said. "Just happy to be on the team."

Tate left without another word, still with that big smile on his face.

Jesse figured he was insulted. He was young. Jesse would have felt the same way back in his rookie days.

But that smile Tate had on his way out the door bothered him. It looked plastic compared to the one he'd shown when he joked about abusing Peebles in the cells.

THIRTY-FOUR

You think you got through to him?" Dix asked.

Jesse sat on his couch at home, the phone to his ear. He'd called Dix. Not about himself this time, he told the psychiatrist. He wanted to talk about Tate.

"I don't know," Jesse said. "I'd like to think so."

"What does your gut say?"

"My gut says he's like a dog testing the chain in the front yard. Seeing how far he can go."

"But you still want to give him a chance."

"Yeah," Jesse said. "I guess I do. I'm not sure why."

"Oh, that's easy," Dix said. "You look at him and you see yourself, just like you did when you looked at the corpse of Phil Burton."

"What?"

"You're afraid Burton is your future. And you're afraid that Tate is your past. You made mistakes as a cop when

194

you were drinking, Jesse. You've struggled with your anger. You want to give Tate every chance to redeem himself. But you should know by now: Some people cannot be helped. Some people should not be cops. Maybe you can't rescue Tate the way you were rescued."

Jesse thought about that. "You think I've got some kind of savior complex?"

Dix laughed. "Of course you do."

Jesse made a noise in the back of his throat.

"Oh, don't be like that. Neither one of us is completely mentally healthy."

"That's not very reassuring, coming from my shrink."

"You're tough enough. You can handle the truth."

"You mean because we're both alcoholics."

"No, but it's related," Dix said. "You and I both went into jobs, *willingly*, where we get into other people's lives. Where we are resented. Where people will sometimes try to hurt us. And we try to fix them anyway."

"You talking about being a cop or a psychiatrist?"

"Mostly about being a cop. Far fewer people have tried to shoot me since I put up my shingle. So you tell me: Does that sound like a completely healthy thing to do?"

"No."

"Right. Most mentally healthy people have firmer boundaries. They don't need to fix other people. They don't need to make sure other people behave. They don't need other people nearly as much in general. They deal with their own lives and let other people deal with theirs."

"I don't know many people like that."

"Thankfully for my practice, neither do I. But we're talking about cops. Cops are *required* to be involved in other people's lives. A good cop always has to walk that line between caring too much and not caring enough. And a bad cop—well, a bad cop doesn't see a line between himself and other people."

"Are you talking about Tate here?"

"Right now, I'm talking about you. Why do you do what you do? Why are you a cop?"

"To do the right thing." No hesitation. Jesse never had any doubt about that, at least.

"Right. That's because you're a good cop, boundary issues aside. You know the difference between right and wrong, and you are constantly policing *yourself* to make sure you stay on the right side of it."

"It's not that hard."

"It actually is," Dix said. "But that's not my point right now. A good cop wants to do the right thing. A bad cop wants everyone to do as he says because he says it. A bad cop figures that if *he's* doing it, it *must* be right."

Jesse knew cops like that. There were cops who looked the other way when things were wrong. And there were cops who actively made them worse.

"And if you challenge that, you're challenging his idea of himself," Dix continued. "You're breaking his identity. That's dangerous. People will do anything to maintain that image. And if it's a lie—if it's not real—they'll even kill to protect the lie."

"Probably not someone who should have a badge and a gun, then."

"Absolutely not."

Jesse thought about that for a moment.

"I'm not sure Tate is that guy," he said. "I just don't know."

"You better decide soon," Dix said. "Like you said, the longer his leash gets, the more damage he can do."

"How do you know so much about bad cops? You run into a guy like that when you were on the force?"

Dix hesitated. That in itself was unusual. For the first time that Jesse could remember, Dix was at a loss for words. Jesse heard him take a deep breath before he spoke.

"I *was* that guy on the force, Jesse," he said. "Why do you think I left?"

THIRTY-FIVE

Jesse had the box of donuts in one hand and the coffees in the other when he spotted the guy.

Molly had told him it was his job to provide food for the station since he was the one who'd screwed things up with Daisy. "An army runs on its stomach," she'd said.

"We're not an army," he'd said. "You said so."

"Shut up and buy the donuts," she'd responded.

So he bought the donuts every day now, because it was easier than trying to cross the Maginot Line of Daisy's front door.

The guy was a dozen yards from the station. He just stood there. Dark hair, thinning in front, medium build, pale. He wore a light blazer. Leaning on a Honda Accord, phone to his ear as if he was on a call, his body against the car as if he owned it.

But he didn't. Jesse knew the owner of the Honda—

Ally Kroener. She worked in the town clerk's office part-time, so she didn't have a regular space. Jesse had instructed his officers never to ticket her when they were on traffic detail; she shouldn't have to pay for the privilege of working for the town—and that guy was not her.

Jesse realized time was slowing down around him, his body and his instincts already working faster than his conscious mind.

The blazer was a little too nice for the jeans and shirt underneath, but long enough to conceal something at the man's waistline. He was also a little too animated when talking into the phone, too much like an actor playing a guy on a phone call.

The guy's eyes flicked up toward Jesse, clocking his progress down the street. He was waiting for Jesse to get closer. Or he was just a guy noticing the chief of police with donuts and coffee.

Could go either way. But one way would get Jesse killed.

Jesse moved.

The guy put his hand by his hip, about to sweep the blazer back.

Jesse dropped the donuts. The coffees he flung straight toward the guy's head. Still scalding hot.

The man ducked, now moving suddenly, smoothly, like a snake uncoiling.

The coffees sailed over his head, dousing Ally Kroener's Honda, splashing the roof and windshield.

The man dropped the phone and turned toward Jesse to plant his feet and assume a shooter's stance.

Jesse saw the gun stuck in the guy's waistband, the

butt of a Glock or a Sig, difficult to tell at this distance, but at least ten rounds in the magazine, the guy's hand already wrapped around the grip—

—Jesse heard the box of donuts hit the pavement—

—as he slammed into the guy with his full weight, pinning him against the door of the Honda, keeping his gun hand stuck tight to his body.

They were face-to-face, nose-to-nose, the guy scowling and staring into Jesse's eyes. He didn't say a word, just brought up his other hand in a fist to punch Jesse in the head.

But, again, Jesse was faster, his left elbow already swinging around in a tight arc, connecting solidly against the man's temple.

The guy's eyes rolled, his chin pointed at the ground. He lost the defiant look on his face for a moment, but he didn't go down.

So Jesse hit him again.

His head lolled back this time, but he still didn't let go of the gun. He tried to push back against Jesse, but Jesse only shoved him harder against the car.

Now they were just stuck together, Jesse holding the guy, the guy desperately trying to wriggle his way out.

Jesse had his right hand on the guy's wrist, locking his gun hand in place, the pistol still jammed into his waistband. Jesse used his left hand to grab the guy's right wrist, holding him still. He squeezed, pushing the bones of the radius and ulna together, trying to break them.

The guy was using all his strength to hang on to the gun, his finger now on the trigger.

Jesse could almost see the bad idea cross the guy's mind.

"You pull that trigger," Jesse said, "and you can say goodbye to pissing standing up."

The guy thought about it for a second.

"Okay," he said. "I give."

Jesse felt him surrender. He stopped struggling, and his right arm went slack in Jesse's left hand.

"Good choice," Jesse said, letting go of the right arm. He then punched him again, hard, in the head.

The guy's skull bounced back against the roof of the Honda like it was on a spring. This time his eyes shut completely and his body went limp.

Jesse took the gun out of his waistband and let him slide to the ground.

The would-be shooter was out cold.

And the donuts were somehow, miraculously, still intact in their box.

Once the guy regained consciousness, he didn't say a word as they put him in the holding cell. Didn't give his name or even ask for a lawyer. He offered only a tight little smile when Jesse asked if he wanted a doctor, shrugging as if to say, *All part of the job.*

His ID was fake, but his fingerprints came back with his real name. If the computer had a flashing light and sirens, it would have lit up and buzzed like a slot machine. MADISON DAVIS, aka MAD DOG, aka MADMAN, among other aliases, with a list of felonies that scrolled down the screen.

Suit took him to the county holding facility. Jesse didn't want him in the cells anywhere near Peebles.

"Are you sure you're okay?" Suit asked, before he left.

"I'm fine, Luther," Jesse said. "Thank you for asking."

While Suit was worried, Molly was angry at Jesse. Even if he didn't have plenty of experience with Molly's temper, he would have known by the way she slammed her desk drawers shut and cursed under her breath as she began pounding the keys on her computer.

"What happened to calling for backup, Jesse?" she said. "What happened to nobody trying to take on these guys *alone?*"

"I saved the donuts," Jesse said.

She glared. "You're not as funny as you think, Stone."

Jesse went into his office and tried to stay out of her way. She hated it when he put his own life at risk, even though she'd been in on the plan. She took it out on anything nearby, including office equipment.

Jesse, however, felt better than he had in a week. His bad shoulder finally stopped hitching up on him, and he felt like he could breathe again. He made the mistake of whistling quietly while he went past Molly to get a refill on his coffee.

"And just what are you so damned happy about?" she said.

He thought about it for a moment.

"I think we're making progress," he finally said.

Molly glared at him. "Because someone tried to gun you down in the street? In broad daylight? In front of the station?"

"Well . . . yeah," Jesse said.

For a second, Molly looked as if she was about to

throw something at him. Jesse cautiously reached across her desk and moved the stapler out of reach.

Molly watched him do it. "You're such a comedian."

"Thank you, I'll be here all week."

"Not if people keep trying to kill you," she shot back.

Jesse smiled. "Yes," he said. "I will."

Molly rolled her eyes. "Yes. I keep forgetting. The bulletproof Jesse Stone. He eats hit men for breakfast."

"I prefer donuts."

"This isn't funny, Jesse," she said. "In what world is someone trying to murder you a sign of progress?"

Jesse stopped smiling. "It means they're getting scared."

Molly looked exasperated. "Who is?"

"The bad guys," Jesse said. "All of them."

THIRTY-SIX

Elliott saw the whole thing from the front seat of his rental car. Damn, that cop was fast. He saw the shooter setting up the hit while he kept an eye on the station house—a little obvious, but sometimes the direct approach worked—and watched the cop walk up the street about twenty minutes later.

He worried, for a moment, that he might be forfeiting the money Mulvaney had promised. He was unsure if he was happy or sad about someone else doing his job for him.

Then the cop moved.

Shit, he covered the ground between him and the shooter like it was one step. He pinned the stupid guy against the car as if someone had phoned him the night before and told him what was coming.

Elliott didn't like cops. At all. He'd never met one he

wasn't happy to kill if they got in his way. He sure as hell didn't respect them. Most of them spent their whole careers hiding behind their badges, counting on their uniforms to do all the work.

But he'd run across a couple of cops who were solid, who were easily as good as he was. He'd learned that some people had the skills to go up against him.

This cop was definitely one of them.

He was going to have to rethink everything.

The more people in his line of work who showed up, the more paranoid and prepared the cop was going to get. None of these assholes Mulvaney had told about the money would soften this guy up. If anything, they were only going to make things harder.

That's when Elliott felt another set of eyes on him. It was an instinct he'd developed over the years. People said you couldn't really tell when someone was looking at you, but Elliott believed in it. He didn't read his horoscope and he thought ghosts and UFOs were for idiots who'd seen too many movies, but that feeling on the back of his neck had saved his life more than once.

He looked around, not too fast, checking the rental's mirrors, scanning the street.

Then he clocked the kid. A young man in his twenties. Slouching at the corner, standing a little too still. Staring right at him, sizing him up.

If this kid was a contractor, like him, at least he wasn't an idiot like the other guy. He was surveying the situation. Planning ahead.

And he was good enough to spot Elliott. Which meant he had to be pretty good.

Elliott waved, partly just to see what the kid would do. The kid smirked and waved back.

Then he began walking toward the car. Hands loose at his sides, well away from his pockets, that smirk still on his face.

Elliott reached under his jacket and gripped his Ruger .357. He preferred revolvers for close-up work, and the .357 was loaded with hollowpoints, so accuracy wasn't a real concern.

The kid stopped at the passenger-side window and knocked on it, shave and a haircut, two bits.

Elliott rolled down the window, the .357 still concealed under his jacket.

The kid grinned and leaned over, a couple of feet away from the car, keeping a respectful distance.

"I've seen you around," he said.

"Really," Elliott said. That was surprising. This was the first time he'd noticed the kid. Maybe he was getting old.

"I have a feeling we might be in the same line of work."

"Why would you think that?" Elliott asked. No sense being an idiot. The guy could be a cop.

The kid shrugged. "Just a hunch. Maybe we shouldn't be working the same territory, you know. Might be bad for business."

"Could be," Elliott said. "You want to move on, nobody's stopping you."

The kid laughed. "You're pretty quick for your age."

"You've got no idea," Elliot said, and laughed, too.

The kid looked away from him, which was a perfect

BURIED SECRETS

chance to shoot him in the head, but Elliott didn't want to do that yet. The kid seemed to be considering his options.

Then he turned back. "We should talk," he said. "You know Daisy's?"

"I can find it."

"You can't miss it. Got a big sign saying NO COPS ALLOWED. Meet me there for breakfast."

"What if I don't feel like talking?"

The kid looked disappointed. "Come on, man. I'm sure neither of us wants to end up like that asshole they just arrested. And it's way too early for bloodshed. Let's talk it out."

He straightened up and walked away.

Elliott eased the hammer back down on the .357, watching him in the mirror the whole time.

He thought about it. He almost always worked alone.

But in this town, small as it was? With every dipshit on the East Coast on their way here to take their shot at the contract and cash?

Against that cop?

He might as well get some breakfast and hear what the kid had to say.

And if worse came to worst, at least he wouldn't have to kill him on an empty stomach.

207

THIRTY-SEVEN

Elliott met the kid at Daisy's.

The kid—it was impossible to think of him as a grown-up, though he had to be pushing thirty—probably would have preferred someplace with neon and cheap tables and greasy food. He probably got all his ideas about the business from *Reservoir Dogs*.

Elliott didn't have any such illusions. He came up in the last days of the Irish Mob, when it was all falling apart and Whitey Bulger was ratting every one of his rivals out to the Feds. All those big, hard men squealing like pigs for whatever scraps of mercy the U.S. attorney would offer. Elliott was just a kid himself then, but that pretty much killed any illusions he had about honor among thieves. They tried to bring him inside one of the gangs, but everything was too chaotic, everyone too scared of the indictments coming down. So he did odd jobs for Mulvaney and the others who were too small or too smart to get caught in the net. It was like a paid internship in killing.

It turned out he was pretty good at it. There might have been other things he could have been good at, but killing people paid a lot more. He went freelance as soon as he was able to, expanding beyond the Irish, doing contracts for the Italians, Tony DeMarco and Morelli, anyone who'd pay him. He'd earned a reputation as someone clean and quiet.

Then Burton found him. He wasn't sure how, but he suspected Mulvaney had something to do with it. It was a good relationship. Burton always got top dollar. Elliott got to travel, put more distance between himself and the work. He liked that. Killing in Boston felt a little too close to home. He eventually saved enough to slide into a comfortable retirement.

But he always kept a line open to the gangsters who knew his real name—if only because he wanted to make sure they never offered him up in exchange for a lighter sentence when they inevitably got caught doing something stupid.

He knew where they lived, too.

Almost forty years in this business, Elliott knew it was nothing glamorous or romantic or exciting. It was garbage work. Maintenance. Sewage disposal. It was hours and hours of boredom with a few moments of cold terror and pure adrenaline.

He really thought he was out of it.

He was happy to sit in a clean, well-lighted place and

enjoy some good food instead of meeting in a dive bar or a strip club. If you were trying to look and act like a hit man, you were probably too stupid to actually be one.

The kid entered, and Elliott grudgingly gave him some credit: Without his leather jacket, he was dressed strictly in catalog wear from L.L.Bean. He could have been a young dad away from his family or a mid-level marketing exec on vacation. He didn't look like a thug.

He waved and smiled at Elliott and headed over to his table like they were old friends. He didn't try to play it cool or tough or sneaky, which were the easiest ways to get noticed.

Good. Maybe he wasn't a complete idiot.

Elliott smiled and shook hands with Raney. Nobody paid any attention to them. A young guy meeting someone for a business breakfast. Or a nephew and his uncle. Or, God forbid, a son seeing his dad again.

They sat and looked over the menu.

"Everything looks pretty good here," Elliott said.

"You talking about the food or the job?" Raney said, smirking.

Elliott held back a sigh. Of course, this kid couldn't wait for breakfast first. He put the menu down.

"Look," he said, "I'm glad you wanted to talk. I appreciate it. Don't get me wrong. But I'm not leaving town."

"I never said you should," Raney said reasonably, pouring himself a cup of coffee from the decanter the waiter had left, along with a fresh mug. "I just don't particularly want you getting in my way."

Well, the kid had balls, Elliott would give him that. He liked his use of the word *particularly.*

"I don't want you in my way, either," Elliott said. "You seem smart enough to want to avoid that, too. Smart people try to stay out of my way."

Raney smiled and leaned forward. "This is great coffee," he said, holding the mug up with both hands, like he was just about to dive into it headfirst. "I mean it. Really good stuff."

"Okay. You're not scared of me. And I'm not scared of you. Glad we've got that established. What now?"

"I don't know," Raney said, shrugging. "I try not to do any jobs I'm not paid for. That's why I thought we should talk."

"Fair enough. Why are you here, then?"

Raney tilted his head toward the small, flat-screen TV playing over the diner's counter. It was on CNN.

"I caught some pictures on TV. I was told they were destroyed. So I need to be here to make sure nothing else was left behind. You?"

"Same thing."

As young as this kid was, Elliott was mildly surprised that Burton had made the connection and was still hiring people out. Elliott thought he would have retired a long time before he died.

But then Elliott thought of a guy he knew who used to repair cars at the dealership where he took his Mercedes for service. He got Alzheimer's, early onset, and the only way anyone realized was when he began forgetting the names of his coworkers. He could still repair an engine, like he was doing it on autopilot.

Some skills don't go away, Elliott thought. At least that's what he hoped.

"So you're not getting paid for this, either," Raney said. "This is cleaning up your old mess. Just like me."

"Well, there is that big pile of money Burton died on."

Raney made a face. "You think they're telling the truth about that? Come on. That's got to be bullshit."

"You think so? Why would the cops lie about that?"

"Bait." Raney said it like it was obvious. "They're trying to get people to come sniffing around, looking for leads. Looking for someone dumb enough to come try to claim it."

Elliott considered that. He might have thought the same thing, if he didn't know better.

"The money is real," he said.

Raney sat back. "You're sure?"

Elliott nodded.

"How the hell would you know?"

"I got a guy."

"Oh, this is one of those old-school gangster things, huh? You got a guy. I bet you got a lot of guys. Sitting around the old folks' home, telling stories . . ."

Elliott rolled his eyes. "Yeah, I know. A lot of those guys are full of shit. Not this time. This guy is the reason I'm here. He doesn't screw around."

"You're sure?"

"I'd be happier if it wasn't true."

"Why's that?"

"You think anyone just gets to walk away with that money? That much cash?"

Raney shrugged. "I would certainly be willing to give it a try."

"The guy I was talking about? He wants it. Or at least his cut."

"What? He didn't do anything for it."

"Welcome to the glamorous world of organized crime."

"That's horseshit. Why should either of us worry about what some ancient Italian—"

"Irish," Elliott said.

Raney made a face. "—whatever—gangster asshole wants?"

"You want to spend the rest of your life looking over your shoulder? Waiting for someone to poison your coffee?"

"Come on. *The Godfather* is just an old movie on cable now. Guys like that don't exist anymore."

"They do," Elliott said. "But now they hire guys like us. You going to tell me you've never done any work for any of them?"

Raney thought about that for a moment. "Well, that's a good point." He thought some more. "Why are you telling me all this?"

Finally, Elliott thought. *A smart question.* "Because the more I learn about this job, the more complicated it seems. You know where they're keeping it?"

"The money? No. Where?"

Elliott smiled and pointed with his chin out the window, down the street.

Raney's eyes lit up and his mouth broke into an involuntary grin. "The police station? Seriously?"

"Yup."

"That's the dumbest thing I've ever heard."

"It's a lot of money. People get stupid."

Raney looked away. Sat there quietly for a moment.

"I guess you're saying we shouldn't be stupid, either."

"That's exactly what I'm saying. You and me, if we race to the finish line, we're only going to get in each other's way. Or, worse, we do something to tip off this police chief, and we both get screwed."

Raney looked skeptical again. "This place barely has traffic lights. How much of a problem can this cop be?"

Elliott did let out a sigh this time, because he thought it helped make his point. He took out his phone. "I thought kids these days knew how to use the Internet." He tapped the screen and a series of news articles came up on Google. They were all about Jesse Stone.

He handed the phone over to Raney.

Raney tried to look bored and unimpressed at first. Then he frowned. His eyes narrowed. He kept tapping the screen, scrolling through more and more pages.

After three minutes of this, he put the phone face down on the table and slid it back toward Elliott.

"Well," he said. "Shit."

"Yeah. That's what I thought."

"This guy seems pretty good."

"He does."

Raney sat quietly again. Elliott did, too. He had time. He could let the kid get there on his own.

"Maybe we could work together," Raney finally said.

"That's what I was thinking, too," Elliott said.

Raney leaned over the table. "All right," he said. "But don't think you're the boss just because you remember when dinosaurs roamed the earth. Don't tell me what to do."

Elliott smiled and picked up his menu. "Wouldn't dream of it," he said. "Now. You want some breakfast? You're still a growing boy."

"Fuck you," Raney said, but he was smiling.

"I'll let you have chocolate milk."

"Fuck you," Raney said, and now he was laughing.

That's right, Elliott thought. He was just a harmless, funny old man.

Until he wasn't anymore.

But until that moment came, he could see some use for Raney.

THIRTY-EIGHT

It was always good to see Rita Fiore, Jesse thought, even if she was a defense attorney. Today she wore a tight, short skirt that showed off her legs to excellent advantage, as usual. She favored him with a brilliant smile as she walked into his office.

On the other hand, it was never good to see Ellis Munroe. He looked at Jesse as if he'd spent far too much time in the station lately. Jesse would agree with that, but probably not for the same reasons. The fact that he was walking in with Rita made it even worse.

"Molly, did I have an appointment with Ellis or Rita today?"

"Jesus Christ, Jesse, what do you want me to do, shoot anyone who tries to get into your office?"

"Thank you, Molly," Jesse said, and gestured to the chairs in front of his desk.

Rita sat and crossed her legs, still smiling. "Jesse, do I really need an appointment to come see you?"

"I'm always happy to see you. Especially up and around again," Jesse said. Rita had been through a lot in the past couple of months. She'd been shot and nearly died. Jesse had wanted to kill whoever had done it. Instead, he'd helped a friend of Rita's take down the man behind the attempt on her life, which had to be enough.

She and Jesse were in the off-again part of their on-again, off-again relationship, and he felt a slight pang at that. She'd been very clear about it.

He knew Rita had to still be dealing with the trauma. But today she seemed almost like her old self again.

"You know me. Can't knock me off with nuclear weapons," Rita said. Although Jesse noticed that her hand touched the spot on her chest where the bullet had almost pierced her heart.

"Well, it's not you. I'm mainly annoyed by him," Jesse said, nodding at Ellis, who made a face back. "But that's usually the case."

"I told you this was going to happen," Ellis said.

Jesse ignored him.

"Coffee?" he asked Rita.

"I'd love some," Rita said.

"No," Ellis said, his voice tight.

Jesse got Rita a cup of coffee. He took his time. Partly to annoy Ellis and partly because he suspected what was coming, and he wasn't anxious to hear it.

"So. Why are you both here? Together?" Jesse said, sitting back down behind his desk.

Rita smiled demurely, which was a bad sign. She was only ever demure when she'd already won.

Ellis went first. He placed a paper on Jesse's desk. "This is a writ of habeas corpus to release Mr. Peebles from your jail."

"He's not under arrest," Jesse said. "He's a material witness being held for his own protection."

Rita's smile grew wider. "That's very kind of you, Jesse, but my understanding is that Mr. Peebles does not want nor does he need your protection. And in either case, the writ of habeas corpus applies here, too. A judge has ruled that you cannot hold him any longer."

Jesse turned to Ellis. Ellis put up his hands.

"Don't look at me," he said. "I told you this would happen. I asked you to consult with me. There's not a thing I can do to stop it now."

Jesse turned back to Rita. "How did you get involved in this?"

"I got a phone call that you were holding a young man without charge in your dinky little cells here and I thought, *That can't possibly be legal.* And then I went to a judge and, what do you know, he agreed with me."

"What I mean is, who hired you?"

"I don't have to tell you that, Jesse."

"Humor me, Rita."

"Well. For old times' sake. It's my understanding that Mr. Peebles's uncle has a retainer with Cone, Oakes."

"When I last spoke to his uncle, Charlie Mulvaney said he was going to let the kid rot in jail."

"Apparently he's had a change of heart."

"I didn't know you still represented mobsters," Jesse said.

"Jesse," she scolded. "You know better than to make wild accusations like that."

"I'll take my chances."

Rita smiled at him again.

"So your firm sent you to deal with me."

"I'm a very good lawyer, Jesse. You know that. Our history has nothing to do with it."

"He's going to kill him, Rita."

Rita shook her head, as if disappointed.

"What did I just say, Jesse? You've presented no proof of anything close to justifying that statement. If I were more easily offended, I might start talking about a defamation suit."

Jesse rubbed his hands across his face. Mulvaney had apparently gotten sick of waiting for Jesse to put Peebles into the system, where he could die in a county holding cell or on the outside if he made bail.

And hence this meeting. Jesse wasn't surprised Rita had gone straight to a judge. She knew the best ways to kneecap an investigation. She *was* a very good lawyer.

Still, he had to try to keep Peebles under wraps. It was the only way to save the stupid kid's life.

"I want to charge him now," Jesse said to Ellis.

"Sure," Ellis said. "I can do that. We can have an indictment ready to go by five p.m. Arrest warrant shortly after that. But it won't keep him from walking out of here today."

"Damn it, Ellis—"

"No," Ellis said. "No. This is not on me. I was prepared to charge him when you brought him in. You wanted to play it your way, I said fine. This is where we are. This is your mess, Jesse. Don't bitch at me because I can't clean it up fast enough."

Jesse hated hearing that. Mostly because he had to admit Ellis was right.

Rita drank her coffee, looking completely unperturbed. "Can someone please go get my client now? He's spent enough time in jail."

"I'll need Peebles to stay close," Jesse told her. "He's still a part of this investigation."

"Of course," she said. "I'm going to drive him back to Boston. From there, I will advise him to make himself available for any further inquiries."

She turned to Ellis. "And if you do issue a warrant for his arrest, I expect you to contact me for his surrender. Mr. Peebles has counsel now, and I want both of you to remember that before you try to sweat him in a little box again."

Ellis shrugged, looking thoroughly defeated. "Of course," he said. "Wouldn't dream of anything else."

He stood. "I'm going back to my office. Goodbye, Rita."

"Always a pleasure, Ellis."

"Oh, how I wish that were true," Ellis said. "Jesse. You gave it your best shot. Sorry it didn't work out."

Jesse didn't respond. He left.

Rita remained seated. "So how you been?" she asked with a bright smile. "You seeing anyone?"

Jesse stood up. "I'm going to go get your client now."

"Oh, don't be like that," Rita said. "We can still flirt, can't we?"

"He better not," Molly interrupted from outside Jesse's office.

"Does she always eavesdrop on your meetings?" Rita asked.

"It's a small station, Rita," Molly yelled back. "I'm gagging on your perfume as we speak."

Rita laughed. "Don't be a sore loser, Molly," she said.

Jesse sighed. "I'll get Mr. Peebles. I just have to do a couple things first. Sit tight. You want any more coffee while you wait?"

"Please," Rita said.

"No more coffee for her!" Molly bellowed.

Rita laughed. "She is *such* a petty bitch," she said. "I really respect that."

THIRTY-NINE

Tate came into the station for his shift just as Rita and Peebles walked out.

He stared at them as they left, then turned to Molly. "What's going on? How the hell is he walking out now?"

"Language," Molly said. She didn't really mind, but she didn't like the way Tate demanded answers of her, like she was a secretary.

"What?" He looked confused.

"Never mind," Molly said. "He's leaving with his defense attorney because Ellis won't charge him."

"Well, that is some bullshit," Tate said, eyes wide.

"Preaching to the choir," Molly said, and turned away from him. She was mad enough as it was. She didn't need the rookie to tell her it was utterly screwed up.

She was about to ask him why he was at the station.

He wasn't supposed to be on shift for another hour or so. And he was supposed to patrol with Peter now.

But Tate was already out the door, on his way to his vehicle.

As Tate got to the street, he saw the hot attorney escorting Peebles down the sidewalk toward a BMW that cost more than he'd made in the last three years.

All right, he thought. Jesse wanted him to patrol. This was perfect. He'd patrol.

This was his chance to show Jesse, to show all of them. He was serious. He was a cop.

And he was not about to let this piece of shit get away, no matter what his fancy defense lawyer had pulled.

Rita didn't particularly like the idea of driving the Peebles kid back to Boston. She wasn't an Uber for criminals. She didn't like spending time in close quarters with crooks fresh out of jail. One of the hazards of her occupation: She knew exactly what her clients were capable of, and she was in no way exempt. But his uncle, Charles Mulvaney, wanted him delivered to the firm, and it wasn't phrased as a request.

Maybe Jesse had a point about representing mobsters, she thought.

She'd tried to winnow them out of her client list, but her firm, Cone, Oakes, had not gotten to the top without incurring a few debts along the way. There were still old-school types in Boston who expected their markers to be honored, and they probably had plenty of buried secrets they could dig up to make life embarrassing for the partners.

Rita tried to make her peace with it. She'd put worse people back on the street. She balanced the scales where she could. Innocent people rarely need defense attorneys. This was her job, and she did it well.

At least Peebles didn't strike her as dangerous. In fact, he seemed almost inert. He sagged against her passenger door as if he couldn't take the weight of gravity. He acted like a dog about to be taken to the kennel—or to the vet to be put down.

Her partners hadn't told her what was going on here, and she didn't ask. Now she wished she had. Maybe Jesse wasn't just blowing smoke about the danger this guy was in.

"You all right?" she asked. He hadn't said more than five words since Jesse had retrieved him from the cell.

He turned his head and looked at her. "Fine," he said.

"I don't have to take you back to the firm," she said. "I can drop you anywhere you'd like."

Peebles laughed like she'd told a bad joke.

"What?"

"It doesn't matter where you take me," he said. "I'm dead sooner or later."

"What?" Rita asked again. "What do you mean?"

But Peebles just gave her a colder look than she thought possible and turned to stare back out the window. "You know what I mean," he said.

She knew she shouldn't get involved. All she had to do was drive.

But she didn't like the idea of being used to deliver Peebles to someone who'd hurt him. Rita did not allow herself to be used.

She tried again. "Why don't you tell me what's going on?"

"If you don't know, you don't want to," Peebles said. "Believe me."

"Try me," Rita said.

Nothing.

"Hey, you're my client. I have an obligation—"

Then Rita checked her mirror, and suddenly she had another concern: There was a Paradise PD SUV tailing her. And not being very subtle about it.

She couldn't believe Jesse would be that dumb.

Well, maybe. Just not that dumb with her. It had been a long time since they'd been together, but surely he had a little more respect for her than to put a car on her like this?

"Oh, you have *got* to be kidding me," she said.

"What?"

"Cop car," Rita said.

Peebles turned to look. "Why are they following so close?"

"It's just a small-town intimidation tactic," she said. "Believe me, the chief is going to hear about it—"

And then the SUV roared ahead as the driver hit the gas and bumped hard into the rear of Rita's BMW.

"Jesus Christ!" she said, and grabbed the wheel as the

BMW tried to slide out from under her. She stomped the gas, cranked the wheel to the right, and skidded to a halt alongside the road.

She realized they were just about a hundred yards past the sign for Paradise's town limits.

The cop pulled to a stop behind them. No lights, no sirens.

This was not normal, Rita knew. There was no way on earth Jesse would ever allow this. Her heart hammered at her ribs. She felt cold. She couldn't catch her breath.

Peebles stared into the rearview, watching. His face had gone slate-gray.

"Just stay calm. Stay seated. We'll see what's going on here."

Rita still couldn't breathe right, but she felt like she had to be calm for him.

Peebles shrugged, as if it made no difference to him whatsoever.

She was terrified, she realized. She felt all the pain and the fear of the hospital and the days after coming back to her.

The cop spoke to them through the PA on the SUV. "Step out of the car. Both of you. Hands in the air."

"You have got to be out of your goddamn mind," Rita muttered.

"NOW," the voice demanded, loud enough to make the windows rattle.

Rita took a breath, then stepped out, hands in the air. Her whole body shook.

Peebles remained in the car, she realized.

"YOU TOO, SCUMBAG," the PA blared.

Rita knew she couldn't let him do this. Not without saying something, not if she still wanted to respect herself. All she had was her voice. Somehow she found it.

"You want to explain what's going on here, Officer?" she yelled.

The SUV's door popped open and a young cop got out. He had his gun drawn, and he fixed it on her.

Rita couldn't believe what she was seeing. This guy was out of control. How had Jesse ever hired him?

"Get on the ground!" the cop screamed, face red, hand on his gun.

"Hey. You hit me." Rita pointed at the sign that marked the start of the Paradise town limits. "And you are out of your jurisdiction."

She hoped he couldn't see how her finger shook while she pointed.

"You get on the goddamn ground now!" he shouted.

"Listen," she said, "I want to know what you think you're doing before—"

The cop's face was red and twisted with anger. He looked demonic.

"Hey," Rita shouted, and reached into her pocket for her phone. "I am going to record this! You have no right to do this!"

"PUT THE GODDAMN PHONE DOWN NOW!" he screamed as he pulled the hammer back on his gun.

Rita suddenly realized she was very close to getting shot—*again*. This cop did not care about what he could and could not do. He would just do it, and worry about the consequences later.

And that's when she lost it.

The terror rushed back into her. All of the pain of her recovery, the days and nights in the hospital, the physical therapy, the *violation*, all filled her as if she were drowning in very cold water.

She dropped the phone instantly. She was very scared. She didn't know what was about to happen. But it wasn't going to be good.

And this wasn't some thug shooting at her from a moving car. This was a *cop*.

The cop turned to her car. Peebles was still sitting inside.

"I said GET OUT OF THE FUCKING CAR!"

Nothing. Peebles stayed where he was.

The cop stomped down the side of the road toward Rita, still aiming at her. Then he grabbed her by the neck and shoved her to the ground. Rita landed hard.

She felt his shoe on her back. "Don't you fucking move," he growled. She turned her head to see him from the corner of her eye. He faced the car, gun pointed at it. "Now you, scumbag. Don't make me tell you again!"

After what felt like minutes, Peebles got out. She could see his feet under the car.

Despite herself, she closed her eyes tight. She couldn't bear to watch.

Don't do anything stupid, she thought. *Please don't do anything stupid.*

Matthew Peebles sat in the expensive BMW for a second. The sound of the cop screaming at him seemed very distant, like a faraway echo.

He didn't really want to stand up. The leather seat was comfortable, especially after sitting on nothing but the cot in the cell for the past couple of days.

The cop had the same uniform as the other officers. He was confused, but only for a moment. Peebles knew Jesse couldn't protect him. Where are you going to hide from the devil?

He got out of the car.

The cop was still shouting.

Peebles turned to face him, even though he was shaking. For a moment, he was a kid again, opening that garage door, looking inside.

He looked at the cop aiming at him down the barrel of a gun. He saw the cold, blank eyes of his uncle Charlie staring back.

He knew what was about to happen.

And he felt no more fear.

Rita heard three gunshots. Her eyes snapped open. Underneath the car, she saw Peebles hit the dirt, his head turned toward her, his eyes now staring and empty.

Oh God, she thought. *Not again. Please. Not again.*

The cop's foot left her back. Rita instinctively curled into a ball and, despite herself, looked up at the cop. She screamed as he pointed the gun at her, certain she was about to die next.

FORTY

Explain it to me," Jesse said again.

"I told you already," Tate said, his voice edging into a whine.

Jesse leaned forward slightly in his office chair and put his arms on the desk. His fists were clenched. It took everything he had not to go over the desk and put his hands on Tate. But he needed to do this right.

For Rita, and for himself. There were rules for policemen.

"Explain it to me," he said. "Again."

Tate flinched slightly. He looked away. "It happened just like I told you. I was following the BMW—"

"Why?"

"What?"

"Why were you following Rita's BMW?"

"I didn't know it was her," Tate said.

Jesse kept a poker face, but that was a new twist on the story. Before now, Tate had not claimed to be ignorant of the BMW or its passengers. He filed that away and listened.

"But she was speeding. And she was almost out of the town limits, so I pulled her over."

"We found both vehicles outside the town limits."

"Really?"

Jesse just looked at him.

"Oh, uh, yeah. She didn't stop right away. I had to follow her a little. Hot pursuit." Tate snickered. "You know what I mean?"

Jesse kept staring at Tate.

"Uh. Well. I guess I must have stopped her just outside the town limits. But she was crazy, Jesse. I mean, that chick was out of her damn mind. Screaming at me. Saying a bunch of shit. So I, uh, well, I know you know her, but I had to put her down."

Jesse said nothing, but his fists clenched a little bit tighter. After all Rita had been through already . . .

"So after that, as I was attempting to put the cuffs on her—and she was scratching and kicking and biting and all that—that's when the guy hopped out of the car. And I thought he had a gun."

"And you shot him."

"He didn't give me any choice, Jesse. Honest."

"Did you see a gun?"

Tate paused.

"No. But—"

"But what?"

"He made a move."

"He made a move? The guy we had in our cells for two days like a coma patient? He made a move?"

Tate nodded. Jesse forced himself to sit back.

"And that's when you put the cuffs on Ms. Fiore."

"Yes."

"And that's when Officer Weathers showed up."

"Yeah. About then. Yeah."

Gabe had been first on the scene. Jesse and Molly weren't that far behind him, followed by everyone else on active duty in the whole town, because Gabe had called in the gunshots.

By the time Jesse arrived, he'd found Rita in the back seat of Tate's SUV, hands cuffed behind her back, scraped and bruised, doing her best to hold it together. Jesse had uncuffed her immediately. He'd let her out of the SUV and tried to place a hand on her shoulder. She shoved him away and walked around the scene for a moment, just breathing deeply.

Then she'd come back to him. "What the fuck" was the first thing she'd said, and it didn't get better from there.

He'd had time to talk to her after they got her checked out at the hospital. She'd told him what happened.

He'd believed her. Not just because he thought he could trust Rita, and not just because they'd been a little in love once. But because he'd had Suit take a statement from Tate. Because he'd had Molly inspect the scene, and none of it fit together the way Tate had said. He saw photos of the cracked rear bumper of Rita's otherwise immaculate BMW. He saw Peebles's body, down on the ground, two in the chest, one in the head. Textbook grouping, center mass, like he'd been caught flat-footed standing outside the car. Not like a man who was lunging for a weapon. And there were other little details in Tate's account that simply didn't add up.

He'd told Rita he would make it right.

"I'm not sure that's going to be enough for me, Jesse," she'd said.

She looked at him as if he was a stranger. She blamed him. He could see it.

Jesse didn't argue with her. Mostly because he thought she was right.

He went into his interview with Tate, and made him repeat his story over and over again like he was a suspect. Because that was the job.

"I really had no choice, Jesse," Tate said. "You gotta know that."

Jesse thought for a moment. Tate seemed to think he'd done everything properly. Or, at least, close enough.

"Is . . . Is the woman all right?" Tate asked.

"Ms. Fiore? You mean the attorney who's probably going to sue the hell out of this department? The one who saw you shoot her client during a traffic stop? No. She's not okay."

"Oh."

"She says her client did nothing but comply with your orders. She says you were the one out of control."

"Come on, Jesse." Tate made a face. "She's a defense attorney. They lie like they're breathing. I mean, who're you gonna believe? A defense lawyer or—"

"I wouldn't have to take anyone's word for it if you'd kept your dashcam on," Jesse said. "Why did you shut it off?"

"Oh, yeah, that." Tate grinned sheepishly. "What can I say? New guy. Don't know how to work everything yet. I thought I was turning it on, and, well, you know. I guess I shut it off instead."

"Right."

Tate looked offended. "You believe me, right?"

"It's a dashcam, Derek. Are you telling me you needed special training for that?"

"Hey, now. Maybe I forgot. In the heat of the chase—"

"In your hot pursuit."

"Right, maybe I just didn't stop to think about the right way to work a little toy on the dashboard."

"In this hot pursuit, how fast was Ms. Fiore driving?"

"Oh, wow, jeez, she must have got up to sixty."

"Sixty."

"Or even seventy. I didn't clock her exactly."

"On Paradise. Which turns sharply about fifty feet toward the 1A."

"That's why it was so dangerous, right? I had to stop her."

"I'm sure the dashcam would show this, though? Right?"

Tate paused. "Yeah, well, it's possible I turned it off before I started following her."

"Right. But you were concerned about safety. You didn't want anyone getting hurt."

Tate smiled. "Yeah, you get it."

"You had no choice."

"Exactly. Exactly right." Head bobbing up and down now, thinking Jesse was on his side, talking him through it.

"So you shot my only witness connecting a known mobster to a series of murders," Jesse said coldly. "And you put a gun on an innocent woman. Because *you had no choice.*"

Jesse let the silence stretch between them. Tate squirmed in his chair.

Jesse wondered, for a brief moment, if Dix was right. If he'd bent over backward to give Tate a chance because he saw a little of his own anger in the younger man. If he was trying to justify the choices he'd made.

But he wasn't that guy. He hoped like hell he had never been that guy.

Either way, he knew what he had to do. It made his decision easy.

"Badge and gun. Now."

Tate jumped in his chair as if he'd been tased. "What?"

"Hand over your badge and gun. You're suspended, pending a formal investigation."

Tate looked stunned. "You're firing me?"

"You're on administrative leave. Standard procedure in any shooting."

"I was just doing my job!"

That was too much for Jesse. "Your job," he said, "is to protect people. And I need to know you can do that safely."

Tate's face went red. He looked at the ceiling, like he was praying for patience, and then he leaned forward and spoke through bared teeth.

"What the hell do you want from me, *Jesse*?" he said. "I am telling you exactly what you need to hear to make this bullshit go away. What else do you want?"

Jesse leaned forward and put his weight on the balls of his feet under the desk.

"I need your gun, Derek."

Tate stood up, his jaw clenched, his eyes blazing. "Maybe you should try to take it," he said.

Jesse stood up. Slowly. He locked eyes with Tate.

"You sure that's what you want?"

God, Jesse wanted Tate to be stupid right then. He really wanted it.

Tate stepped back, his eyes widening a little. His hand went to his gun.

Jesse tensed for a moment, ready and waiting.

He suddenly knew, without a doubt, that Tate had not been making mistakes. He hadn't been overzealous or inexperienced. He'd made these choices deliberately. He'd been testing the chain.

Jesse knew one other thing: He was finally seeing the real Derek Tate peek out from under his mask.

Tate seemed to consider his options. He looked at Jesse and realized, maybe, that he would not win this particular showdown. Or he was afraid to try.

Something changed on his face, and he looked at Jesse with scorn. He took the gun from his holster and flung it on the desk. Then he unpinned the Paradise PD badge from his shirt and put that on the desk, too.

"Keep it. Whatever makes you feel better," he said.

Jesse put the gun in an evidence bag. "I asked you

what kind of cop you wanted to be, Derek," he said. "Now I know."

Tate laughed in his face. "You've got no idea who I am," he said. "But you're going to find out."

He turned and walked out of the office, slamming the door as he left.

FORTY-ONE

Jesse waited for a moment, then called Gabe Weathers into his office.

Gabe came in and sat down.

As soon as Jesse realized they'd have to cut Peebles loose, he'd left the office and told Gabe to follow Rita back to Boston. He'd wanted to find out who picked Peebles up at Cone, Oakes. That was why Gabe was first on the scene.

Great plan. Simple, Jesse thought. *Until Tate rolled up.*

Now Peebles was dead, and Rita was traumatized and his case was in pieces.

Great plan, Jesse thought again. *Real genius.*

"You hear all that?" he asked.

"Caught the highlights," Gabe said. "You think Tate was going to take a swing at you?"

"He might have been a little caught up in his righteous indignation," Jesse said. "I impugned his honor."

"You pulled his badge."

"He didn't give me much choice."

"You should have just hit him," Gabe said. "Everyone here likes Rita."

"If I wanted to punish him for Rita, I'd give his name and address to a couple of friends in Boston," Jesse said. "But that's not the job. We're cops. We don't always get to do what we want. Before I do anything else, I need to know what happened out there."

"Do you think he killed Peebles deliberately?"

"If I did, I wouldn't have let him walk out of here. But we don't have any witnesses aside from Rita, who was mostly looking at the ground, and we don't have any dash-cam video. What I need to know now is what you saw."

Gabe shrugged. "Not enough."

He leaned forward, placing his elbows on his knees. He looked exhausted. Jesse realized he was already punishing himself. Gabe was conscientious. A good cop. If there was trouble, he wanted to be there to stop it. And in his mind, he'd failed.

Jesse knew because he felt the same way. Especially today.

"What happened?" he asked quietly.

"I did what you told me, Jesse," Gabe said.

"I know you did. Tell me what you saw."

Gabe straightened up in the chair and pulled himself together. "Right. You told me to follow Rita and Peebles when they left. I took a GPS tracker and tacked it on Rita's BMW. Like you told me."

Paradise was a small town. It was hard to avoid being seen. So they had a box filled with GPS trackers in one of the desks at the station. Anytime a Paradise officer needed to follow someone, they could just stick one under the wheel well of a car and hang back and follow the vehicle with a phone.

Jesse didn't like technology, but he had to admit it made surveillance a lot easier. True, they were supposed to have a warrant before they did anything like that. But he hadn't expected anything they found out by following Rita to wind up in court. He just wanted Gabe to keep an eye on Peebles, keep him safe.

Obviously, that hadn't worked out.

"She went out by the high school. Probably wanted to get straight to the 1A."

"So you hung back."

"I didn't want them to see me. I let them get about a mile ahead."

"Did you see Tate at all?"

Gabe shook his head. "No. He must have come up one of the other streets before they got to Paradise Road."

"Okay. Then what happened?"

"I saw the car come to a halt. I figured they'd stopped for something. I didn't want them to see me. I stopped, too."

"How far?"

"It took me a minute to realize they weren't moving. So I'd almost caught up. I was maybe a tenth of a mile back by then. Not even that. You know, near the country club." Gabe took a deep breath. "It's a nice day. I had my windows down. I heard the gunshots."

"Then you went to them."

"I figured you wouldn't care about maintaining a tail at that point."

"You're right. You did the right thing."

"When I came up, he had his gun on Rita. Peebles was already dead. He told me he was just covering her. Basic shooting procedure, in case she had a gun."

"Not sure where she would hide one in that skirt."

Gabe didn't laugh. Which was fair, Jesse thought, because it wasn't that funny.

"Do you think it was a good shooting?"

"I wasn't there. I can't tell you if the shooting was good or not. I didn't see it."

"You're the closest I've got to a neutral eyewitness. I've got Suit out there looking for security cameras or any video that shows the road. Maybe at the gas station. But they were behind the trees and the sign. You saw that."

"Yeah."

"So give me your impressions. Tell me what you saw."

"I don't know, Jesse."

"Your gut instinct, Gabe."

"I don't know, okay?" Gabe looked up at Jesse. "We've both been there, you know? When you have to make the call? You have to decide fast. You don't know what someone has in their hand or their pocket."

"That's not what I'm asking," Jesse said. "What did you see when he had Rita on the ground?"

Gabe thought for a moment. He stared at the wall. "He had his gun pointed at her head."

"Why do you think he did that? Did she seem like a threat to you?"

"He's new. He doesn't know Rita the way we do."

"That's not what I asked."

Gabe shrugged. "I can't read minds, Jesse. I don't know what he would have done if I hadn't been there."

"Me, either," Jesse said. "That's what worries me. What I want is your opinion, Gabe. You know I trust you. So tell me: What do you *think* would have happened?"

Gabe looked away.

Jesse sat quietly, waiting.

"Jesse, I really think if I hadn't shown up when I did, he would have shot her."

They were both silent for a moment.

"Thank you, Gabe."

Gabe shook his head, as if trying to shrug away what he'd just said.

"I could be wrong," he said. "I mean, I don't know. Why the hell would he do that?"

"I have no idea," Jesse said. "But I'm glad you were there."

Gabe snorted. "For all the good it did."

"He didn't call it in," Jesse said.

"What?"

"Tate. He didn't call in the traffic stop. He turned off the dashcam. He didn't tell anyone where he was going. But he had to have followed Rita and Peebles as soon as they left the station to catch up with them like that."

Gabe thought about that. "Holy shit, Jesse. What does that mean?"

"I don't know yet," Jesse admitted. "But I think you might have saved Rita's life."

FORTY-TWO

Peter drove his own car to the apartments where Tate lived, instead of using one of the department's vehicles. He wasn't in uniform, either. He wanted Tate to know this wasn't an official visit.

He knew the kid was having trouble with Jesse, and he'd heard about the mess with Peebles and Rita.

But Peter thought of the department as his only family now. He'd lived alone since his wife passed away a year before. Cancer. Molly had arranged the funeral and a meal train that kept him fed until he got his feet under him again. Truth be told, that was probably why he kept putting off his retirement. He didn't know what he'd do alone in the house.

Peter had never had kids. Maybe that's why he wanted to help Tate fit in. Maybe he could be a father figure to him.

He was sure the kid hadn't meant to screw up so badly.

He was sure if they talked it out, he could help Tate make Jesse see that.

Peter walked up to the apartment door. It was small and cheap-looking—it was hard to get anything in Paradise, with rents the way they were—and the door opened directly to the parking lot, which was going to be pretty damn cold in the winter.

Peter smiled when Tate opened the door. He stared at Peter like he'd never seen him before in his life.

"Hey, kid," Peter said. "Thought maybe you could use a sympathetic ear."

Tate took a step forward, forcing Peter back. He'd never really realized how broad the kid was before, how much of his body was stacked with muscle.

"What?" Tate said, his voice tight and angry.

Peter gulped. "I thought maybe you'd want to talk about it. You know. The shooting. Maybe we can—"

He didn't get to finish the sentence. His breath was taken away by Tate's fist, buried deep below his sternum. The punch was quick and short and hard, coming up from Tate's hip.

Peter couldn't breathe. He saw spots dance before his eyes.

He realized he was on his knees in the doorway, desperately trying to suck air into his lungs.

Peter knew that kind of punch. Most cops do. It was meant to incapacitate a suspect without warning, to end the fight before there was a fight.

What he couldn't figure out was why Tate had hit him.

Tate kneeled down and roughly grabbed Peter by his thinning hair, pulling him up so they were face-to-face.

Tate smiled at him. Peter, despite himself, tried to smile back, like this was some kind of terrible prank.

"You think I don't know this trick?" Tate said. "You come over all sympathetic, get me to say shit? Get me to incriminate myself? You a spy for Stone?"

Peter shook his head. Not to indicate agreement, but because he still couldn't speak, and because he wanted to tell Tate, *No, no, you've got this all wrong.*

Tate's face seemed to ball up with frustration.

"I tried," he said. "I really did. I tried to follow his chickenshit rules and say all the right things. But you know what? Why fucking bother? Why even *be* a cop if you have to follow the same rules as anyone else? I am done. From now on, nobody tells me what to do. You got that?"

He shook Peter as if that would make him listen harder.

"You tell Jesse Stone if he wants me, he's going to have to come and get me himself," Tate said, still gripping Peter's hair. "He needs to do better than send a sad old man. Understand?"

Peter wheezed, trying to say something.

Tate released his hair and slapped him with the same hand. Peter blinked hard as tears began streaming from his eyes.

"Just nod," Tate said. "That's all I need from you."

Jesus Christ, Peter thought. He finally understood. This kid was a psycho. He'd kill Peter right here, right on the front steps of his apartment.

Peter had never thought of himself as vulnerable. He knew he wasn't as brave or as tough as Jesse or Suit or

Molly, but he wore the uniform and he'd gone through doors where he expected to get shot.

But he'd never felt this frightened before.

Peter nodded.

Tate looked at him for a moment that seemed to stretch for minutes.

"Good," Tate said. "Glad we had this talk."

He stepped over Peter's body, carrying a duffel bag. He didn't even bother to close the door.

Peter tried to sit up and found he couldn't.

Tate drove away just as Peter curled into himself and closed his eyes. He lay in the doorway and did not move.

FORTY-THREE

You did everything you could," Dix told Jesse.

"Doesn't feel like it," Jesse said.

Jesse had shown up at Dix's office at the end of a long day. Dix was on his way out, but, seeing Jesse, he had turned around and opened the door again.

Jesse had told him about Peebles and Tate. He expected Dix to tell him he'd done everything right, to try to soften the blow of a man dying on Jesse's watch.

But it didn't help, because Jesse didn't believe him.

"You think you didn't do your job? You think you failed?"

"The kid is dead, isn't he?"

"Yes," Dix said. "But are you telling me you didn't do everything you possibly could to keep him safe?"

"Maybe you should ask Rita that question."

"I'm asking you."

"I think the results speak for themselves."

Dix was quiet. Then he asked, "You remember that game where you busted your shoulder?"

"Only every day."

"Right. It changed your life. Set you on a completely different path. I recall you once told me you thought your friend—"

"He wasn't my friend."

"—your *teammate* set you up with a bad throw. Made it so you had to leap to make the catch and that's why you fell, and you landed badly."

"Right." Jesse didn't know where this was going. But he knew he usually didn't like the destination when Dix arrived at his point.

"Was that an important game?"

"Considering how it turned out, yeah, I'd say so."

Dix chuckled. "You know what I mean. Was that game important to your team's chances that season? Was it going to keep you in contention?"

"No," Jesse said, still mystified.

"Was it a playoff? Or the championship?"

"No."

"Anyone from the Dodgers organization in the stands watching?"

"No."

"So, really, nothing was riding on this game."

"I guess not."

"Then why did you sacrifice your body and your career for a crap throw in a nothing game?"

Jesse felt like he'd just run smack into a brick wall. He couldn't answer the question.

"Jesse?"

"I don't know." He was suddenly angry with Dix, and he couldn't understand why. He knew enough about therapy and himself by now that this meant they'd touched something important. But it didn't stop him from feeling the anger.

"Why would you throw yourself into harm's way, Jesse?" Dix asked, his voice surprisingly gentle.

"Because you don't let things go," Jesse said. "You don't give up when it's tough. You don't quit."

"Lots of people quit," Dix said. "Lots of people stop doing something when they could get hurt."

"Not me," Jesse said.

"No. Not you," Dix said. "You never quit. You never do anything less than your best, even when you were flat-on-your-ass drunk. No matter what it costs you personally. So I'm going to say you did the best you could for Peebles, too."

"It wasn't enough."

"Jesse, how many people would you say you've helped in your life?"

"I don't keep count."

"I'm not surprised. I've lost count myself. I try to keep track, just by following your career, and I think I stopped when I got into triple digits."

"Why would you do that?"

"Because by helping you, I like to think I helped those people, too. I help you keep your head together. I keep you in the fight. And I think you should give yourself more credit for the good you've done in the world."

"Tell that to Peebles."

Dix made one of his rare gestures of annoyance, waving away Jesse's words like flies at a picnic. "Oh, don't be an ass, Jesse. You're a hero. And what's more, you like being one. You and I know it. You try to save people. It's what you do. And thank Christ you do. You can't save everyone, but there are a lot of people who'd be dead without you. Why don't they count? Why do you work so hard at punishing yourself?"

Jesse shrugged. He hated it when Dix didn't give him the answers, but sometimes he hated it more when Dix led him with the questions.

"I don't punish myself."

"Really?" Dix began ticking counts off on his fingers. "You've tried to drink yourself to death several times. You run headlong into bullets and fights. And your relationships? In the past, you stuck with Jenn, even though you knew she was unavailable, both emotionally and physically. You stayed with Sunny when she was committed to someone else. Because you knew they would disappoint you, but they'd never surprise you."

Jesse had to admit that made a lot of sense.

"And the one time you did let go of your fears and commit to someone—"

"I don't want to talk about that right now."

"Fair enough. We both know what happened. I understand how you'd be reluctant to relive that. Ever. And that's a choice you can make."

"I'm not making any choices. I'm just getting through the day. You make it sound like I plan this stuff out."

"Jesse, refusing to choose is still choosing."

"I think I saw that on a bumper sticker."

"All right," Dix said. "Let's try this another way. You like Westerns."

"Sure." They were the only movies Jesse did like. It didn't matter that they were set more than a century in the past. They were still about people facing hard moments and hard choices. Everything else, he couldn't really see the point.

"What happens to the hero in most Westerns?"

Jesse thought about that for a second. "He rides off into the sunset."

"Does he?"

"Well. Shane did."

"Interesting choice. Wasn't Shane dead at the end of the movie? Just stuck on his saddle as the horse took him away?"

Jesse shifted a little in his seat. "Some people think of it that way."

"Do you?"

"I guess not."

"But he is alone."

Jesse thought about that. "Yeah. Yeah, he is."

"He turns his back on a woman who could love him, a boy who could be his son, a town that could be his home."

"Sounds like you like Westerns, too."

"They should make more. But what does that tell you?"

Jesse shrugged again.

Dix asked another question, not letting him off the hook. "Does being a hero mean you've got to die alone, Jesse?"

Jesse felt that one all the way down to his gut. He'd taken punches that hadn't landed that hard.

"I don't know," he said at last.

"I'm going to suggest you think it does. And that's why you've been so angry—so enraged—since you saw Burton dead in that house."

"Maybe."

"Maybe it doesn't have to be that way. You can change the script, Jesse. You don't have to ride off alone into the sunset. You can turn things around. But it's got to be your choice. You have to let people into your life. You have to take chances, open yourself up."

"I don't think I can change who I am," Jesse said.

Dix shrugged. "You have a good, noble place to put your anger. You stop bad guys. They deserve it. You have this duty you carry around. Like a knight with his armor. And you take the weight, Jesse, you really do. I don't say things like this often, especially to a patient, but I admire you."

That might have been the nicest thing Dix had ever said to him. It put Jesse on his guard. "I'm sensing there's a 'but' coming."

"But. Do you ever think about what carrying all that weight means?"

Jesse just looked at Dix, which was answer enough.

"Right," Dix said. "So I'm asking: If this is your job, what's it pay? All jobs have a paycheck. You must get something from yours. What is it?"

That stopped Jesse cold. He'd never thought about it. Not really.

"There has to be something more than the pain and the rage and the risk and the loss," Dix said. "Otherwise, what's the point?"

FORTY-FOUR

Jesse was still thinking about Dix's last question as he walked out to his Explorer when his cell rang. Molly.

"What is it?" he asked.

"It's Peter Perkins," she said. "Jesse, it's bad."

Jesse never let his officers use the lights and sirens. They scared people, and they didn't actually move traffic enough to make a difference in a town as small as Paradise.

But this time, he hit the lights and sirens and reached ninety on his way to the hospital.

Dr. Lowenthal was on call in the ER again. She spoke to Jesse calmly, professionally.

"The surgeon did everything he could," she said. "Officer Perkins's spleen ruptured from the impact of the blow. It caused a great deal of internal bleeding before he was found by a neighbor."

Jesse looked down at the bed where Peter rested.

"I should have . . ." Jesse began. Then he stopped. He honestly didn't know what he should have done.

But he should have done *something*. And done it better.

Dr. Lowenthal touched his arm. "I don't think you would have gotten to him any sooner," she said gently. "He couldn't have been on his front step for more than twenty minutes or half an hour, at most."

"Is he going to make it?"

"He's an older man," Dr. Lowenthal said. "There could be complications. But we've given him blood and repaired the damage. He's got a good shot at a complete recovery."

Jesse nodded and felt a weight lift from him.

"Okay," he said. "Thank you."

"Of course. I'll be here to monitor him all night. Call if you have any questions."

"Thank you," Jesse said again, and left the room.

Outside, in the hallway, Jesse saw Gary Armistead approaching with a bouquet of flowers.

"Jesse," he said, looking solemn. "Terrible thing. I wanted to come by and pay my respects."

"He's not dead yet, Gary."

"Of course. You know what I mean."

Jesse looked past Armistead and down the hallway. Ty Bentley waited at the nurses' station with a cameraman.

"Election in November, isn't it?"

"I always care about the officers in my police department," he said loudly. Armistead then leaned in and spoke quietly, only to Jesse.

"Which is more than you can probably say, isn't it, Jesse? A veteran officer hurt by the guy you recruited. Such a shame. And on top of that riot outside Daisy's. Which is a place you're not allowed anymore."

He smirked. "You're having a real bad run lately, aren't you, Chief Stone? Might be time for some new blood in the department."

Jesse's face was perfectly blank.

Armistead attempted to walk past him. Jesse grabbed his arm.

"About that," Jesse said. "I'm not sure you're any more qualified than I am to pick a new cop for the department. After all, you recommended Tate to me."

Armistead flushed. He tried to pull his arm away. He couldn't.

Jesse let it go.

"I'm not sure I like what you're implying, Jesse."

"I'm not implying. I'm asking. Why did you want me to hire Tate?"

Armistead made a face like he'd heard a bad joke. "Come on. You've been complaining about manpower since before I got this job. Now you're going to complain I sent a candidate your way?"

"That's not what I meant," Jesse said. "I've been asking for money for new hires for years, like you said. Then you fast-tracked Tate over to me. So why did you want this particular man in the department?"

"I saw this kid and I thought he'd fit in here in Paradise. Big-city training, like you, but younger. I was thinking of the future."

"Were you?" Jesse asked.

"I do care about Paradise. No matter what you might think of me."

"What do you mean he'd 'fit in'?"

"What?"

"Fit in how? What would make him a good fit for Paradise?"

The mayor looked at Jesse with an expression like a dog trying to solve a math problem.

"I don't understand."

"I think you do."

Armistead tried to wait Jesse out.

Jesse stood, blocking his way. He was far more comfortable with silence than the mayor was. Armistead couldn't take it for longer than thirty seconds.

"You know why," he said.

"I don't."

"Come on."

Jesse said nothing.

Finally, Armistead made a little groaning noise and rolled his eyes. "Fine. Fine. He's the kind of cop some of our older, more traditional residents would respect."

"Because he's white."

Armistead sighed. "You going to make me say it? Sure. Yeah. He's white."

Just when he thought his opinion of Gary Armistead couldn't sink any lower . . .

"Looks like we both picked a winner, Mr. Mayor."

He stepped past Armistead.

Armistead laughed. Hard. It sounded a little forced, to be honest.

Jesse stopped. Looked at him.

"You find that funny?"

"No, I find you funny, Stone," Armistead said. "You know what bothers me about you?"

"There's just the one thing?"

Armistead made a face. "Aside from your questionable sense of humor, your hardass attitude, and your lack of respect, it's the fact that you're such a goddamn hypocrite."

That genuinely surprised Jesse. He'd been called a lot of things, many of them less polite than the words on the mayor's list. But "hypocrite" wasn't one of them.

"How do you mean?"

"Don't play dumb. You and I both know you've done a bunch of shit worse than this kid. You bend the law whenever you damn well feel like it. You've hurt people. I've heard the stories. And I bet there's even more out there that nobody knows about, because you're smart enough to keep it quiet."

Jesse didn't respond to that. Didn't feel the need to. He knew Armistead was just repeating rumors he'd heard without any solid facts. But it was all true. He'd hurt people. He'd taken the law into his own hands more than once.

Armistead took Jesse's silence as an admission of guilt. He smiled. "So tell me, Chief Stone: What makes you so different than Tate?"

Jesse turned to leave again. He had better things to

do. But he wasn't about to let Armistead have the last word.

"He thinks what he does is right because he's the one who does it," Jesse said. "I do what I have to because it's the right thing."

"What's the difference?" Armistead asked.

"If you don't know, Gary, there's no way I can tell you."

Molly waited outside the entrance to the ER. She fell into step alongside Jesse as he walked out of the exit.

"Where the hell is Tate?" he asked.

"Suit is on his apartment. Gabe is out on the street looking for him. Nobody has seen him since he left the station."

"We're going to find him," Jesse said.

"Bet your ass we are," Molly said.

FORTY-FIVE

Mulvaney woke up, although it was hard to say he'd ever really been asleep. Most of his nights passed in a kind of twilight now, where eventually the world grew dim but he never really rested. He'd worked his whole life to be a survivor, and he'd put plenty of other people in the ground to do it, but sometimes he wondered why he'd bothered living so long. He couldn't remember the last time his body didn't hurt or he'd been able to take a steady piss.

Stacy, his nurse, stood by the door of his room. He appreciated her. He had to admit he'd hired her only because she was the best-looking of the women the agency had sent over, but she'd turned out to be good at her job and fiercely loyal. Her dad, as it turned out, had grown up in one of the neighborhoods Mulvaney had helped run for the organization, way back when. Her dad told her that in those days, everyone knew their place. They looked out for each other. The gangs kept everything in order.

At least until the Feds began rounding up everyone and it all went to hell.

Mulvaney was smart and quick and always willing to make a deal. He turned in the people bigger than him, gave the cops and the Feds just enough to eliminate his competition, and so he managed to stay on the outside of a jail cell for most of his career. (Except for one fall for receiving stolen goods when he was just a kid. Which that prick Healy had known about, of course. He'd have to do something about that retired cop when all this was over.)

There were people who tried to shop Mulvaney, too, but that was why he had people like Burton. Burton would hire someone who'd pop the bastard in the head, and he'd learn the details only when he read them in the paper. Mulvaney subcontracted his dirty work, and nobody in town would know about it. No trails ever led back to him.

Until now.

Who knew Burton was sitting on a whole house full of evidence? Who would have believed that bastard would be able to finger him even after death? Now he was scrambling to keep that tourist-town cop from putting him in a cell for the remainder of his days. And the tools he had weren't enough. He was supposed to be retired, for Christ's sake.

Stacy waited for him to get his bearings. He always needed a little time upon waking. More and more each morning, it seemed.

"What is it?" he said.

"There's a guy here to see you."

"What? What guy?"

"I don't know. He just said he was the one who killed your nephew."

A sudden spurt of fear replaced Mulvaney's anger. He thought of asking Stacy to get her gun. It was a .38 Special she kept in the sideboard, an untraceable old model Mulvaney had given her when he decided he could trust her. He still had a cache of weapons with no serial numbers stashed in the house. You never knew when you'd need a gun that couldn't come back to you.

But no, someone coming to kill him wouldn't announce himself at the front door.

"Are you all right?" Stacy asked. "Your blood pressure okay?"

She actually was a good nurse, he was reminded. "Gimme my phone," he said. "I need to make a call."

She put the phone in his hand and he squinted through his thick glasses at the screen. He dialed the number from memory. He could still do that, at least.

"Get your ass over to my place now," he told Elliott. "Somebody did your job for you."

The cop—Tate—didn't seem at all worried.

That worried Elliott.

Raney and Elliott had seen the whole thing from the front seat of Elliott's rental, from a safe distance.

The day before, Mulvaney had called Elliott on the burner, telling him about the plan to use the lawyer to get his nephew out of jail. He was instructed to pick Peebles up in Boston, and then, after a brief conference to find out what he'd said to the cops, deal with him. Elliott figured Raney could come along for the ride, since they were working together now. He could deal with the lawyer, if it came to that.

But instead, they watched as the cop rolled up and shot Peebles as soon as he got out of the car. Then he looked like he was about to do the same to the lawyer.

"Wow," Raney said.

"Yeah," Elliott said. "Did not see that coming."

That's when they heard the sirens in the distance, very close and getting closer.

"We should—" Raney said.

"Already gone," Elliott had said, putting the car in gear and steering away.

They found a place to park and wait. They didn't know what to do. They decided to wait to hear from Mulvaney.

Then he'd called and summoned them to Boston, where the cop who'd killed Peebles was waiting for them in the living room. Mulvaney's tame thug watched him. So did the nurse. The nurse, frankly, looked meaner.

The cop seemed weirdly glad to see them. "You guys work for Mulvaney?" he'd asked.

Raney ignored the question. So did Elliott. He didn't know what was going on, so he stayed quiet. It was a strategy that had kept him alive so far.

This was Mulvaney's problem, Elliott decided. Let him figure it out.

Maybe they'd take the cop out back and put one in his brain. Killing a cop was always a hurricane of blowback, but he'd done it before. He could do it again.

But Elliot would have felt better if the cop would stop smiling all the time. Like he was exactly where he wanted to be.

It took Mulvaney a while to get shaved and dressed, but he eventually steered his electric wheelchair into the parlor, where Elliott waited with the cop, still in uniform, and another kid. Both of them looked too young to Mulvaney, children playing dress-up. Everyone was younger than he was now.

Even Elliott looked almost the same as he had the last time they'd seen each other more than twenty years ago. Hair gone gray, but still wound up like a coiled spring, and those creepy dead, cold eyes. He seemed to barely have aged, while Mulvaney felt like he was teetering on the edge of the grave every day. He was reminded why he had never liked Elliott.

"Who's he?" Mulvaney asked, pointing to the new kid.

"Raney," Elliott said. "Another one of Burton's subcontractors."

The kid looked mildly annoyed. "Hey. Tell the world, why don't you."

Elliott gave him a face. "We're way past that now."

Raney shrugged, conceding the point.

"Huh," Mulvaney said, looking at him. "Well, the more the merrier, I suppose. Christ."

He looked at the cop, who sat in one of his leather club chairs, purchased a long time ago by his dead wife to class up the room. The cop had his feet on the coffee table.

He stood up quickly and offered his hand like he was a salesman.

"Mr. Mulvaney. I'm Derek Tate. Pleasure to meet you."

Mulvaney looked at the hand like it was a dead rat on a stick. "Are you serious?" he asked. "Why the hell are you here?"

The cop's smile only grew wider. "Because I did you a favor. I killed the one guy who can connect you to the Burton house and everything left from it."

"I thought you were a cop."

"Well, I'm in the process of changing careers," Tate said. "I think I can help you out."

Unbelievable, Mulvaney thought. He looked at Elliott. "You searched him for a wire, right?"

Elliott nodded.

Mulvaney still looked at the door like he expected a squad of cops to bust it down at any second. Then he turned back to Tate.

"Explain," he said. "Quickly."

"That was on the house," Tate said. "Consider it an audition. Or a demonstration."

"For what?"

"I want to work with you."

Mulvaney laughed. Well. He wheezed. Laughing, like sleeping, was hit or miss for him these days. "You want to work for me?"

"*With* you," Tate said. "Not *for* you. I can make all your other problems go away. I can get you the money that was in the house. And all I want is half."

This time, Mulvaney got out a real laugh. "How about

CHRISTOPHER FARNSWORTH

a pony? Or a blowjob? You're about as likely to get either one of those as you are the money. And as for my problems, the only problem I've got right now is you standing there, wasting my time."

Mulvaney pressed the joystick on his chair and began rotating away from Tate. "We're done here," he said to Elliott. "Get him out of my sight."

"I can get you into the police station," Tate said.

Mulvaney rotated back to look at him again.

"I know the codes to the keypads to enter the cells. I know the system. I can shut off the alarm and the cameras. I know where the only remaining evidence from Burton's house is kept."

Mulvaney considered Tate for a moment.

"And I know when Jesse Stone will be covering the night shift again," Tate said. "Alone."

Ah. There was the reason. He hated Stone. Mulvaney could see it. Stone seemed to be the kind of guy who made enemies easily.

"So why come to me? Why not just grab the money and run?"

"Because I know you'd come after me. Or you'd send someone. You think that money belongs to you."

"It *does* belong to me."

"There you go. That's why you've told every thug on the East Coast about it," Tate said. "But if you let me get it—if you sign off on this—I don't have to spend every day looking behind me."

Mulvaney looked at Elliott, who shrugged. Could go either way.

"I could have my friends here get that information out of you."

"I promise you," Tate said. "They would not."

Mulvaney saw something hard there, just below the surface. This guy wasn't exactly smart. But he was willing. He'd killed Mulvaney's idiot nephew, and then he'd come looking for a way to make it pay.

Mulvaney could use that.

"You really want to be a bad guy, don't you?" he said.

Tate smiled. "I prefer to think of it as going into business for myself."

"Why?"

"I tried to do the right thing. I tried to be a cop. Stone wouldn't let me."

Mulvaney thought it over a little more. It made things simpler.

"All right," he said. "But you're not getting fifty percent."

"Hey, if you take out Jesse Stone, everything else is pure profit."

"Sure. Why not." Mulvaney put out his own hand, and Tate shook it.

He gave Elliott a look over the cop's shoulder.

Elliott nodded slightly. They'd just have to kill the cop later. But until then, he could be useful.

"Welcome aboard," Mulvaney said.

Tate smiled and shook the old man's hand again. He knew they'd try to screw him. He knew they looked down on him. Like Jesse Stone, they didn't know who they were dealing with.

He felt the red mist descend like it always did when someone underestimated him or condescended to him.

But for the first time that he could remember, he felt in control. Like he was using his anger instead of letting it drive him over the edge.

Because he'd finally found the people who would let him do *whatever* he wanted to do, *whenever* he wanted to do it.

Before, he thought that meant being a cop. Now he knew better. He was right where he belonged.

It was, honestly, the best Tate had ever felt in his life.

FORTY-SIX

J esse walked into the Helton PD's station. The officer at the desk took a long time to notice him from behind the screen of bulletproof glass, and even then he didn't go out of his way to greet Jesse. He finished scribbling on some paper, checked his phone, looked at Jesse, looked at his phone again, then pressed a button to activate a speaker.

"What," he said.

Jesse pulled his badge. "I need to talk to your chief."

The desk officer thought about that for a few seconds, then pressed the button again. "Wait here," he said.

He heaved himself off his stool and disappeared into the back of the station. Jesse had to admit, maybe Gary Armistead had a point about putting a barrier between the Paradise PD and the public.

Ten minutes later, the desk officer returned. He looked

at the surface in front of him like it might have changed in his absence, then checked his phone again. After a moment, he glanced up at Jesse as if surprised to see him.

Jesse smiled and waved.

"You can go back," the cop said. He pressed a different button and the door to the back unlocked. Jesse caught it just before the buzzer ended.

Jesse found his way through the hall into the office of Helton Chief of Police Bill Fawcett.

Fawcett got up and shook Jesse's hand. "Sorry to keep you waiting," he said with a grin that said he wasn't sorry at all. He pointed Jesse to a chair.

Jesse and Fawcett didn't really get along. Fawcett, like Jesse, was a refugee from a big city and a big department—Boston, in Fawcett's case—but he'd come to Helton looking for a way to retire while still earning a paycheck. Helton was a little collection of villages along the 1A that grew into one place as they got bigger, but still never quite coalesced into a town. It was mostly quiet, as far as Jesse knew, but he wondered how much of that was because Fawcett didn't put much effort into the job. Unlike Jesse, he believed police work should be low-impact. And he never looked for a second explanation if the first one fit.

They'd spoken on the phone about Tate. Helton had given him a glowing recommendation when Jesse was checking Tate's references.

Now Jesse wanted to look Fawcett in the eye and see if the story remained the same.

"So you wanted to talk about Derek, huh?"

Jesse nodded.

"How's he working out over there?"

Jesse thought about that. "How do you think?"

Fawcett kept a straight face for another ten seconds, then burst out laughing. *Well,* Jesse thought, *that didn't take long.*

"Sorry," Fawcett said, wheezing. "Sorry. I heard about the café owner shutting you guys out of the restaurant. Figured Tate was being his usual charming self."

"So he wasn't the really outstanding young officer you told me about?"

"Is that what I said? Well. You know how it is."

"Let's say I don't," Jesse said. "Why don't you tell me?"

"He never did anything illegal here," Fawcett said quickly. "I want you to know that right off the bat."

"You'll forgive me for thinking that's a pretty low bar for a police officer."

"Aw, hell, Jesse, you know what I mean. He never hurt anyone. Or if he did, he didn't leave any marks and he didn't do it on video. Never had any complaints that we had to investigate. He did the job. Far as I could tell, anyway."

Jesse took a deep breath. "But you didn't want him here anyway."

"Kid's wound pretty tight," Fawcett said. "Got into a couple shoving matches with some of the other guys. We're a pretty close bunch here. He didn't fit in well. Couldn't take a joke. You know he wanted to give himself a nickname? Wanted us to call him Slate. You can't give yourself a goddamn nickname."

"Why do you think he's like that? Why so angry?"

Fawcett shrugged. "Who the hell knows. I thought it might be PTSD—he's a vet, you know—but I looked up his record. You know he never even saw combat? He was on the supply chain. He loaded trucks."

"But he really wants to be a fighter," Jesse said. "He wants to prove he's tough."

"Yeah, well. Maybe. Maybe he's just an asshole."

"What else happened?"

"Nothing. He just didn't fit in."

Jesse waited.

"Seriously, Jesse, nothing. I swear."

Jesse waited a little more.

"Okay," Fawcett said. "There might have been something else. This kid we brought into custody. He'd been tagging police cars. Not even gang shit. Just graffiti. You know. 'ACAB.' 'Fuck the police.' That sort of thing."

"And?"

"Tate made the arrest. Kid fell down the front steps on his way into the station. Broke his front teeth."

Jesse rubbed his face with both hands.

"What did you do with Tate?"

"What do you think? I pulled Tate aside, told him he wasn't working out here. I didn't want to have to write him up, put a black mark on his record. So I told him to find another job and I'd give him a good recommendation."

Fawcett's whole face turned into a shit-eating grin.

"And then, luckily, I found this self-righteous SOB who was willing to take him off my hands. It all worked out."

"What happened to the kid?"

"We paid for his dental work, sent him home to his parents. No charges. No lawsuit. It worked out fine."

"It wasn't on video?"

"We don't use body cameras here. And the camera out front was glitching that day."

"Yeah. I'll just bet."

"Oh, fuck you, Stone. You think I should keep evidence that can be used against me? Against my guys? I'm not that stupid. What would you do?"

"I'd like to say I wouldn't have a cop who'd commit crimes in my department. But you made a liar out of me on that."

Fawcett laughed. "As soon as he left the town limits, he stopped being my problem. Guess you should have checked his references a little more carefully."

Jesse stood up slowly. He leaned forward, placing both hands on the desk, looking down on Fawcett. The other chief recoiled, his face going pale.

"Tate went after one of my officers. Put him in the hospital."

"Ah, hell, Stone. Sorry. I didn't know. I never thought he would have gone after a cop."

"But you were fine with him going after anyone else."

Jesse glared down at him. Fawcett's hands trembled a little on the desk.

After a moment, Jesse decided it wasn't worth it. "Do you know where I can find him? Any friends? Any places he hangs out?"

"No," Fawcett said quickly. "No, sorry, I don't. I'd tell you if I did."

Jesse nodded and turned to go.

Fawcett called after him at the door, defiant now that Jesse was leaving.

"Hey. Don't tell me you wouldn't have done the same thing, Stone. There's us and them. That's all."

"I'm not part of your 'us,'" Jesse said. "At least, I hope like hell I'm not."

FORTY-SEVEN

Elliott, Raney, and now Tate all found another hotel, halfway to the New Hampshire state line, far enough away from Paradise that they didn't think anyone would spot Tate there.

Then they started planning. Tate's last look at the duty roster said Jesse Stone would be alone in the station on Saturday night, covering the eight p.m. to eight a.m. shift, fielding any calls from the county 911 dispatcher and keeping an eye on all that money. The department was even more understaffed since Tate left and took out Perkins on his way, so he knew Stone would be stuck covering that shift.

They had to hit the Paradise station that night. The problem was, none of them trusted the others enough for any plans to stick.

The simplest thing would have been to get a rifle and

put one of them on a roof somewhere in Paradise and then wait for Jesse Stone to emerge from the station and put a bullet through his head. Death from above. Hard to avoid a shot you can't see coming.

But none of them wanted to do that, each for their own reasons.

Tate wanted to see Stone's face when he died, which struck Elliott as a little dramatic.

Raney said he wasn't much of a shot from a distance, even with a scope.

And Elliott didn't trust either of the other two to split the loot with him if he was the one stuck up on the roof. In fact, he thought they'd leave him there and deal him to the cops, who'd inevitably descend, like flies on shit, when one of their own got killed. And he told them so.

"This town is going to be locked down the minute we get Stone. They're going to have State Police, Boston PD, probably the FBI, all showing up, going door-to-door looking for us," he said. "We've got two roads out and the ocean on the other side, in case you hadn't noticed. I am not going to be trapped here while you two figure out how to divide two million dollars in half."

Raney smiled like this was funny. "You have trust issues, you know that?"

Tate scowled. "Are you saying you think I'd stab you in the back like that?"

Elliott and Raney looked at each other. "Yes," Elliott said.

"It's nothing personal," Raney said. "It's just you're already betraying your boss. Not hard to see you deciding to screw both of us, too."

Tate thought about it for a moment, then shrugged. "Yeah, all right, fair enough," he said. "But that would mean cutting Mulvaney out, too. And I personally am not dumb enough to piss him off, even hooked up to as many tubes as he is. No, thank you."

Tate was right to be scared of Mulvaney. That was the only reason Elliott was here. He did not want any ghosts of his past coming back to haunt him, and he certainly did not want Mulvaney or any of the people in the organization viewing him as a loose end to be snipped. People who said organized crime was nothing in America anymore hadn't been on the wrong side of it. The organization might not be what it once was, but it still took revenge seriously.

So Tate was thinking clearly, at least about this. Elliott had noticed that Tate could fly off the handle over the smallest slights and perceived insults, but then he'd turn around and be rational in other moments.

It made Elliott wonder how much of Tate's personality was an act and how much was genuine stupidity.

It didn't make him any more trustworthy, but he was the only one who could get them into the station, so they were stuck with him.

"Well, that leaves us where we started," Elliott said. "How do we get Stone away from the station? And who handles him?"

"I've got nothing personally against the guy," Raney said. "That seems like a job for McGruff the Crime Dog here."

"Yeah, but he knows me," Tate said.

"All the more reason," Raney said. "He'll try to talk to you. He'll want to give you a chance."

"Not anymore," Tate said. "Not after Peebles. Believe me. He sees me again, he's going on full alert."

Raney wiped his hands over his face. "I thought this was what you wanted. You and him. Showdown in the middle of the street. Like an old Western."

"I want him dead," Tate said. "I'm okay if someone else does it, as long as it happens."

"Sounds like you're scared."

"Please. I could take him, but then who's going to get you into the cells?"

"And you want the money," Elliott said.

"We all want the money," Tate said. "Don't you? I mean, we're all in this to get paid, right?"

Elliott wondered if Tate was baiting him. There was no way the three of them were riding off together like the Three Musketeers when this was all over. He had to know Elliott or Raney was planning on putting a bullet in his brain as soon as they had the cash out of the station.

He wondered if Tate thought Mulvaney would protect him from that because he'd made his deal with the old man personally.

If he did, then maybe he really was stupid. Mulvaney and the organization protected only themselves. It was how a guy like Mulvaney managed to live as long as he did.

Elliott shook it off and got back to the problem at hand.

"We need Stone out. We need in. And we need the evidence he still has."

"Yeah, you've been saying that for an hour," Tate said to Elliott.

"Haven't heard you come up with any brilliant plans," Raney said.

"You haven't, either," Tate shot back.

Toddlers, Elliott thought. Maybe he could just shoot them now and figure out something else entirely.

"Look," he said, struggling for patience. "This isn't that hard. It's a small-town cop with a Podunk police station. We get the money and the file. And we make sure he's dead so everyone is busy dealing with that instead of following us. We don't need some elaborate *Mission Impossible*-style bullshit here."

"Okay. Tate and I go in," Raney said. "He's got the code to the keypad for the cells. I can watch him and help get the money out."

"You think I trust you more than him?" Elliott asked. "What am I supposed to do while you're getting the money?"

"You're the best shooter here. We know that," Raney said. "You've got the experience. You're the only one with a chance of taking Stone down."

"You trying to flatter me?" Elliot said. "You think my ego is so big I'm willing to go up against Stone just to prove something?"

"I'm saying it because it's true, isn't it?" Raney said. "Between the three of us, honestly, who would you bet on?"

Elliott had to admit Raney was right. He was better, even at his age. It was just a fact in his mind, as fixed and immobile as granite.

"At some point, we've got to trust one another enough to get this done," Raney said. "You know I'm right."

Raney and Elliott stared at each other for a long

moment. Elliott was trying to read the younger man like they were across the table at a poker game. He got nothing from Raney's face. No tells.

"We need a place to hit him," Elliott said. "I can't just do it on Main Street. We've already seen what happens when he faces someone head-on. We need a quiet spot. Out of the way."

"Ambush," Raney said.

"Yeah," Elliott said.

"Like in Iraq," Raney said. "We'd walk into a home or apartment, looking to get people out. We couldn't go in shooting. The insurgents knew our rules of engagement. So they'd wait for us in the places where we'd have to go. Like when we were clearing a building of civilians."

"Not a bad idea," Elliott admitted. "Where can we hide out in Paradise? Someplace he won't see it coming?"

"Wait," Tate said. "I got it. I got an idea."

This ought to be good, Elliott thought.

"I know exactly how we get Stone out of the station," Tate said, beaming like he'd just invented the lightbulb. "We make him come out for the one person he can't turn down."

He explained his idea.

Elliott considered it. He looked to Raney. "What do you think?"

"I'm getting bored sitting around here, going over and over the same problem. This is worth a shot."

Elliott was surprised, but it seemed like it could work. It *would* work.

"You know what," Elliott said. "You're right. It's a good idea. We can do this."

"Don't sound so surprised," Tate said. "We're going to take Stone down. And we're going to get the money. This is the start of a whole new adventure."

Once again, Elliott looked closely at Tate. No way he was that stupid. He had to be planning to kill Elliott and Raney, just like Raney was planning to kill Tate and Elliott, and Elliott was planning to kill them.

Pretty soon, they'd all have their guns pointed at one another's heads.

But that was the future. They'd get there soon enough.

"Okay," Elliott said. "Let's map it out. This is how it's going to go down."

FORTY-EIGHT

Jesse sat in his office and looked out the window, watching the dark clouds gathering over the ocean in the distance. The early-spring warmth had given way to a cold and wet storm front coming down from Canada, soaking everything in its path.

Paradise would be inundated before nine p.m. He expected he'd get more than a few calls to rescue stranded drivers or help someone with a flooding house.

There had been no further word about Tate. Jesse had pursued every lead he could think of and come up empty. Tate's parents hadn't spoken to him in years, or at least they said they hadn't. He didn't seem to have any friends in Paradise, and hadn't made any in Helton, either. The Philadelphia PD had put up a stone wall when Jesse called them, preferring to keep Tate strictly in the past.

Jesse didn't have to wonder how a guy like Tate found

himself so alone. But he did wonder where he found shelter when he'd finally gone too far.

He got up and poured himself more coffee just as the storm broke overhead. It sounded like someone had turned a firehose on the station's roof. He hoped the building would stay dry. After his last argument with the mayor, he didn't think they'd get any money for emergency repairs.

Peter Perkins was out of the hospital, at least. He was at home recovering, minus his spleen. He was going to have a hard time fighting infections without it. Jesse had been to see him once. Peter had been quiet. He said he didn't blame Jesse. Maybe he even meant it.

"You think he's coming back?" Peter had asked, just before Jesse left. The home health aide wanted him to go; Peter needed his rest. But the thought of Tate clearly terrified Peter.

So Jesse lied. "I think he's as far from Paradise as he can possibly get, and if he's smart, he won't come back."

But that was the thing. Tate wasn't smart.

In his gut, Jesse knew that he wouldn't have to find Tate.

He knew Tate would be coming back for him.

He just didn't know when.

At that moment, Tate sat with Elliott and Raney in Elliott's rental outside the station, under the rain streaming down from a big tree in the corner of the public parking lot across Atlantic, next to the park. In high summer, Raney figured, they never would have gotten a spot like this. But the hour and the rain kept everyone off the streets except for a few other cars that looked abandoned.

They could see a light on in the station window.

"That's got to be him," Tate said, looking out the windshield.

Elliott sat in the back seat. "Okay." He checked his watch. "Time to go."

"Showtime!" Tate whooped, bouncing a little in his seat like a kid at a carnival.

Christ, what an asshole, Raney thought.

"Yeah," Elliott said. "Sure."

He popped the door open and slipped out, moving like a shadow in the rain.

Then he vanished into the darkness without a trace.

FORTY-NINE

Daisy finished wiping the counter where Jordyn had missed a spot. He was doing better. Another six or seven months and he might actually be competent to lock up on his own.

Not for the first time, she missed Cole, Jesse's son. Law enforcement's gain was a loss to the world of fine dining. Say what you will about that kid, but he could really bus a table.

She was on her way to the back door to the alley where she parked her car, pleasantly tired.

She took one last look around the café before leaving. She'd be back here in six hours, doing it all again, baking and cooking and serving and cleaning.

Then her eyes snagged on the sign she'd put in the window when she was so enraged. **NO PARADISE COPS ALLOWED.** *Jesus.* What a shit show that had turned into. She'd heard they'd suspended Tate because he'd shot someone. She'd resisted the urge to call Jesse and shout "I TOLD YOU SO" at the top of her lungs.

Probably not what he needed to hear right now, honestly. But she was still so damn mad at him.

They'd work it out. She knew it. Whenever they got the time. Until then, he could eat at the Gray Gull. He wouldn't starve.

She turned to go then. And heard something. A scraping noise.

Daisy walked carefully toward the back door. It was locked, but she hadn't set the alarm yet.

There was the scratching noise again. Then the deadbolt began to turn on its own.

For a moment, it was so strange, she could think only of a haunted-house movie. But her mind put it together even while she stood there, staring.

Someone was breaking into the café.

Daisy had a baseball bat under the front counter, a souvenir of the bad old days when someone from Hasty Hathaway's idiot militia liked to throw rocks through her plate-glass window or tear down her pride flag. Now she mostly kept it for sentimental reasons, and anyway, it was too far away for her to do any good.

But she was right in the kitchen, surrounded by dozens of expertly sharpened knives.

She wasn't moving fast enough, she knew. She couldn't take her eyes off the lock as it slowly turned.

But Daisy forced herself into gear, ran over to the nearest prep station, and grabbed the closest knife. By all bad luck, it was a short paring knife, the one she had Jordyn use.

She'd just gotten it when it occurred to her that the smarter thing to do was run out the front door. Escape was a hell of a lot better plan than a knife fight.

Again, her mind and body seemed to be weighed down by quicksand. She'd heard Jesse talk about this, how when the adrenaline hits, when you're in danger, everything slows down. Including your reaction time, sometimes. You freeze.

Daisy had been in fights before, but this was different. Then she had her anger on her side. It erased any fear.

Now all she could think about was someone coming into her place for God knows what reason.

In the time it took her to decide to run, the lock snapped open. The door slammed wide and a man rushed through, seeming impossibly quick to her, his movements sure and unhesitating. He made her feel slow and stupid by comparison.

She just had time to shove the knife away under the sleeve of her sweater.

He was across the kitchen in two big steps, one hand coming up and shoving her down to the floor.

Daisy landed hard on the tile. It hurt.

When she looked up again, an older man with graying hair stared down the barrel of a very big gun pointed at her.

"This is not how I wanted this to go," he told her.

Elliott pressed a button on his phone, activating the three-way call that Raney had set up earlier.

He kept the gun on the woman without looking at her.

"I'm here," he said into the mic connected to his own

phone in his pocket. The call was not actually going through his phone, but through an app Raney swore was "end-to-end encrypted" so no one else could listen in like they would on a cell. Elliott had only just figured out how to work the earbuds his wife had gotten him for Christmas so that he could make calls and listen to music while out golfing, so he had to take Raney's word for it. One more sign he was too old for all of this shit.

"Copy that," Tate replied, too loud in his ear. "We're holding here."

Idiot, Elliott thought. He hated people using military jargon like they were in some kind of action movie. *You're not James Bond,* he wanted to say.

But he needed to talk to the café owner instead.

"Daisy Dyke, right?" Elliott said. "A pleasure to make your acquaintance."

Daisy remained silent, glaring at him.

Elliot reached down, gun in her face, and searched her pockets until he found her phone. He put it in her hand and stepped back.

"Call your friend Jesse Stone," he said.

Daisy gave him a look that wasn't sufficiently frightened for a woman facing a bullet. "Why should I?" she said.

Oh, this goddamn town, Elliott thought. He would be happy to have it in his rearview mirror. Did everyone here have to make everything so difficult?

He pulled back the hammer on his Ruger .357, which was one reason he always loved revolvers. The sound of the gun being cocked clarified so many arguments.

"You're going to shoot me?" she said. "Like you're not planning on doing that anyway."

Her voice trembled. He could tell she was frightened. But she didn't make any move to dial the phone.

Elliott crouched down to get closer to Daisy, keeping the gun in her general direction. He spoke softly so she'd have to listen.

"I don't want to shoot you," he said. He meant it.

"But I can shoot you without killing you. And then you'll be in more pain than you've ever felt in your life, and I'll ask you to make the call again. So. It's up to you at this point."

He meant that, too.

He saw her shake. Involuntary fear. He'd seen it so many times. The body betraying people even when they were trying to be brave. He'd seen hardened killers shudder like that, just before he put one into them. He'd seen it in cops. The body knew when death and pain were close, no matter how the brain tried to deny it.

"Then I guess you better quit screwing around and shoot me," she said.

Her voice was almost inaudible by the end of the sentence. Her mouth had gone dry and he could tell she was having a little trouble breathing.

But he gave her credit for saying it.

He sighed and cocked the hammer back again so the gun didn't go off accidentally. Then he whipped the revolver across her face, knocking her flat on her back.

A Ruger .357 weighs almost twenty ounces fully loaded, which is about the same weight as a claw hammer.

It feels exactly the same when getting hit with one in the face. Elliott knew from experience on both ends.

He picked up Daisy's phone from the floor where she'd dropped it and stood over her. She was not unconscious, but she was stunned. He held the phone in front of her face, hoping the blood would not mess up the face ID too much.

It didn't. The phone opened and he had access to her apps and contacts.

He frowned, momentarily confused. How could he possibly have the wrong phone? He'd just taken it off her.

"Who the hell is Flora Patterson?" he demanded, shoving her a little, showing her the name on the owner's contact card.

"That's me," Daisy said. "Flora Patterson. Always hated it. Sounds like a housewife from Jersey."

Elliott looked at her.

"What, you didn't think my real name was Daisy Dyke, did you?"

"Shut up," Elliott said. *This goddamn town.*

He scrolled through the directory, looking for the right name. He found it. Then he hit the button on the screen and waited as the phone rang.

FIFTY

His phone buzzed on his desk. His personal number, not the one he gave out for people looking for the chief of police.

The caller ID said **DAISY**.

He picked up, already alert. There was no good reason for her to call at this hour.

"Daisy?" he said.

"No," a man's voice said.

"Who is this?" Jesse was already on his feet, clipping his holster to his belt, moving toward the door.

"I'm the guy telling you how things are going to be. I'm monitoring your radio. I've got people watching your station. You make a call for help, you get on the police band, you do anything but what I tell you, and she dies."

Jesse stopped. "I'm listening."

"Good."

Elliot put his own phone on mute, shutting off his mic and effectively cutting Raney and Tate out of this part of the conversation. He wasn't so technically inept that he didn't know how to do that.

"I want you to get the file of the remaining photos and papers from the Burton house. The ones that were not in the fire. The ones you showed on TV. Do you have them?"

"They're at the state evidence facility."

Elliott smiled. "Nice try. They're locked in the small safe behind your desk. You sent the copies to the state evidence facility, but you like to keep the original evidence where you can look at it. That's strike one, Chief Stone. You played baseball. I sent that one past you just to see if you'd swing. And you did. Now, believe me when I say we know what you've got and what you don't. You can try lying to me again, but I don't think you want to see what happens to Daisy here when you strike out."

Shit, Jesse thought. Whoever the guy was, he knew exactly where Jesse kept the Burton file. Which meant he had inside help.

It didn't take a genius to figure out who that was. It just didn't do Jesse a lot of good in this particular moment.

"Okay," Jesse said. "The file is here. What do you want?"

"Come to the café. Leave your gun. Bring the file. Call anyone else, call for help, she dies. Anyone but you shows up, she dies. Take longer than a minute to get here, she dies."

Jesse finished gearing up and closed his office closet. He put his backup piece, the .38, in his ankle holster and pulled his pant leg over it.

"Put Daisy on," Jesse demanded, shrugging into his jacket, the phone stuck between his shoulder and his ear.

"She can't come to the phone right now. But I think she's got a message for you," Elliott said.

The next thing Jesse heard was a shot followed immediately by a scream.

"There he goes," Tate said, as if Raney were blind and couldn't see the cop burst out of the station and sprint toward the café. Raney had never liked cops, even ex-cops. Being this close to Tate was a chore even when he wasn't saying stupid shit like that.

Just a little longer, he reminded himself.

Raney watched Stone disappear down the street. He moved pretty fast for an older guy. Must have been scared. Scared was good. It took him a little while to get out of the station, but they heard nothing from the app that monitored the police bands on their phones. No calls for help, not even a click for a coded message.

A little weird that Elliott was so quiet, too, all that time, but that was Elliott. Getting two words out of the guy was a triumph.

Tate, on the other hand, wouldn't shut up even when he wasn't talking. Right now, he shifted and creaked in the passenger seat of the car. He sniffed and cracked his gum and blew bubbles, like a kid with ADHD.

Raney really could not wait to kill him. He was reasonably sure the Mob guy in Boston would be fine with another body in the final count when this was all over, no matter how helpful he'd been. He wasn't as sure about Elliott, but that would come down to what the old guy did when they split the money.

He had no intention of letting his share go without a fight.

But Elliott was right about one thing: First things first. Do the job, then deal with the other problems.

So he waited until the cop had vanished. Then he didn't say anything to Tate other than "Let's go."

They ran wide across the street, circling around the station to the back door, avoiding the cameras on the front and on the streetlight. Even though they were both wearing hoods and masks, they wanted to leave as little evidence behind as possible. Raney had read there were algorithms now that could analyze your walk and match it against a video, identifying you by your gait like it was a fingerprint.

It was getting harder and harder to stay anonymous these days.

But with any luck, he was about to retire.

They couldn't avoid the camera above the back door of the station. But Raney was quick. He dropped the crowbar he was carrying from his sleeve and leaped up and swung, all in one smooth motion.

The crowbar hit exactly where he'd aimed and knocked the camera cleanly from the wall. He heard it land in the back parking lot.

Tate was already punching numbers into the keypad on the door, his gun in his other hand.

Raney came up behind him, crowbar in his right, nine-millimeter in his left.

Tate opened the door and Raney followed him through. "We're in," he said.

"We're in," Elliott heard through the earbuds. He stood over Daisy and waited, eyes darting back and forth between the front door and the café's owner on the floor.

She sat there, mouth shut, shivering like she was out in the freezing cold.

She'd screamed only once when he'd fired the gun into the floor near her head. *That was enough,* he thought. He really did not want to shoot her. Despite what everyone sees in the movies, he'd learned long ago that it was easier to kill someone with a bullet than to wound them. You never knew how someone would react to eight grams of lead entering their body; he'd seen people walk it off, and far more drop dead from the shock, or a sudden arterial bleed, or, one time, go into cardiac arrest.

Keeping her alive as a hostage was tricky, but it was better than giving up his only leverage over Stone.

Maybe this was arrogant. Maybe he had too much faith in his own skills. But he was sure he could take Stone and get out of here.

More than anything, Elliott needed that file.

He just had to be ready when the cop came through the door.

FIFTY-ONE

Jesse skidded to a halt just outside Daisy's café, feet slipping on the wet sidewalk, the file close to his chest, under his jacket, where he'd stuffed it to protect it from the rain.

He tried to crane his neck to see through the front window without being seen himself. *No good.* It was too dark inside. Nothing but light reflected from the streetlamps dancing against the glass as the rain poured down from above, soaking him to the skin despite his jacket.

He saw the sign in the front: **NO PARADISE COPS ALLOWED.**

He could go around the back. The door there opened into the kitchen. But it was possible that whoever had Daisy had that covered as well.

Daisy could be bleeding out, dying inside.

He forced himself to take a deep breath. To think.

The man said no calls for help. Jesse assumed he had a
police scanner to hear anything that went out over the
radio.

Truth be told, there was a part of him that wanted to
do this alone. To be the only cowboy dealing with the bad
guys in his town.

But he wasn't alone.

He took out his phone again and dialed.

Listened to it ring, alone in the rain. And heard it ring,
faintly, inside the café.

Elliott looked at the phone. *What the hell?* Why was Stone
calling back? Did he think he could negotiate his way out
of this?

Elliott let the call go to voicemail.

Nothing happened. Stone didn't enter the café. There
was no call for police on the scanner app Raney had in-
stalled on all of their phones. There was nothing but the
sound of the rain and the woman on the floor breathing
heavily.

What the hell was Stone up to?

"How's it going?" he asked.

"We're on our way into the cells," Raney said. "What
are you doing? I thought we said we'd keep the line
clear—"

"You're sure Stone isn't there?"

"What? No, why would he be here?"

The phone rang again.

"Never mind," Elliott said, and muted his own phone
again.

Daisy's phone kept ringing.

This time he answered it.

"I'm here at Daisy's," Jesse said. "Front door."

"Come on in," Elliott said.

"Why should I? Is Daisy even alive?"

Elliott, inside the café, kicked Daisy in the chest, almost impersonally. Her grunt of pain was audible over the phone.

"Still breathing for now," Elliott said.

"Is she hurt? Should I call an ambulance?"

"Stop stalling, Chief. You want to see her? See how she is? Well, the door is open. Next move is up to you."

"Okay," Jesse said. "I'm coming in."

Elliott hung up on him.

Jesse moved toward the front door of the café and hoped his message was clear enough.

Halfway across town, Suit looked at his phone dumbly as he heard all this. He was sitting wrapped in a sheet in his bed, still wiping the sleep from his eyes. The call had been from Jesse, but Jesse hadn't said anything to Suit. He'd just started talking to someone else.

"I'm here at Daisy's," Jesse had said. "Front door."

Suit shook his head to clear the grogginess, and it slowly occurred to him that Jesse had patched him into another call.

Then he heard Daisy grunt in pain, and it all became clear to him.

Holy shit, he thought.

Molly rang on the other line as Suit grabbed his pants. She was already shouting at him.

"Goddamn it, Suit, get moving, Jesse is all alone over there, it's going down now—"

"Molly, what . . . ?"

"He *conferenced us in on the call,* you moron!"

"I knew that!" Suit protested.

"They've got Daisy! Get your ass up and down to the café, I'll meet you there—"

That was as much as Suit heard because he knocked the phone to the floor as he pulled on his vest and Elena yelled at him from the other side of the bed.

But he didn't have time to stop. He splashed his way to the car, rain sheeting down on him as he struggled to buckle his gun belt and open the door at the same time.

Raney had to admit that at least Tate knew what he was doing inside the station. They went into the conference room and he moved methodically and systematically through all the evidence on the table, piling it into the garbage bags they'd brought, ripping down photos of the Burton house from the wall, taking an old mug shot and rap sheet of Charlie Mulvaney and wadding it up with the other trash.

Tate moved into the chief's office while Raney gathered up every other scrap he could find and bagged them all.

Tate came back from the office empty-handed. "The file is gone."

"What?"

"The original photos. The file Stone's been carrying around like it's a damn baby. It's not in the safe. It's not on his desk. It's gone."

"Shit," Raney said. That file had the pictures from his job as well as the others. Nobody had connected him to it yet, but that was the whole reason he was here. The money didn't mean shit if he was stuck in prison for murder.

Tate kicked a trash can across the room, sending it bouncing off the wall. "Damn it, what did he do with that file?"

Raney clicked over to the line with Elliott. "We can't find the file," he said into his mic. "You get that? We can't find the file."

No answer. Elliott's phone had been iffy since the start. Now he wasn't responding at all.

What the hell was going on over at the café?

Jesse opened the café door slowly. It didn't creak ominously or squeal with rust. Daisy ran a tight ship. There was only the cheerful little jingle of the bell attached as it swung.

He stepped inside the café. The light from the street was enough to see the man with the gun standing over Daisy, who was huddled on the floor. They were in the space between the booths and the four-top tables. Jesse wouldn't have had a clear run at him even if the guy didn't have a gun aimed at Daisy's head.

Jesse stood there, dripping, for a moment.

"Daisy, are you okay?"

"*No, I'm not, Jesse*," she said, in a tone that implied Jesse ought to be able to see that for himself.

"She's fine," the man said, the gun absolutely rock-steady in his hand. Aside from his lips, he didn't move an inch. "At least she is for now."

Jesse looked at the man. He thought he'd seen him around town a couple of times. Casual dress. Graying hair. Anonymous. An early tourist, a guy up from Boston for the weekend or for a lunch.

Now he seemed like a different kind of creature altogether. Something that had been bred or even manufactured. Jesse had seen Vinnie Morris exhibit this kind of stillness. Crow, too. Like a trap about to spring.

Jesse reached toward the top of his jacket. The gun in the man's hand moved like it was on a swivel, coming up from Daisy to target Jesse center mass.

"Easy," the man said.

"I'm easy," Jesse said.

"Drop your gun on the floor."

"I don't have one."

"Bullshit. You're not that dumb."

"Appreciate the compliment, but you said come unarmed, so I came unarmed."

"I assumed you'd do it anyway. I told you, you had three strikes. This is strike two. Take out your gun and drop it on the floor, then kick it away."

"I don't have—"

The man aimed his gun back at Daisy, centering it on her head.

Daisy did not look up. Her eyes were locked on Jesse's.

"You sure you want to take a swing on strike three, Jesse?" the man said. "I will put a crater in her skull right here, right now."

"Okay," Jesse said quickly. He reached, slowly, under his jacket and took his Glock out, holding it by the handle with two fingers. Then he placed it on the floor and kicked it across the tiles to the man.

It hit a table leg and skittered away in another direction, disappearing into the shadows under a booth.

"Close enough," the man said. "I assume you've got a backup piece. Toss that, too."

"You didn't give me enough time to get fully dressed."

The man smiled, but his eyes looked like the glass marbles of a crocodile in a taxidermy shop.

"I told you I'd shoot her."

"Come on over and search me if you want."

The man shook his head. "And get that close? No, thanks."

They both waited for a moment.

"All right. Let's pretend you don't have a backup at your ankle. I don't think you can get to it before I kill her—"

Daisy made a little sound at that.

"—so we'll call that ball one. But you better have the file."

Jesse unzipped the top of his jacket and pulled out a plastic file folder, tied shut with a string, stuffed with papers and photos.

"This is it," Jesse said, holding it in front of his heart.

"How do I know that's not just the pictures from your summer softball league and old parking tickets?"

"You know, at some point, you have to extend a little trust in any transaction," Jesse said.

The man smiled again. "They were right. You are funny." He gestured with his .357. "Place it on the table over there. Open it and spread out the contents. I want to take a look."

Moving slowly, Jesse did as instructed. He opened the plastic file and pulled out the pictures and the pages from Burton's weird encoded records. The dead people stared back at him as they had since he'd first seen them, scattered among the stacks of garbage.

"Step back," the man told him.

Jesse backed up to his place by the door again.

Keeping his gun pointed at Jesse—an impressive amount of control, considering the length of time he'd been holding it—the man went to the table and scanned the pictures and papers.

"You don't seem to care that much about the money in the cell," Jesse said.

"This is more valuable," the man said.

"Why are those so important to Mulvaney?" Jesse asked.

"Not just Mulvaney," the man said, watching Jesse only from the corner of his eye.

"You, too," Jesse said. "They matter to you, too. Personally."

The man's eyes snapped back to Jesse. "Yes," he said. "They do. This is my insurance policy. Mulvaney almost never got his hands dirty. But, well . . . this one was personal. This is why he owed me."

"So why not use it? Turn him in. You could offer state's—"

The man's laughter cut Jesse off before he could say another word. "I'm sorry, did you think I was looking for a way out? That I'm anxious to enter witness protection and spend the rest of my life waiting for a bullet or a car bomb? I am fine where I am, thank you. This is just so I can go back to my life and never have to see this godforsaken corner of the country again. I'll finally be left alone."

"Because one of those killings could bring Mulvaney down," Jesse said.

"You have no idea," the man said, grinning for the first time with what looked like genuine glee. It was not a happy expression, or a comforting one.

It occurred to Jesse that the man was giving away a lot of information. As if he never expected Jesse or Daisy to repeat it to anyone.

"Okay, you've got me and the file. Let her go."

"You think that's how this ends?" the man asked. He looked thoughtful.

"You can keep me here. I'm a better hostage, anyway. Anything goes wrong, you can always threaten to kill the chief of police. Just shoot me," Jesse said, tapping his chest. "Right here."

Daisy stirred in her position on the floor. "Jesse, don't," she said.

The man shook his head. "Come on, seriously? Doesn't this hero bullshit get a little old after a while?"

"What do you mean?"

"Look at that sign," the man said. "She told you what she thought of you. She said she doesn't need you. She said screw the police. And yet here you are. Offering your life for hers. Tragic."

"Jesse—" Daisy said again.

"Shut up," the man told her, and turned back to Jesse before he could blink. "Why do you do it? Why take the risk for people who don't even thank you?"

"It's not about thanks," Jesse said.

"I've known cops all my life. That's bullshit."

"Not here," Jesse said. "Not to me."

The man scowled. "You'd really take a bullet for her even though she told you to go fuck yourself?"

"Yeah," Jesse said. "That's the job."

The man looked like this was either the funniest or the saddest thing he'd ever heard, but he couldn't tell which.

"Suit yourself," he said, and fired at Jesse, hitting him dead center in the chest.

FIFTY-TWO

Tate and Raney gave up on the office. The file was gone, or it was in the safe, and Tate didn't have the combination to that. Either way, they weren't getting it.

So they might as well get the money, they decided.

Tate led Raney past the cells. There was someone in the first cell at the start of the corridor, away from the money. Some homeless drunk, from the look (and the smell) of him. He seemed more like a pile of rags on his cot than a person. But he didn't move, so Tate assumed he was sleeping or passed out.

"I could shoot him," he said to Raney.

Raney gave him that look. The one Tate was getting really tired of, to be honest. Like he was some kind of idiot.

"Can he get out?"

"No," Tate admitted.

"Then let's get the money," Raney said.

"Just trying to be sure," Tate said.

"Whatever you say, killer."

Delivered in that same superior tone. Tate was really sick of that, too. He might not be a big-time contract hit man like these guys, but he knew he was going to add at least one more body to his count before this was over. He could damn well guarantee that.

Tate entered the code on the keypad for the final cell, the farthest from the exit door, where the duffel bags sat on the cot.

The cell door opened. They both hesitated.

Tate didn't want to go in first, leave his back open and unguarded with Raney behind him.

Raney grinned at him, probably thinking the same thing.

"You want to do rock-paper-scissors for it?" Raney said.

"What?"

"Never mind. I'll go."

"Wait," Tate said. "Why should you get the money?"

Raney rolled his eyes. "So do you want to go in there?"

Tate was torn. Either way, there were disadvantages.

"Clock's ticking," Raney said.

"Shut up, I'm thinking."

"Because we have that kind of time."

"I said *shut up*."

Tate thought for a moment. Either way, he was taking a chance.

"What's going on with Elliott?" he asked, stalling.

"It doesn't matter," Raney said. "Elliott can handle himself."

Elliott watched the cop stagger and fall backward to the floor.

After all that, the great Jesse Stone died like pretty much anyone else.

But then, nobody died well, in Elliott's experience. There was no such thing as a good death. He took a second look to make sure Stone wasn't getting up.

Then he turned to put his next shot into the café owner. Time to clean up and move on.

But to his surprise, she wasn't a quivering wreck anymore.

Before he could squeeze the trigger, her arm swung up from her position on the floor. He caught a glint of steel in the murky light.

Then it vanished as she buried the knife deep in his thigh.

He'd been knifed before, but this time it felt like she really knew what she was doing. She pulled the knife out and stabbed it back in three more times before he'd finished screaming. She twisted and carved and dragged. It was like fighting a bobcat with metal claws. He felt steel dig into him in his back, his gut, and his arm. He couldn't get free.

It was all he could do to swing the .357 around and club her in the head.

That sent her sprawling on the floor. Elliott struggled to stand up and pointed it at her.

She looked at him with defiance. Not scared at all.

Good for her, he thought, and prepared to squeeze the trigger.

Then something—someone—belted him hard in the back of the head and grabbed his arm.

Elliott saw spots. He managed to turn and saw—impossible—the dead cop. Stone. Very much alive, his hands wrapped around Elliott's arm, trying to get the gun away from him.

Elliott had had about enough of all of this. He was bleeding and outnumbered. The cop didn't know enough to stay dead.

He twisted his wrist as far as it would go and fired another shot in the cop's direction.

At this distance, he was deafened and half blinded. But the cop let go. There was a lot of blood. Elliott assumed most of it was his, but maybe he got lucky.

He grabbed the file with the papers and photos, then ran out the back door.

He was finished. He didn't even care about the money or Mulvaney anymore. He just wanted out of this goddamn town.

Daisy could hear the guy with the gun winding himself up. Maybe Jesse couldn't. Maybe with all his cop experience, Jesse had never heard this particular routine before. Daisy had. Daisy had been caught out late at night more than once by guys who took her existence as an insult. They had to talk themselves into it. They needed to grant themselves permission, to paint themselves into a corner where they could say they really had no choice.

So they asked questions, like this guy did. There were no right answers. There was only one end to the conversation.

Daisy tried to warn Jesse. But the guy told her to shut up.

And Jesse, big fucking idiot that he was, wouldn't stand down, wouldn't turn away. Just stood there with his chest out, proud and stupid.

Daisy slid the knife into her hand and waited for her moment. And waited. She knew the guy would turn the gun on her immediately as soon as she lunged. Maybe that's why she waited too long.

She was still frightened.

But when she saw Jesse go down—the flare from the muzzle burned into her retinas and the sound of the gunshot ringing in her ears—she somehow forgot to be afraid anymore. Suddenly she was a teenager, a young woman in her twenties again, fighting those guys who came after her and her friends in the streets of Boston, no matter that they didn't have a chance of winning.

She found her rage. The bastard had killed her friend.

She stabbed him over and over in the leg. She was a chef, and the muscles and bones in a human leg aren't really that different from a big joint of meat. She sliced and carved, going deep, hoping to get an artery, the puny little paring knife going as far as she could force it.

The guy hit her with the gun again, and this time the

world went a little black around the edges. She didn't
care.

When she could see straight, she saw he was aiming at
her. She was on the floor. And he was going to shoot her.

Daisy didn't want to die. But she wouldn't let him
see that.

He smirked at her.

Then, somehow, Jesse Stone rose from the floor and
tackled the gunman, slamming him into the nearest table.

Daisy sat there, stunned. She couldn't believe what she
was seeing.

They struggled for the gun. Daisy tried to rise, but
found she had trouble getting her legs out from under her,
and the room was still spinning.

Then the world exploded again, and she realized the
guy had fired another shot. It was like another punch to
the head.

A second later, she sat there with Jesse, on the floor,
both blinking.

For a moment, she thought she'd been shot. But she
realized she was only aching and sore from the kick to the
chest.

She looked around the café. The man was gone, fat
drops of red blood leading toward the kitchen and the
back door.

And there was Jesse, somehow, miraculously, not dead.

They were both breathing heavily. Jesse got to his feet
and extended a hand to her. Daisy took it, and he pulled
her to her feet.

"You okay?" he asked.

She nodded, still gaping at him.

"How are you alive?" Daisy asked Jesse.

Jesse pulled open his jacket completely, then his shirt. Underneath, his bulletproof vest was punctured by two shots. One dead center in the chest. The other off to the side.

Jesse tapped the vest.

Daisy's mouth dropped open. "How did you know he wouldn't shoot you in the head?"

"I didn't," Jesse said.

Daisy thought about that for a second. Jesse let a man shoot him. For her.

"Jesus Christ," she said. "You are such an idiot."

Jesse took a deep breath, then bent over and retrieved his gun from his ankle holster.

"Stay here. It's not over yet."

Before Daisy could say anything else, he loped out the rear kitchen door, following the trail of blood.

FIFTY-THREE

Raney yawned. He was tired of Tate making this more complicated than necessary. He put his gun into its holster and walked into the cell.

"Hey," Tate said.

"Shoot me if you want," Raney said. "Then you've got to carry both bags on your own."

"I could do it," Tate said.

"Yeah, yeah, you're a big, strong man," Raney said, and went over to the duffel bags on the cot.

He grabbed the first bag. It was heavy.

And why not? That was his future in there, Raney thought. That was a whole new world in there.

Suit and Molly pulled up outside Daisy's at almost the exact same time as Jesse emerged.

They leaped out of their vehicles, but Jesse was already waving them off. "Check on Daisy! I've got this!"

He ran off before they could argue.

They didn't like it, but they did as they were told. They followed orders.

Jesse did not want them following. If anyone was going to run into the night after a killer, it would be him.

If anyone was going to die tonight, it would not be them.

Elliott ran, the folder under one arm, his gun in his other hand.

He went as fast and as far as he could, which wasn't very fast or very far. His right leg dragged where he'd been stabbed. He couldn't quite lift it properly, as if she'd cut some vital string inside him.

He couldn't catch his breath, either. He still ran five miles every day at home, but now he had a hitch in his chest and his vision narrowed to a tunnel.

It took him a second to realize he was losing too much blood. He wasn't thinking clearly.

He made a blind turn around a building, just trying to get distance between himself and the café and the police station. He wanted to turn on his phone again and call for help, no matter how much it galled him. But he had the file in one hand and his gun in the other, and he didn't want to let go of either. Elliott needed a safe spot where he could regroup.

He made another blind left turn, thinking this would

take him farther away from downtown. Maybe he could boost a car. He still knew how to do that. Well, provided he could find an older model in this town full of Mercedeses and Range Rovers and those electric things that looked like the Batmobile.

Elliott suddenly came to a skidding halt on the wet pavement. He looked up.

The alley ended in a brick wall.

He had nowhere to go.

"Well," Elliott said out loud. "Shit."

"Yeah, these alleys can be tricky until you've been here awhile," a voice behind him said.

He knew the voice. Stone.

Son of a bitch. For the first time in his life, he'd been caught.

He turned, very slowly, but didn't drop the gun.

Stone didn't shoot him, but he could have. The cop had him lined up with a .38, the barrel aimed center mass.

"How the hell are you alive?" Elliott said, and then answered his own question. "Vest. Damn it."

"It was still a good shot," Stone said.

"Thanks," Elliott said. "Must have hurt like a son of a bitch."

"It didn't tickle. That a .357?"

"Yeah."

"Felt like it. You going to drop it now?"

Elliott considered his options. At this range, there was no way Stone could miss. And unlike the cop, Elliott wasn't wearing a vest.

He played the only card he had left.

"You could waste your time with me," he said, "but right now, someone is robbing that two million from your jail. You ready to let all that money go?"

The cop smiled at him like this was funny.

"Yeah," Stone said. "About that."

Raney opened the first duffel bag.

"Jesus Christ, what are you doing, just grab it and let's go," Tate said.

"Oh, now you're in a hurry?"

"Quit screwing around!"

Raney ignored him. He wanted to see what a million bucks in cash actually looked like. He pulled back the zipper.

For a moment, his eyes couldn't quite process what he was seeing.

He wanted to see money. Lots of it. Lots and lots of it. He wanted to see it so badly that for a moment, he could almost turn the yellow-and-white paper into green stacks of cash.

But he couldn't ignore what was actually there.

There were very thick, bound books of yellow-and-white pages of some kind stuffed into the bag.

He read the covers. "Greater Boston Telephone Directory?" he said, almost to himself.

Holy shit, he knew what these were. He'd seen them as a kid. "Phone books," he said.

He tore open the other duffel, even though he knew what he'd find. He ripped out several of the heavy, thick stacks of thin pages.

They were both packed with old phone books. Nothing else.

"I'm fine, damn it, stop poking me," Daisy said, as Molly examined her cheek. The gash from the man's gun was wide but not deep. The real problem was the broken cheekbone. That would hurt a lot.

"We've got a paramedic team on its way," Molly said.

"I'm not the one who needs it! Jesse got shot, for chrissakes!" Daisy said.

"He what?" Molly asked.

"Hey, what's this?" Suit said. He'd found Jesse's gun on the floor when he turned on the lights, and then he saw something else.

A burner phone, still active.

"Must have belonged to the gunman," Molly said.

"He was talking to some other guys while he was talking to me," Daisy added.

Suit held the phone to his ear.

He looked puzzled at first. Then his eyes went wide.

"We've got to get to the station. Now."

"What the hell?" Raney said. Quietly at first. Then louder. Then he was screaming.

He couldn't believe it. He'd been right all along. The money was only ever bait.

He wasn't taking it very well.

Tate heard him bellowing and crowded into the cell to

see the problem. He looked into the duffel bag. Phone books.

In this moment, for this one second at least, Tate was smarter than Raney. Maybe because he'd worked with Jesse Stone, if only for a short time. But he realized he'd been played—they all had—and he didn't waste any time getting angry about it.

Instead, he shoved Raney down toward the floor and turned and stepped outside the cell.

Then he slammed the door shut.

"The hell do you think you're doing?" Raney screamed at him.

Tate didn't reply. He turned to leave. He hoped Raney would put up a fight, that he'd try to shoot his way out of the cell. That might give him enough time to get out of Paradise.

"Hey," the drunk said from the nearby cell.

Tate turned to tell him to shut up.

And saw Gabe Weathers, wrapped in the thrift-store clothing he'd used as a disguise, holding a gun on him.

"Tell me something, Derek: Who's stupid enough to break *into* a jail?" Gabe asked and grinned.

That was too much for Tate. He saw nothing but red. He didn't care that Gabe had the drop on him. He began pulling the trigger of his gun, spraying bullets all over the corridor and the cells.

The older man laughed.

"The money isn't there?"

"Nope," Jesse said. "There's nothing here worth dying for. Come on. Put the gun down. Let's get out of the rain."

The man didn't drop his gun. His pant leg was soaked, and not from the rain. Jesse thought he might fall from blood loss if they stayed out here much longer. He stood a safe distance away, perfect shooting stance, muscles and body locked into place by reflex, sights trained. He had him.

The older man didn't move. Just breathed, deep and quickly, like a dog panting when it's scared.

"It's over. Put the gun down," Jesse said. "Then step away."

The man looked up at Jesse and squinted as if seeing him from a great distance.

From a couple of blocks away, there was a faint noise. A sound like firecrackers going off in rapid succession.

The older man looked at Jesse. "Sounds like gunshots. You wanna go see about that?"

"I'm fine here," Jesse said.

"You sure?"

"Absolutely," Jesse said, and hoped he wasn't lying.

Gabe was no idiot. Unlike Jesse, he did not stand around, waiting to be shot. As soon as Tate brought up his gun, Gabe fired and then dived out of the way, ducking into the cell for cover.

Gabe's bullet went wide of Tate. Tate missed every one of his shots and, surprisingly, managed to avoid getting hit by his own ricochets.

But he made a clear path to the door and ran at it as fast as he could. Tate burst out of the cell area into the station, convinced he was home free.

That's when Molly clotheslined him with her baton, dropping him flat on his back.

Eyes unfocused, he bent at the waist, struggling to get back up.

Suit leaped onto him and grabbed his right hand with both of his own, squeezing hard enough to crack the ulna in Tate's forearm.

Tate yowled in pain and dropped his gun.

Suit rolled off him and then flipped him onto his stomach, pulling on one arm to cuff him at the wrists.

Tate threw a wild punch that caught Suit in the side of the head. Suit was stunned, but didn't let go.

Tate struggled. He thrashed. He flopped on the carpet like a fish on the deck of a boat.

Molly thumped his skull once again with the baton. And then one more time for good measure.

Half conscious, Tate finally stopped struggling.

Working together, Suit and Molly put Tate's arms behind his back and zip-tied him at both his wrists and his ankles.

"Bastards," Tate said, the word slurring slightly as it left his mouth. "Knew Jesse was too scared to face me himself."

Suit laughed. "Jesse is busy with real problems. He only sends us to handle pest control."

Tate told Suit to do something anatomically impossible.

Molly finished hog-tying Tate's wrists to his ankles. "Hey, Derek," she said. "How's my ass look now?"

———

Elliott stood there in the alley, tired and numb. The gun in his hand felt unbelievably heavy. All those years, all those guns, they had always felt just like an extension of his arm, a part of his body. Now it felt like a cinder block, dragging him under the water.

Getting old, he thought.

There were sirens in the distance, getting closer. It sounded like a lot of them.

Elliott heard the cop's voice, didn't quite catch the words, but he was sure he knew the tune. Put down the weapon. Hands on your head. Come along quietly. Something like that.

Even if he won this little gunfight with the cop—and, honestly, he knew he didn't have a chance—he'd be surrounded. Stuck in this goddamn town.

Trapped in Paradise.

He wished he had a cigarette. He'd never smoked, but he thought that would be a cool move, lighting a cigarette. Maybe, like Raney, he was a little in love with the idea of the hit man from the movies.

He wondered if Raney would get away. Or if that idiot Tate would get them both killed.

Elliott didn't regret it. He'd made his choices.

Elliott didn't regret anything, really.

Everything seemed to be moving in slow motion now.

The cop said something again, but Elliott's mind was somewhere else. He thought of Kate.

He had multiple IDs on him, but none that went back to her, or to the accounts he'd set up for them. He didn't have life insurance—he smiled a little, thinking of a Mob that offered health and life and pension—but the mortgage was covered. She had her Social Security checks and enough in the bank.

It wasn't $2 million, but she'd be fine. And they'd never trace his steps back to her.

But she'd never know what happened to him. She'd stay up nights wondering. He knew how she worried.

She'd call his phone, and then the hotel where he wasn't, and then, finally, the fake numbers of the companies he'd set up years ago, and find them dead or disconnected.

And she'd be baffled and scared, probably for a long time.

It would hurt her.

"I said put the gun on the ground and step away now. Last chance," Jesse said.

Jesse didn't pull the hammer back on his gun or anything like that. Those were moves for people who saw gunfights only on TV. The older man would do what he wanted to do. He knew his options here.

Jesse wanted to shoot the man just for hurting Daisy. But he managed to stow his anger away. When the anger faded, he always remembered he didn't like killing people.

So he could give the guy a moment to turn this around. To change the story. It was a risk, sure. But Jesse figured it was his life to risk.

"It doesn't have to end like this," Jesse said.

Elliott heard that loud and clear. It came through even though everything else sounded muffled by cotton in his ears.

He wondered if this was what having a stroke felt like. Maybe he'd end up in a hospital before prison. Or maybe this was just his time.

God, he hated the idea of being an old man on a cell block. He'd seen those guys, inside and out. Husks of themselves. Scared all the time. Hollow men.

Kate would be fine, he decided.

He lifted his gun. It felt heavier than ever.

"Yeah, it does," he told the cop.

Even for an old guy, he was pretty fast.

Jesse put three into him from a standing position, but the older man got a shot off anyway.

It went wide of Jesse and shattered the wall near his head. A couple fragments of wood and masonry sliced open his forehead and cheek.

Jesse blinked away blood as he walked over to the body. He kicked away the gun, but he knew it didn't matter. The man was dead.

It was over.

FIFTY-FOUR

But what if he'd shot you in the head?" Suit wanted to know.

"No great loss," Molly said.

"Thank you, Molly," Jesse said.

Molly, Suit, Gabe, and Jesse sat around the conference table after cleaning up the scene. It was two-forty-nine a.m. Elliott's body had been taken away. Tate and Raney were in the county holding facility, officially someone else's problem now. The news vans were long gone, although Ty Bentley told Jesse he wanted a full sit-down interview in the morning.

They'd found some stale donuts in a box on the table and ate them anyway. Sugar and starch were the best medicine for the inevitable adrenaline crash.

"Seriously," Suit said. "How did you know he wouldn't go for the head shot?"

"I kept drawing his attention to my chest. Tapping there, like it was a target. I didn't know if it would work, but I couldn't come in wearing a helmet."

"You took an awfully big chance, Jesse," Suit said, looking as mournful as a schoolkid who'd lost his homework. Jesse couldn't help smiling at him.

"That's the job," he said.

"What I want to know is," Molly said, "where the hell did you get all those phone books?"

"One of the clerks had them at the Staties' evidence facility," Suit said.

"From the Burton house?"

"No, he had a whole cabinet full of them. They'd been piling up for years, apparently, and he'd never gotten rid of them."

"Maybe that guy is a bit of a hoarder himself," Molly said.

"Well, I took them off his hands."

"Pretty smart," she said.

"I'm more impressed Jesse finally figured out how to work the conference-call feature on his phone," Gabe said.

"Thank *you*, Gabe," Jesse said.

"So where's the money?" Molly asked.

"Still locked in the safe with the State Police," Jesse said. "I knew it would be safer there."

"You disobeyed a direct instruction from the mayor and the district attorney?" Molly said. "And their neat little court order?"

"Funny, they don't seem to be worried about it now,"

Jesse said. "They would rather believe they were in on the brilliant trap all along."

"It does make them look smarter," Suit said.

"I'm just glad I can finally stop sleeping in the cells," Gabe said, "and wearing these stinking clothes as pajamas."

"How did you get them to smell like that, anyway?" Molly asked.

"You don't want to know," Gabe said.

"Sure I do."

"Well, I don't want to tell you," Gabe said. "You were right, Jesse. Leave a big enough piece of bait, and eventually the rats will show up."

"It's easy to be a genius in hindsight," Jesse said, wincing a little as he took the wad of paper towels away from his face. They were bloody, but not soaked. He still felt something under his skin.

"You should get that looked at," Molly said. "Don't be such a tough guy."

"You're right," Jesse said, and got up.

"Wait, where are you going?"

"To the ER," Jesse said.

"Seriously? No fight? No manly grumbling about how it's not that bad and you'll be fine?"

"Not this time."

"Maybe I should drive you," Molly said. "It might be worse than it looks."

"If it makes you feel better," Jesse said.

Now Molly looked alarmed. "Holy crap, Jesse, are you dying?"

"Never a bad idea to ask for help now and then," Jesse

said. "By the way: Thank you all for being there when I needed you. I don't say it enough. You're good cops."

Molly narrowed her eyes at him. "Okay, not dying. But definitely a blow to the head."

Jesse smiled. "I'm sure I'll get over it."

"Now, that's the Jesse Stone I know."

FIFTY-FIVE

Did you think your skull was thick enough to deflect bullets?" Rachel Lowenthal said.

"I hoped he'd aim for the heart," Jesse said.

The ER was quiet. Three a.m. was usually busier in an emergency room, at least in Jesse's experience. But Rachel—Dr. Lowenthal, he reminded himself—had taken him back to an exam room as soon as he walked in.

Maybe she liked him a little after all.

"Well, congratulations. It's definitely the stupidest thing I've seen in a long time, and I work in an emergency room where people show up with lawn implements inside them."

Then again, maybe not.

Sitting on the exam table, Jesse winced as she thumped his ribs. Large purple bruises were already flowering on his chest where the vest had caught the bullets.

"You're lucky the Kevlar held, too," she said. "I read it's not great with multiple shots."

"I had plates under the Kevlar."

She thumped his chest once more, which seemed a little unnecessary to Jesse. "Your ribs aren't broken. You're going to hurt a lot, though. Maybe you'd have done better with more body fat. Give you a little padding."

"I'll try to eat more donuts."

"All right," she said, pointing to his forehead. "Lean forward and I'll clean that wound."

Jesse ducked down so she could reach the spot on his brow where the ricochet had hit.

He held still while she plucked with tweezers. She placed splinters of bloody brick and wood and dirt into a metal basin while she talked.

"You know you don't get anything for being a repeat customer, right?" she asked, as she plucked with the tweezers. "We don't have a punch card like a coffee shop."

"I'm only here for the cafeteria food."

"The food in there is awful."

"I was misinformed."

She smiled. "You're pretty charming for someone people keep trying to kill."

"They just haven't gotten to know me."

Lowenthal dug a particularly big piece out of Jesse's head. It came free with a slight shucking noise.

"You're allowed to say ouch," she said.

"Ouch."

"You want something for the pain?"

"I'll be okay."

"Right," she said. "Tough guy. How could I forget. By the way, your friend Daisy was in here earlier."

"How is she?"

"Alive. Although that cheekbone is going to hurt like hell for a while, and she'll have a lovely black eye to show people."

"I'm sorry," Jesse said.

Dr. Lowenthal looked him in the eye. "Don't be," she said. "You didn't do it. And you saved her life. Believe me, I heard all about it."

She nodded, as if that settled the discussion, and then turned her back on Jesse while she opened a drawer.

"I'm going to give you antibiotics and a tetanus booster," she said.

"Is that necessary?"

"Don't tell me you're scared of needles, Chief Stone."

"It's Jesse."

"Right."

While she swabbed his arm and jabbed him, Jesse thought of what Dix had said. How you have to make an effort to let people into your life. How you have to risk little things to win big things.

He took a breath. It hurt his ribs.

"Hey, Dr. Lowenthal," he said. "I wonder if I could ask you out for coffee again sometime."

"What did I say last time?"

"Hard to recall. I've been hit in the head a few times since then."

"I think I said I wasn't interested in being another notch on the bedpost of a guy trying to get himself killed before he had to face retirement."

"Is that what you said?"

"Well, it still applies."

"I'm not that guy," Jesse said. "Or, at least, I'm trying to do better."

Lowenthal looked at Jesse for what felt like a long time. She narrowed her eyes, as if he was an X-ray and she might be able to spot something if she squinted hard enough.

"Okay," she said. "Why not? Let's take a chance."

Jesse smiled.

"My thoughts exactly."

"So when should I clear my schedule?" she asked. "I have to be back here at eight tonight."

"How about tomorrow," Jesse said. "I still have a couple things I've got to finish up today."

FIFTY-SIX

Healy and Jesse stood outside the townhome on Beacon Hill. Technically, neither one of them had a right to be there. They were invited only as a courtesy. But once the warrants had been drawn up, Lundquist asked if they'd wanted to watch. It was the file Jesse had salvaged from the Burton house—and his testimony about what Elliott said about it—that had enabled the State Police to close a thirty-five-year-old cold case.

Jesse and Healy drank coffee and leaned against a federal sedan. It looked like they were the only ones not on duty. Boston PD, the FBI, and the Staties were all lined up on the steps, wearing their windbreakers and vests, loaded with enough artillery to take a small country. Lundquist was in the lead. He knocked once, then kicked in the door.

"You wish you were going in?" Healy asked.

Jesse stretched, feeling the muscles pull in his back, feeling every one of the last twenty-six hours he'd been awake. He was getting older.

But he was still alive. That was the important thing.

"You know what, I'm willing to let someone else play hero on this one."

"Eh, you did all the hard work," Healy said.

Actually, it had been Healy who'd put the last piece of the puzzle together. Jesse had called him and told him how Elliott said the photos implicated Mulvaney personally. That triggered a memory for Healy: a cousin of Mulvaney's in the Irish Mob who'd been shot. He'd been ahead of Mulvaney in the line of succession, and they'd been fighting over territory and earnings. When he'd been killed, Mulvaney was the obvious suspect. But Mulvaney had an alibi, and there was no other obvious connection.

But with the file and the photo, Healy had been able to get Lundquist to open the case again. The photo matched the crime scene where they'd found Mulvaney's dead cousin in an alley with a neat gunshot wound in his forehead. And they were able to match a payment in an old, crumbling check register to Phil Burton, which had been meaningless thirty-five years ago.

But it was now proof of conspiracy to commit murder.

Not that they really needed it. Tate and Raney were both singing to the U.S. attorney and the DA and anyone else who would listen.

Mulvaney's pretty, angry nurse came out of the townhome, although not on her own. She was carried by two big FBI agents, both of whom were bleeding freely from cuts and bruises. She thrashed and cursed and kicked despite being zip-tied at both wrists and ankles. The big agents looked a little embarrassed.

A moment later, Mulvaney's bodyguard walked out, hands cuffed, head down, practically polite by comparison.

And then Lundquist pushed the old man in his silk pajamas and his expensive wheelchair out through the front door and down the ramp to the sidewalk.

Mulvaney looked sick and gray and lost, his mouth open. He looked as if he was stuck in a nightmare and couldn't wake up.

Then he glanced across the street and saw Healy and Jesse watching, and his face twisted into a mask of pure hate.

Healy laughed out loud and toasted him with his coffee cup. They lost sight of him as he was placed in a special transport van that could hold his wheelchair.

"What do you know," Healy said, still beaming. "Sometimes the good guys win one after all."

FIFTY-SEVEN

And miles to go before I sleep, Jesse thought. That was the only line of a poem he could remember by heart. Probably because it was the only one that ever really applied to his life.

But he still had one last thing to do. The most important thing, really.

On his way back to the station, Jesse walked to the front door of Daisy's café. He stopped at the threshold, however.

Daisy was busy wiping down the counter. She spared him a glance, but finished her job. She put the towel and cleanser away and washed her hands before turning back to him.

Everyone in the café pretended to pay serious attention to whatever was on their plates. But Jesse could feel them listening. This was going to be good gossip in Paradise, no matter what happened, and they were all in the front row.

Daisy stood before him. Her eye was swollen and black, just like Dr. Lowenthal had said, but she stared at him clearly.

"So are you coming in or what?" Daisy asked.

Jesse shook his head. "I'm sorry, Daisy," he said. "I should have listened. I should have paid attention. I should have been a better friend, and a better cop. And I will do my best to make sure what happened to you never happens again. To you or anyone else in Paradise."

Daisy nodded. "That it?"

"Yeah," Jesse said. For him, that was the equivalent of a filibuster in the U.S. Senate.

Daisy didn't say anything, though. She only kept looking at him, as if trying to figure something out.

Jesse had said what he came to say. He'd owned his mistakes, just like he always did. He turned to go. He needed to call Cole and tell him he got shot again.

"Wait," Daisy said.

Jesse could almost feel the people straining not to look at them. He turned back.

Daisy crossed the café and stood right in front of Jesse, looking up at him.

He decided if she took a swing at him, he'd let her. He probably had it coming.

Instead, Daisy threw her arms around him and pulled him close. And held him.

"I know it's not easy being our hero all the time," she said. "You big idiot."

Surprised at the sudden catch in his throat, Jesse put his arms around her, too, and patted her on the back.

They stood like that for a long moment.

Then Daisy broke the hold, pushing him away, using the sleeve of her shirt to wipe her eyes.

"Now get your ass in here. You look like you've lost ten pounds. Can't you even feed yourself without me."

Jesse went to his usual table. No one was seated there. He wondered if that was a coincidence.

"You really were an asshole, though," Daisy said, clearing her throat.

"I was," Jesse said.

"Don't do it again," she said, retreating to the kitchen. "We depend on you to be the good guy around here. Don't forget that."

"I won't," Jesse said. "I promise."

Daisy stopped at the kitchen door. "Jesse. Do me another favor?"

"Sure."

"Take that goddamn sign out of the front window and chuck it in the trash."

Jesse smiled. "Yes, ma'am."

ACKNOWLEDGMENTS

Many thanks are due to Alexandra Machinist and Esther Newberg and the Estate of Robert B. Parker for giving me the chance to follow in the footsteps of Robert B. Parker, the dean himself. I've been reading him since high school, and I hope I did right by his legacy here. Thanks as well to Ben H. Winters, who read an early draft of the manuscript and, as always, gave invaluable advice. And finally, thank you to Tarini Sipahimalani and the entire team at Putnam for their effort and support.